Jezebel

came striding toward Ahab, her magnificent breasts moving rhythmically, the flesh of her thighs quivering.

"Yahweh, forgive me! I cannot resist her beauty," he prayed. Then he swung her up against his armor and threw his cloak over her nakedness as he kissed her lips.

In his arms she felt his maleness respond to her touch— this big man who had just smashed the forces of Aram —and laughed in the delight flooding her veins. "This night we worship Baal-Melkart. The men and women shall drink and know each other to the glory of Baal."

Jezebel

JEFFERSON COOPER

WILDSIDE PRESS

Jezebel

Published by Wildside Press LLC
www.wildsidepress.com

BOOK ONE: The Book of Ahab

One: The Night Of Revolt In Tyre

1.

A naked woman postured before the brazen statue.

Glowing torches made a carpet of fire below her across the wharfside square as armed men shook their bronze spears and bellowed at her words. The torchflames touched the metal helmets of the warriors, their shirts of chain-mail and the upper rims of their wooden shields where they were edged with copper. There was a madness in the salt air blowing in from the roadstead between the island palace of Tyre and its mainland city, and as men breathed deep of it, set their blood to boiling.

"Baal-Melkart," screamed the woman.

The torches lifted, shaking. The soldiers roared an answer.

"Baal-Melkart—hear us! Turn your eyes toward us, your worshippers. Give us this night the victory over Phales!"

"Victory over the tyrant. Victory over Phales!"

The great god towered high above them all, its horned head almost in darkness where the torches failed to light it. Baal-Melkart sat upon a golden throne, high on a wagon of massive wooden beams and wooden wheels. The woman—young, with skin the color of dark cream, slim of waist and shapely of legs—threw back her mass of heavy black hair so that it tumbled below the twitching buttocks gleaming in the torchlight. Her arms went wide. Muscles tightened her sweat-wet flesh as she arched her back, proffering the swollen bowls of her heavy young breasts.

"God of all! Father of our race, hear us!"

"Hear us," roared the men.

"Phales is evil in your eyes!"

"Evil! Evil!"

"Touch our swords, our spears! Bless them with your god-hood!"

A thousand points rose into the night sky and were held there in the torchlight so that the jeweled eyes of the mighty Baal-Melkart might see and seeing, bless them with his own omnipotence. The girl stared up at the god, giving herself to its gaze, her loveliness covered neither by scarf nor veil. She was wanton, pagan, as she posed shamelessly, showing her god and any man who cared to look the secrets of her womanhood.

High the image towered, of beaten gold inlaid with silver and lapis-lazuli, grim and silent, in the shape of a man with a great crown upon his horned head. It sat with strongly thewed legs apart, hands on its knees. It had been carved in realistic detail, so that it might indeed be said to hunger for the woman posing so lewdly before it.

In the shadows of the docks that stretched outward into the harbor waters toward the rocky island that held the great stone palace of Phales, king of Tyre, three men pressed their backs against a wall. They were tall men and strong, being clad in mail-shirts and leather jerkins, with military boots on their feet. Each of them carried a long sword in a scabbard at a plain leather belt; over each shoulder, almost hidden beneath the folds of a brown wool cloak, was a small shield.

"Saw you ever such a woman?" breathed the tallest of the three. His face was hard, with high cheekbones; a sparse black beard was trimmed close to the line of his jaw. His black eyes blazed with feral lights under downpulled eyebrows; he seemed about to spring.

The man who stood to his left was shorter, not so bulky through the shoulders. There was no hair on his face and he seemed younger than the others. His hands, where they clasped his belt, were white and their long fingers supple as snakes as he moved them continually in a steady motion over the leather.

He said, "She is perfection, Ahab. Compared to her, my Ruth is like wheat after the thresher has beaten it flat."

"Well, didn't you come to Tyre to drop a few oats before your marriage?" rumbled the third man, not taking his eyes from the woman on the great dais that held the golden image.

"But to arrive now—in the midst of a rebellion!"

"You're too sensible, Rael," rasped Ahab. "This is the time to strike, when emotions are fever-hot and passions run like water in a spillway."

"Aye, the women will be weak as newborn kittens," grunted the third man, who was almost as tall as Ahab but bulkier by far, with shoulders so wide they seemed grotesque. His hairy legs and long arms bulged with muscle. "They'll tumble to our pull like wool to the shearers' knives."

Rael smiled thinly, almost envious of the sheer animal spirits of the heavier, stronger Jehu. He wished in his heart he could be more like him, but there was a sensitivity in him that was absent from his companions. He could admire the beauty of the naked woman posturing above them, yet be aware of his own inadequacy before it. Neither Ahab nor Jehu were so affected; they saw in the priestess only a woman with whom to slake their lusts.

Ahab clamped a powerful hand on his wrist. "Be ready, you two. They're breaking up—getting ready to cross the harbor."

"Where Phales waits like a fly for the spider, helpless to escape. Ithobaal is a smart man. He lets his king hole up in the one spot from which there can be no running."

Rael chuckled. "Always you see things with the eye of a soldier, Jehu. Is there no perception of beauty in your heart? To turn from the sight of a lovely girl to—well, to killing— smacks of an abtuseness which—"

Jehu bellowed laughter and hugged the slighter man against him with an arm like the bole of a cedar. "Rael, you are answered out of your own words. You're a physician. You see in that shameless little tart a fine body full of health and vitality. Beauty, if you will, since that makes up beauty in your eyes."

Even Ahab chuckled. "Each to his own. And now, since I am a prince in Israel, I think it's time I gave the orders. Jehu, Rael—be ready. The men are thinning out. They're starting across the mole. The girl will be alone with her god very soon, now."

"Aye, she's done her work. She's roused the blood in them."

"To kill," commented Rael.

"To kill, to rape—they're brothers of a sort," snapped Jehu, still looking at the girl. "Frenzies which overtake a man in his blood heat."

She was turning away from the statue to stare at the river of armed men flooding into the boats which would carry them across the harbor to the island palace of King Phales. Perspiration covered her slim body; her thick black hair was plastered to her smooth shoulders and upper arms; her jutting breasts rose and fell in rhythm to her labored breathing. In the light from the few remaining torches, thrust into copper holders around the brazen statue, she made a barbaric sight to the three men staring from the shadows.

Ahab sighed and stood away from the wall, tugging his

swordbelt around in front of him so the braided hilt of his longsword was ready to his hand. He shook out his woolen cloak and slipped the shield from the thongs that held it suspended from his shoulders.

"No," he said quickly, without looking behind him.

They made a wedge of mailed flesh and muscle, striding forward. Most of the rebels were being rowed in boats across to the palace; only a few remained and these were gathered about a bronze arm, lifting its harness clamps and fastening them to the traces on small grey asses. In a moment greased hubs were creaking as the heavy ram began to move onto a flat barge.

Ahab waited until the ram was gone.

Then he moved swiftly, approaching the brazen statue, putting a hand on a painted ornament of the wheeled dais, drawing himself upward. His scabbard clanked against its chains; at its sound the woman turned to stare down at him.

"You're no Phoenician," she said suddenly.

Ahab grinned up at her. From this position he could look along her sleek thighs upward beyond her mounded belly to the thrusting breasts. Aie, she was a beauty! Lovelier by far than any girl in his father's palace at Samaria. Or at Jezreel either, for that matter. It was hard to breathe, staring up at her like this.

"Not I," he agreed lightly and renewed his climbing.

There was no fear in her. She must have seen Rael and Jehu behind him, climbing also—like men pursuing a strange, impossible dream, the thought came to him—as they rose upward to lay hands on this Tyrian harlot.

"Israelites," the girl said suddenly, and laughed.

Her palms clapped together, imperiously.

The great dais lurched forward, jerkily. It was a wide, broad wagon, that mighty pantechnicon, and inside it was a hollow space. There were men in that space, Ahab realized suddenly; slaves, brawney black men from Africa and bearded Hittites and Aramaeans—war prisoners—whose duty it was to transport the god from the Temple into this city square. Now they were taking it back to the Temple.

The sudden movement of the dais shook his handholds loose. Desperately Ahab and his companions scrabbled for new grips. Pressed to the wood, they fought to keep from falling.

The god-wagon was moving faster. Faster.

Ah, but—

Not toward the Temple! No!

Ahead of the swiftly rolling wagon was a stone wall.

Rael shouted and fell away, landing on a hip, rolling to avoid

8

the mighty wooden wheel that towered high above him. At the same instant he saw Jehu flash past as he leaped.

"Ahab! Jump!" he screamed.

Ahab clung to the wooden dais, knowing his death was upon him. He could not climb fast enough to avoid the stone wall against which the heavy dais, weighted now by the golden image of Baal-Melkart, soon would crash. Nor could he jump safely from this angle as Jehu had jumped, far enough from the rotating hubs to avoid the crushing wheels. He was caught between wall and wood like a grain of wheat between mill-stone and grinding wheel.

The breath rasped harsh in his throat but he never looked away from the girl bending above him and smiling cruelly. Her black eyes were alive with the lust to kill and her full red mouth twisted into a grotesque imitation of its former loveliness. Forgotten were her breasts and loins, forgotten the silken sheen of her soft flesh and the shapeliness of her thighs. All he could see were those eyes.

He drowned in them, lost in their glistening wonder. It seemed he looked into depths of lust so evil that his skin crawled, not with disgust but with a strange, hot eagerness to know those depths of degradation, those nameless delights which this woman alone could give. She was too far above him to reach or he would have put a hand about her ankle and drawn her down to die beside him.

Her laughter rose mockingly, as though she could see inside his eyes to his mind benumbed by the vision in her own. "You will never know, Israelite," she breathed. "You die—without knowing."

The wall was at his back.

"Ahab! My prince!"

The words rose up from the tortured throat of a man who would have given everything he owned to be where the prince of Israel now clung, inches from a grinding death. Rael stared with the horror clear to read in his eyes. Jehu was yanking out his iron sword, running to mount the dais from the side, shouting oaths.

"Prince?" whispered the girl staring down at Ahab.

She cried out suddenly, rising and waving a hand.

Feet slid. Men flung themselves on wooden brakes, to force and hold them against the wheels. There were torturous squeals of wood on wood and smoke came where the friction started tiny fires.

The god-wagon slowed, lurched.

Ahab felt the stones at his back, biting in. The pressure was

9

tremendous; it seemed that Baal-Melkart leaned his golden weight against him so that he could not breathe; his ribs bent and he expected to hear them snap. He was like a beetle crushed between the thumb and forefinger of a scholar.

Held helpless, unable to keep his face from twisting in pain, he watched the girl kneel above him. "Who are you, Israelite? What is your name?"

"Ahab, son of Omri. I am prince of Israel."

She called down to the men in the dais hollow, "Back, draw it back. Release him. But—be easy. I don't want him hurt." She smiled at Ahab then and his senses reeled at the pleasure her smile gave to him.

As the pantechnicon backed from the wall, Jehu and Rael ran between its timbers and the stone wall and began to climb. Their hands reached upward, caught Ahab under his armpits. As he eased the strained muscles that held him to the jousts, they lowered him to the cobbles.

When they looked up, the girl was gone.

They leaned Ahab against the wall of a dockside warehouse that stared out over the harbor waters, letting him get his breath back. Rael was probing his deep chest—his mail shirt and leather jerkin lay on the street—with delicate fingertips, forehead furrowed in concentration. As his fingers moved, the tenseness went out of his muscles and his features eased their hardness.

"No bones broken, for which give thanks to Yahweh."

"I shall dedicate a dozen golden bowls for His worship, I swear it," he panted. The sweat stood out on his forehead, ran down into his eyes and along his ashen cheeks; the touch of death was still on Ahab.

He leaned his head against the stone wall and drew deep breaths. Jehu took a corner of his cloak and wiped his face. Ahab opened his eyes and smiled wolfishly, showing even white teeth.

"I will have that woman, that priestess," he breathed.

"Some other time," Rael nodded, handing Ahab his garments.

"This night, before the sun rises."

"Ahab, be reasonable," protested Rael.

"She thinks she has—beaten me. No woman can do that to me and not—suffer a little in consequence. Just give me a few minutes. I'm all right."

Jehu said nothing. His eyes were occupied with the distant palace of Phales, who would be king of Tyre no longer after this night. From the open sea behind the palace ships were moving in, low pentecosters with catapults hurling fireballs and mighty stones. Across the harbor other boats, filled with men armed with bows and quivers of iron-tipped arrows, were firing steadily at the palace walls, sweeping them clean of life. The palace quays held spearmen drawing back to give the bronze ram room to swing; its hollow poundings at the brazen gate made a booming noise which echoed and re-echoed across this corner of the city.

The rebels under Ithobaal would be a few hours at their fighting, Jehu knew. Phales would be unlikely to give up his crown without a battle to the death. If Ahab were intent on bedding a Phoenician harlot, the time to strike was now. His hand touched his swordhilt, then fell away.

"The temple will be well guarded," he growled.

Ahab nodded. "I don't want the temple. I want a woman. There'll be ways to come at her. As a worshipper, if need be."

Rael gasped at the suggested sacrilege, and was troubled. Although Ahab, like his father Omri, was no intimate of Yahweh as David and Solomon had been fifty years and more before, still he was heir to the throne of Israel. If word got out that Ahab had joined in the worship of Baal-Melkart, there would be trouble in Samaria, where the prophet Elijah was preaching these days.

He was about to protest when Ahab pushed away from the wall to slip the mail shirt over his head. As he tied the strings of his leather jerkin, Ahab said, "You two can remain behind. When I'm done I'll find you at the inn where we're staying."

Rael looked at Jehu, who shrugged. Rael said, "We won't desert you." He would have stepped forward except that Jehu put a hand on his shoulder and held him.

"Let him go. He wants to be alone with her. We'd only be in the way." Jehu whispered so that only Rael might hear him; aloud he said to Ahab, "Go, then. I'll be busy myself this night. There's a serving wench at the inn who caught my eye earlier, when we were eating."

Ahab nodded, smiling faintly. He turned and was soon lost in the shadows, with only the swaying motion of his cloak to show where he walked. In a moment he turned the corner and was gone.

"If you think I'm going to . . ." Rael began.

Jehu silenced him with a fierce motion of his hairy hand. "Oh, we'll follow him, never fear. But let him go first, and alone. He came to Tyre for adventure, where he isn't known. Let him find it."

11

"But a priestess of the god! Won't the Phoenicians think it's a sort of—well, sacrilege?"

Jehu snorted, "Baal-Melkart is brother to Astarte, isn't he? And to the harlot goddess any sort of embrace is holy."

Rael growled, "It's a funny kind of religion that makes sacred the most intimate relations between a man and woman."

"It goes back a long time, Rael, this worship of Astarte. You find her everywhere. They call her Ishtar in Babylon and Assyria, Ashtoreth in Philistia. In Egypt she's known as Isis."

"But why worship a harlot?"

"It isn't a harlot they worship but the creative principle. As a physician, you should understand that."

"Oh! Life and the generative powers of a woman."

"And of a man." Jehu's glance was sly. "If you'd lived a little instead of burying your face in scrolls and medical texts, you'd understand even better than I the theory behind it."

Rael grinned in embarrassment. "I understand the theory. Ever since man began to realize he was man, he realized that his safety and his comfort depended on having a lot of people in his tribe. As a result, that which gave him people—the phallus and the yoni—came to be sacred in his sight." He added wryly, "The theory I know, it's the practice that confuses me."

Jehu nudged him with an elbow. "Come on, it's time to go after him. But don't let him see you. Let him think he's completely on his own."

They walked swiftly through the Phoenician night, cloaks up to shield their faces. Behind them the palace of King Phales began to glow with fire.

2.

Ahab paused in the shadows of the basalt pillars surrounding the mighty bulk of the twin temples of Baal-Melkart and Astarte, his heart hammering under his bruised ribs. There was an enchantment in the moon-drenched night, a sense of anticipation that ran like wildfire in his veins.

There, beyond the granite incense bowl!

Someone or something had moved a little. Moonlight flashed on metal, was quickly gone. He stepped forward. As if in echo to the slap of his boots on the paving stones of the pathway he heard another, softer footstep.

"Are you the priestess?" he called softly.

"Are you the prince of Israel?"

He grinned and moved forward confidently. He had been right about the wench. She wanted him just as badly as he wanted her. A spark had come to life between them; it was up to him to nurture it to flame.

She backed away from him slowly as he advanced. True, he could see her only as a shadow but his heart told him this was the woman who had posed naked before her god. His arm ached to enfold that nude white body. His lips itched to cover that smooth flesh with kisses.

"Wait," he called.

"Follow me," floated back her answer.

A door in a high wall opened. For a moment he caught sight of a garden enclosed by those walls, filled with statuary and with flowers, fragrant in the springtime night. The woman slipped inside and closed the door; he did not hear the sound of any bolt.

He ran, big and strong in the pride of young manhood, straight for that barrier. His hand went out for the latch. It lifted and the door opened.

Ahab went into the garden and closed the door behind him. His hand drew the bolt while his eyes moved this way and that, seeking out the Temple harlot. The garden could be a trap, he knew. Among the shrubbery, half a hundred soldiers might lie in wait. He did not see them, nor any twinkle of moonlight on a burnished helmet or spearpoint, however, and so his tension eased.

He moved along the path, away from the garden door. The heavy scents of mimosa and roses made the night swim in languor. An ache was forming in his middle as he moved deeper into the garden. Behind him was the Temple of Baal-Melkart, ahead the smaller Temple of Astarte.

Between the two temples and set like a jewel in the center of the walled garden was a small sanctuary, like a summerhouse. It was the only place where the woman could be hiding.

Ahab slipped between the pillars.

She was lying on a low couch, wrapped about by a silken garment. Ahab paused, staring. The woman was different, somehow. More regal. Proud. Imperious. She wore a golden fillet in her hair from which dangled tiny golden hyacinth flowers, shaped like bells that tinkled when she moved her

13

head. Her slim white arms were clustered with golden armbands. There were khalkhals around her ankles.

"What kept you, Ahab?"

Her voice made music in his ears.

"I came as swiftly as I could. It was no mean embrace in which I found myself, between that stone wall and the god-wagon."

Her laughter tinkled. She raised slim arms into the moonlight and made caressing motions with her hands and fingers. Not once had she looked at him; she seemed enchanted by the bottom of the domed roof.

"Come. Let my embrace wipe out the memory of the other. I promise you, though—that mine may be a harder one from which to escape."

He needed no encouragement. His long legs took him to the couch so that he stood above her, filling his eyes with her loveliness. The silken robe she wore was only a mist over her nudity. Earlier he had looked upon her nakedness and known excitement; now he realized that excitement had been as nothing. Veiled by the black gauze through which the tints of her nipples and the even darker smudge of blackness at her groin could be seen stark against white skin, she was enough to choke the breath from a man.

He knelt and bent his head, touching her warm thigh with his lips through the robe. She made a contented sound in her throat and put a hand on his head. Lazily she ran her fingers through his hair.

"Ahab, do you know my name?"

"You are beauty," he whispered.

"Oh, sweet. I like that, but—I'm not just beauty, you know. I'm a person. I do have a name, a certain sort of rank."

"You are Astarte."

She laughed at that, turning her head to stare at his intent face. "This from you? An Israelite? Your god is my god's mortal enemy."

"Gods are never enemies. It is only their worshippers who make them so."

Her eyes widened. "Are you so wise, so young?"

He grinned at her, nodding. "Like Solomon himself."

His hand was on her thigh, sliding upward to her belly. Under his fingertips he sensed the smooth fire of her flesh, felt the tremble that showed her awareness of his exploration. Slowly he began to unwrap the robe that only pretended to hide her body.

She permitted his attention, breathing more rapidly when

14

the silk slid away to bare the swollen mound of a breast. Ahab bent to touch its jutting nipple with his lips. Under her breath she whispered words which he could not make out.

"My name, Ahab," she panted. "Who am I?"

"Does it matter?" he wondered. "You're a woman, I'm a man. We are together in the gardens of your love goddess. Worship her with me."

Her fingers caught his thick hair and held his head motionless above her belly. "You are wise with the wisdom of Solomon, as you say. To get what you want you tempt me with my own religious beliefs. Ah, but you! Isn't it a sin for you to forsake Yahweh in order to slake your desire in the body of a Phoenician girl?"

"I am a prince," he told her.

Her strength was as nothing against his heavily muscled frame. She was further weakened by laughter. Fingers tangled in his hair, she drew his mouth to the pouting nipples of her breasts, held him to his devotions while her hips squirmed lazily.

"As you say, you are a prince. And I—what shall I be after this night?"

"What greater rank can you have than that of goddess?"

A sullen roar seemed to be his answer. It came from the direction of the royal harbor. The woman drew strength from it, half sitting up and listening with her head tilted to one side. Ahab saw her ripe red mouth parted expectantly, felt her breast move against his cheek as she breathed in and out with excitement.

"Can you make out what they say?" she panted.

"Something about a new king in Phoenicia."

"Ahab! Is that right? Are you sure? Listen again!"

To humor her, he drew away and concentrated. Yes, he could hear their words now, the words they shouted to the night sky. Ithobaal! Ithobaal was king in Phoenicia. The tyrant Phales was dethroned! The attack of the palace was a success. The king had been dragged screaming from his sleeping covers where he had hidden himself, to form a human pincushion for the spears of the rebels. Ithobaal ruled in Tyre!

He could make out the screams of women.

"Phales' wives and concubines," breathed the girl beside him. Her hand dug into his arm so tightly her silvered nails were drawing blood. "They will be raped to death before the goddess!"

Ahab growled in his throat. She turned an amused face to him. "It is the unwritten law of the conqueror. An old law,

15

true—but one which Ithobaal decided to uphold. He wants no unborn child of Phales to rise in later life and plague him."

He nodded grimly, saying, "Such was the law in the old, old days. Things are different now. We are barbarians no longer."

She sank her teeth in his earlobe. "We are still barbarians here in Tyre. Tonight, you will be glad of it. Come with me to the Temple. I want to see what happens to proud Shubadad who was queen in Phoenicia before Phales lost his crown."

He might have refused, might have pulled her down to slake his flesh hunger on her body but there was an excitement about this woman that was like heady wine. Soft, warm, fragrant, her skin smooth to the touch of his hand, she was an allurement he could not resist.

"All right," he nodded, lifting her to her feet. "Show the way."

She ran ahead of him along the garden walks—while outside the tumult of the crowd and the screams of the terrified women were growling louder—toward the columned portico of the Temple of Astarte. Ahab found himself caught up in the excitement that flushed her cheeks and made her eyes sparkle.

He gave no thought to the fact that this was a pagan temple, forbidden to him as a worshipper of Yahweh. All he saw was a naked woman under a thin black robe through which he could see plumply quivering buttocks, and when she turned to urge him onward, the bouncing of her ripened breasts. She waited for him before a blue door on which was set the carving of the wheat sheaves which were sacred to the god.

When he came up to her, she moved against him, clutching his shoulders with her arms, her open mouth lifting to his own. He held her, shuddering in the passion that gripped him. For this woman, he would dare anything. All she need do was beckon.

"Come quickly," she called, catching his hand.

They ran side by side into the darkness of the great colonnade and up a flight of stone steps to a gallery that bordered one side of the temple. Below them in the vast open space before the goddess, men and women were thronging, crying out as the doors opened to reveal armed men in bloodstained mail shirts, their metal caps awry on their heads, as they came forward into the candlelit Room of Altars. They moved forward between the golden pillars past the great ablution bowl in a shouting wave, carrying four helpless females to the gigantic block of obsidian that was the Altar of the Gods.

Ahab stood by the rail, the woman holding him by his arm, staring down in horrified fascination. Two women were being dragged forward between the opening ranks of jeering soldiers, together with two young girls. They had been stripped naked in the palace, he assumed. All the way from the dockside quays, over the city cobblestones, they had been forced to walk on bare feet. Now their feet left bloody stains after them as they were pushed forward to the altar.

They were not screaming now; their throats were raw and painful. All they could do was roll wild eyes at the grinning men hemming them in. Hands clutched at their loins and their breasts. Voices cried out lewd invitations to them.

The woman in his arm stirred expectantly. Her breath was coming fast and her hips quivered where they pressed into him. "Proud Shubadad," she whispered. "She who was queen in Phoenicia."

Ahab stared down at a struggling, writhing woman whose face was streaked with tears and grime. Her hair had become disarranged during the nightmarish walk from the harbor but it showed traces of the gold dust that had powdered it and a few chains still gleamed between her thick black hairs. The greedy hands that had snatched her jewels and garments from her had left her little else.

She mewled in terror as rough hands dragged her to the altar, struggling weakly and crying out against her degradation. Her eyes sought the ivory and gold statue of the goddess looming tall and gigantic in the torchflame and incense smoke rising from the tripods.

"Mercy, great Astarte. Mercy!" she screamed.

A row of priestesses stirred at her words. The foremost of them, a tall woman in a high tiara wound about with jeweled ropes, lifted her arms, palms outward. This was the high priestess, she who officiated at all the sacrificial ceremonies.

"Who is this who comes before me?"

"Shubadad, queen of Phoenicia," the woman panted.

"No longer queen," a man bellowed. "Phales is dead by twenty spears. Shubadad is here to be sacrificed that the rule of Ithobaal may be a good one."

The throng pressed closer, roaring. Unseeingly the priestess stared out over their heads. "Shubadad is no longer queen in Tyre. Let her make sacrifice to the goddess."

Triumphant laughter rose into the vaulted ceiling. Shubadad screamed, mouth open, muscles strutted against the arms that held her, that turned her across the altar. Ahab saw her legs lifted before she was almost buried by the men crowding about the great high altar.

Shubadad screamed and screamed.

The young woman pressed her buttocks back against him, moved them gently. She whispered a command. Ahab put his hand to her robe and parted it.

"Yes," she whispered, "yes, Ahab, prince of Israel. Take me now, for I am Jezebel, daughter of Ithobaal—and this night I am a princess, heiress to the kingdom of Phoenicia."

He gasped in surprise and at the insane pleasure of her flesh. Below them, they were bringing forward the sister of Phales and his two young daughters, throwing them to the ground and falling on them. It was a scene of nightmare, Ahab thought, though only briefly, for he was too concerned with his own delight to be philosophical. Vaguely he felt disgust at what he witnessed but it was a disgust that excited the primal instincts that are in every man.

This night a man had won a kingdom. Another man had failed to keep his power. Now he lay dead and his women paid the penalty of his failure.

Ahab's pleasure went on and on. . . .

Rael stared into the thick wine in his leather cup.

Across the winewet tabletop, Jehu was cuddling a serving woman. Jehu would enjoy himself with her. And that was all that mattered to Jehu.

He wished fiercely that he could be more like his friend, but there was a sensitivity in him that made him yearn for something better than a sweatstained tavern wench. Something better? Ah, why lie to himself?

The woman—priestess, rather, he guessed—who had posed so shamelessly before the image of Baal-Melkart was the one he wanted. Ah, there was a woman to set fire to a man's blood! He saw her in the air before his eyes as she had been then and his heart beat more swiftly. His long fingers tensed, closing.

To get his hands on her. Just one! It would make his years of study, the sacrifice of time when he had passed up the antics of his friends to become a physician, all worthwhile. He lifted the leather jack and drank.

When he put down the cup he saw that Jehu and the redheaded woman were moving toward a curtained doorway that offered entrance into the little cubicles that held a bed, a table and a basin of water. Sourly he watched them, faintly envious.

Jehu could be satisfied with substitutes.

He could not.

After a while he forgot the woman in the wine.

Jehu sat on the edge of the cot and watched the serving woman lifting off her worn woolen tunic. Instead of the loose breasts and overwide hips, his staring eyes were seeing the woman on the pantechnicon. The breath scratched his throat. His hands itched to stroke and fondle.

"Hurry, hurry," he rasped.

She smiled down at him, tossing aside her tunic, throwing back her long red hair. Oh, she was fortunate, this night. The Habiru from Israel was young, thewed like a working ox. She did not wonder what made him so eager for her flesh; she accepted his lust for what it was, and knew contentment.

The woman would have posed for him but he was too impatient for niceties. His hand stabbed out, caught her wrist, yanked her down on top of him. Astarte! He was eager. Wild. Kind of crazy, almost. She giggled and let him do what he wanted, knowing he would not be through with her until the dawn.

Jehu groaned out his frustrations.

Always he had stood in the shadow of his prince. As long as he could remember, Ahab had always taken first choice. He was prince in Israel; Jehu was only an officer, the youngest son of a grain merchant. He had seen no future in industry with two older brothers already taking over the management of the grist mills, and because he was naturally strong and quick, had turned instead to the war chariots for his career.

He did not regret his choice, no. But he was cast into close association with Ahab who was a soldier and a good one, and soon the two were fast friends. He might hope to be commander of the armies were it not for Ahab, who took the poled banner of leader as a matter of his rank.

Ahab also took the choicest loot when there was a war, and the loveliest of the women who had been made prisoners. Just once, just once Jehu would have liked to make the first selection. Like tonight. The woman on the god-wagon had chosen Ahab. Not because of his good looks, nor because of his princely bearing. Only because Rael had howled out his rank to her in the stark fright that gripped him.

"Damn her," he growled.

"Who, honey?" panted the woman.

"The bitch on the dais of Baal-Melkart."

She trailed laughter into the night. "Oh, her. A wild one, that Jezebel. You'd think she'd be satisfied with being a rich man's daughter, wouldn't you? But not her. She has to play at being a priestess, too."

"Jezebel? You know her?"

"The whole city knows her. Oh, you're a stranger. I forgot. Her father is Ithobaal—honey, you all right?"

"I'm all right. Ithobaal? Isn't he the one leading the revolt?"

"And if it succeeds, he'll be king in Phoenicia. Some people have all the luck, don't they?"

Jehu began to laugh. The woman rolled her hips at him, felt his laughter turn to harsh sobs. Her arms drew his head down so she could whisper in his ear.

"People like us, honey, have to take what we can get. There's a kind of destiny about women like Jezebel."

"And about men—like Ahab."

Destiny. Maybe that was it. Destiny waited on Ahab and placed his feet where he would walk so as to fulfill it. He, Jehu, was doomed to walk forever in the shadow of such a man. It would do him no good to rail against his fate.

He must accept the leavings, like any other servant of royalty. Like this woman panting and surging back and forth beneath him. She was no Jezebel but she was a woman and she could bring him forgetfulness of a sort.

He gathered her in his arms and brought her in closer to him, feeling her respond with soft, erotic cries. A moment later her teeth were biting into his shoulder. Jehu wondered if Ahab would have toothmarks in his flesh by morning.

Two: A Bride Comes Into Israel

1.

Omri stared from the high window out across the plain of Jezreel. He was a man of medium size, balding now with age, but there was still an intense vitality in him. Twelve years had he reigned in Israel, ever since overthrowing the former general of the armies, Zimri, who had in turn achieved kingship by murdering young Elah, son of Baasha.

They had been good years. He had done much for his people, his kingdom. As far away as great Nineveh in Assyria, he had made trade treaties with its king, mighty Assur-nasir-pal. In Assyria they knew Israel as the House of Omri, and his wisdom was known and respected. It annoyed him, therefore, that his own flesh and blood should not also honor that wisdom by bowing before it.

"A pagan woman," he growled. "A priestess of Baal."

"And the princess of Phoenicia," added Ahab, from a bench before the cedar table that held a score of scrolls. He had spread out one of them—it contained a listing of war chariots stabled at Megiddo—but his eyes were on his father.

When Omri snorted, Ahab smiled. He said casually, "An alliance with a powerful neighbor like Phoenicia is not to be shrugged away so easily, father. Such a dowry is better than any other I can think of."

Omri turned from the window to face his son. Pride beat strong in him at sight of Ahab. His son was tall and strong, a good soldier, a wise man. He would extend the boundaries of the lands he would inherit when Omri died. By conquest or by statesmanship, it made no difference; Israel would be a power in its world, and Ahab, son of Omri, would sit its throne.

But a pagan woman!

Omri shook his head. They thought their own thoughts, this younger generation. In his youth, when Baasha had been king in Israel, the young men were subservient to their elders. Oh, there were times when he had been rebellious, though he had not carried it quite so far as Absalom against King David, nor Adonijah, who could not wait for his father to die before attempting to seize power.

He supposed he might make concessions. It was true that Ahab would rule Israel in his place when the grave-bands were tied about his wrists and ankles; Omri did not like to think of death but a king must make preparations for such eventualities; it was the duty of a king to think of his people even after he was in his grave. If by doing so he might guard them against disaster, Omri was all for it.

Aloud he said, "If it will make you happy, Ahab—take this woman to wife."

Ahab gave a shout and raised high his arms. "Father, I thank you. Jezebel is the fairest of all women. You too, will come under her spell."

He threw his arms around Omri and kissed him on both cheeks. He broke free and danced a few steps, turning and whirling as did the dancers during the rites of Ab. He had never known such happiness, except for that night in the Temple of Astarte when he had taken Jezebel over and over again, in his mad attempt to match the frenzy of the blood-stained soldiers who were raping Shubadad and her daughters to death. It had been a night of wild excesses, of insane passions. He was eager to know such pleasures again.

He would know them, with Jezebel.

She had as good as promised as much, in the early hours of the dawn before they had slept together in the garden summerhouse, when the Temple was quiet, inhabited only by the bodies of four dead women. Her perfumed fingertips had toyed with his black curls while her tongue had chattered on about what their life together would be like, when he was king and she was queen in Israel. He seemed to hear her voice once again, langorous, sleepy.

"There will be no end to our delights, Ahab."

He closed his eyes, remembering, and his body yearned for her embrace. She was so soft, so smooth of flesh, so fragrant and good to kiss. Ahab almost groaned in his want for her.

Omri growled and waved a hand at him.

"Go do your mooning somewhere else, boy. I have work to do. Aye, I'll write this day and despatch a courier to Ithobaal."

"The date must be soon for the marriage, father."

Omri grinned at him. The boy was in heat to bed the wench, any fool could see. Well, let him get her out of his system as fast as possible. Then he could turn to the pursuits of kingship. Israel needed a strong man on its throne, not a lovesick youth.

He began to feel better about Jezebel.

2.

Jehu was packing his war gear.

"Not that I expect to use it in Babylon, you understand," he said to Rael who sat and watched him in the small bedchamber which had been home to Jehu all his life. "I'm going to enjoy myself, not fight anybody."

"You're running away from Jezebel, that's what you're doing. Why don't you admit it?"

Jehu planted his fists on his hips and glared. "If you were anyone but Rael, I'd break your nose for that. Since friends have a certain freedom with one another, I'll permit your fatheaded comments."

Rael grinned at him. "I wish I were coming with you."

"Why don't you?"

The young physician shook his head. "Ruth would have a fit. We're to be married ourselves, next year. No, I'll go with Ahab to Tyre and watch him take his vows. One of us ought to be with him."

Jehu paused, his sword and scabbard in his hands. Glowering down at the inlaid copper sheath and the silvered hilt, he muttered, "I suppose you consider me a traitor?"

"Not I. Omri wants to know what makes the Assyrians such great soldiers. He has to send someone who can make a sensible report to him. You've been a soldier all your life. You're a good choice."

"You think I ought to wait, though."

"Ahab does. He wants his friends at his back when he rides into Tyre. And yet he doesn't want to stand in your way. This is a rare opportunity for you to see the world. He knows well enough you can't wait until after the ceremony. It would be winter, then. No fit time for travel. Better to go now, in the good weather."

Jehu grunted, unconvinced. Secretly he felt guilty, as though he were running from a duty. In a sense, he was; but it was a duty of friendship, not of occupation. He tossed the sword aside; he would wear it at his belt on the road, wayfaring being what it was these days, where robbers crouched behind almost every big rock. The rest of his stuff, the war mail and his shield, even his spears, he could carry in his baggage. A leather purse heavy with gold coins would hang at his belt. There would be more monies waiting for him in Babylon; Omri had made arrangements with some merchants for credit.

All in all, he ought to be happy. He would be gone a year, maybe even two. By the time he got back Jezebel would be a settled matron, perhaps with a child to keep her confined to the palace. He would be in her company very little. Time would heal the hunger in his heart for her.

Jehu was not happy. He felt like a traitor, not only to Ahab but to himself. A man should face up to his troubles, his temptations, not run away from them. He glanced at Rael from the corners of his eyes.

The young physician would stay here. He would see Jezebel every day, might be called to attend her in childbirth. In his heart he envied him for his even disposition. Rael could face up to temptation, could conquer it. He could not. Jehu had the feeling that, despite all his own muscular bulk, Rael was the stronger of the two.

A man was what he was. Jehu sighed.

"I'll send messengers from time to time," he said. "I'll let you know how I'm making out."

"Ahab is waiting to say goodbye," Rael remarked.

Jehu swung his pack onto a shoulder. "I know, I know. Let's go get it over with." He did not like farewells. They smacked a little of dying to his way of thinking and a soldier faced death often enough without going about looking for it when it wasn't necessary.

They found Ahab in the courtyard, brooding. He came to his feet at sight of his friends and forced a smile.

He would miss Jehu very much. He put his hand on Rael's shoulder and stood beside him while Jehu had spoken and then left. At least he had one friend to stand beside him in the palace of Ithobaal when he claimed Jezebel as his wife.

Rael was thinking, Jezebel has come between the three of us already. And she is not even a bride, yet. He might have hated her, did he not lust for her so much.

3.

Jezebel stood before a toy temple, touching it with rouged fingertips. All around her was the confusion and excitement of the royal palace preparing for her wedding. She alone was calm. Her ears did not hear the wheels moving over the cobbles, bringing meat and bread for the feasting, nor the stamping feet of the dancers, the sounding balag drums, the reed pipes and flutes of the dancers and the musicians readying their entertainment for the occasion. Her every sense was occupied with the little structure resting on the ebony table before her.

"Such a temple will I build to Baal-Melkart, once I am queen in Israel," she told her slavegirl, Alanna.

Alanna was an Elamite girl who had been born into slavery of a Hittite mother and an Elamite father. She had known no other life but the service of Jezebel and so she considered herself privileged to speak her mind upon occasion.

She said now, "Israel worships Yahweh. He dislikes graven images or so I've been told."

Jezebel moved her shoulder idly. "Pooh! Did not the Habiru worship a golden calf while Moses was leading them out of Egypt? Did not Solomon permit his many wives to worship the gods they chose? And Jeroboam, when Solomon died and he took the northern kingdom for his own—did he not build temples and put golden calves in them for his people to adore?"

"Yes, but . . ."

"The Habiru have a weakness for graven images, despite what their Yahweh says. It's a failing I mean to exploit." Her face dimpled into a smile. "Ahab will do whatever I want him to do. He likes his pleasures, does Ahab."

"Yes, mistress."

Jezebel turned and regarded her thoughtfully. "I always wanted to be high priestess. My father would never permit it, though he allowed me to practice the worship of Baal in the temples almost as if I were a priestess. In Israel, there will be no one to forbid me from doing as I please."

"There will be Ahab," Alanna pointed out.

Jezebel laughed, "I can handle Ahab."

She turned back to the toy temple and caressed it. Such a building would she make in Samaria, and in Jezreel, which was a sort of summer capitol for the nation she would rule. Priests without number she would bring from Tyre and Sidon into Israel, to worship her god.

In such a temple as this all Israel would bow down in worship before great Baal.

Living babes would be cast screaming into the holy fires built before the golden statue of the god. Let their mothers wail and tear at their hair, as some Phoenician mothers were wont to do, it made no difference to Jezebel. Men and women taken in war would be brought for sacrifice into his temple, held down for the sacrificial knife that their deaths might bring the blessings of Baal-Melkart on Jezebel and Ahab.

She put her hands to her breasts under the thin muslin tunic, lifting them up as she felt a flood of desire stab her loins. Ah, and after the sacrifices, when the blood-lust was upon both men and women, when men forgot their heritage and were no better than animals in rut, these were the moments which were best of all.

She and Ahab would watch and then take part in the orgy. Jezebel was glad she had saved the young Israelite from death on the timbers of the god-wagon. He was young, strong, filled with hungers as vital as her own.

After a while she would tire of him, but that was only natural. She would procure, pretty slavegirls for him, or handsome noblewomen if he wanted them, while she herself would . . .

25

She smiled dreamily as her eyes narrowed. Those two companions of his, the one who was built like a stallion, Jehu, and the other one, the more slender Rael: they liked her. She had seen their eyes on her as she posed before the golden image of Baal. It might be fun to see how passionate she could make them.

Oh, it would be marvelous, being queen of Israel!

4.

The high priest dipped the myrtle twig into the golden basin and scattered drops of water from a spring dedicated to Baal over the persons of the young man and woman standing under the ornate canopy of white linen and gold brocade, the silver spears supporting it being held by two friends of the groom and two friends of the bride. The myrtle was a flower sacred to the gods; because of its eternal freshness, it symbolized affection and constancy.

Jezebel blinked when the spring-water touched her. Baal-Melkart was the god of weather, of rain and sun and wind, and water was a sign that he rained his blessings on this couple who stood before his altar. She wondered why she shivered at its touch. Certainly there was no need to shudder; she was gowned magnificently in a tunic of Cos linen so sheer her body could be seen and admired beneath it, and the value of the gems sewn into it exceeded the price of a small caravan. She was radiant with beauty, and no woman in all Tyre might match the glory of her long black hair.

A young boy knelt with a cushion in his hands; on it rested a tiny shoe. Jezebel reached for it and with her eyes cast down, handed it to Ahab. This was an evidence of good faith, an admission of the dependence of Jezebel upon her husband. In return, Ahab lifted a small coffer from another page —it was filled with gold and jewels—and passed it beyond Jezebel to the boy who reached for it; Jezebel merely brushed it with her fingertips in token acceptance of the bride price. As she turned her head to follow him, she saw the young physician from Israel, the good friend of Ahab, staring at her.

Jezebel smiled at him. He was so handsome! Not big and strong like her husband but slim and with wide, thoughtful brows. An intense type, with that full mouth and dark, piercing eyes. She wondered if she might develop a little ache or pain after the rites, in order that he might examine her. No; she must not give Ahab reason to be angry with her, just to gratify a whim. In her own way, she loved the prince of Israel and was determined that their marriage should be a good one.

The high priest was moving around in front of her, blessing her and her bridegroom. The ceremony was complete.

Jezebel put her hand on Ahab's wrist, smiling up at him. He was so tall, so powerful. His arms were used to the heft of a shield or the tug of a brace of chariot horses on the reins, but they also served to crush her softness against him when Astarte goaded his loins. Her senses swam when she remembered the night—how long ago it seemed!—which they had spent in the Temple watching the deaths of Shubadad and her little girls.

She hoped that night would live again this night.

Rael tossed the nuts he held at the bridal couple, keenly aware of a tightness in his chest, of a slow sullen fury deep in his mind. Not Ahab but he should be walking the Temple floor tiles with Jezebel on his arm. His should be the right to strip her garments from her. His should be the body to crush her softness. His should be the power which would make her his own and fertilize her flesh for motherhood. A man nudged him and Rael for the first time realized that he was trembling.

He understood also that he hated Ahab.

Jehu had been smart. He had run away to avoid trouble over Jezebel. Rael wished that he had gone to Babylon with him. On the other hand, in Babylon he would not be able to see the woman whose image appeared in all his dreams; as he filed out with the other merrymakers bound for the feasting, he wondered if those strange dreams would ever prove prophetic.

His flesh leaped at the thought.

Omri died while the marriage cortege was in Cabul on its way to the cities of the plain, that the prince might show his people their future queen. A dusty rider threw himself from his foaming mount into the dirt where Ahab sat in the crimson saddle of a white mare, and rubbed his face on the ground. From the litter where she lolled at ease on fluffy cushions, Jezebel sat up straighter and lifted a brocade curtain the better to hear what was being said.

"Hail Ahab, king of Israel," cried the rider.

The men closest to Ahab turned to one another with startled faces. Ahab himself scowled and quieted his unruly horse with a hand at its glossy neck.

"What nonsense is this?" he demanded harshly.

"Omri died last night, my king. Now Ahab his son rules in Israel."

"Hail, Ahab," shouted an officer, clanging sword on shield.

"Hail, Ahab king," echoed a hundred tongues.

Jezebel put a hand to her throat, knowing the thick pulse of intense pleasure. So soon to be queen! So soon to sit on a throne, lording it over these adopted people of hers, these Israelites! Her eyes squeezed shut in her excitement and her red mouth curved into a smile. Just for a few seconds did she revel in her exaltation; then she smoothed out her features with an effort of will and pushed wide the brocade curtains.

A slave came running to help her from the litter. Other slaves dropped cushions on the ground so that she might walk on them as she crossed to the white mare where Ahab sat like a man stunned by a terrible blow. His face was blank, his eyes glazed.

She understood that he had loved his father. They had been close in the years of his youth and young manhood. He would be grieving deep inside him.

He started when she touched his knee. "You will want to ride for Samaria at once," she said.

Ahab blinked. "You are understanding, my wife."

"Go now. Fast and straight. Take only enough soldiers to guard you from harm. Leave the others to protect me. I will follow you at once." She saw him glance at the litter, and shook her head. "I would slow you, even if I rode a horse. It is better that you go alone, that you may take power at once. It is not good for a land to be without a king."

Startled, he glanced down at her. She had made him understand by her words that with Omri dead, the land of Aram under Ben-hadad its king, might rise against Israel as it had risen up against David and later against King Solomon. The Aramaeans were troublemakers, as were the people of Bashan to the east, the Moabites and Ammonites to the south. Israel stood surrounded—well, not quite surrounded, since Phoenicia was its ally—but certainly uncomfortably close to easy attack, on several sides.

Omri had a reputation as a soldier who had held his neighbors to a restless peace. His son Ahab was unknown either as ruler or as warlord. Men like Ben-hadad of Aram and Mescha of Moab would scarcely wait to test him.

Ahab was constantly finding himself amazed by his bride.

28

He had married her for her physical attractions alone, heightened by the memory of a night spent in her embraces; now he was learning that she was more than a sensualist, that she had a keen mind, quick to leap to judgment, alert to seize at weakness.

Already, she had captivated the cities of Israel by her beauty. The people delighted in her loveliness which she enhanced by the arts of her exotic Tyrian garb, in her generosity which prompted her to unlock the coffers carried on great wagons in the rear of their cortege and to distribute handfuls of silver shekels to the screaming, laughing crowds. The merchants she charmed by her knowledge of their problems, suggesting that they form a private army with which to patrol the caravan routes against robbers and promising to use what influence she might have with Omri to lessen their taxes.

Now she was demonstrating that she understood statehood.

"Leave someone with me you can trust to follow you swiftly and without pause. Zubral, perhaps, who is captain of your guards, or even Aael."

Ahab nodded. "Rael, then. I'll need to arrange military matters while I see to the burial of my father and Zubral will be a help."

No expression touched her face, but inwardly Jezebel laughed. She could have told him which man he would choose to take, which man to leave behind. There had been no need for her even to hint. She would have hugged herself with glee if she had not been so concerned with decorum. This big husband of hers could be managed very easily.

She waited there in the hot sunlight while he called his orders. He came back to her, the white mare dancing sideways, and leaned from the saddle to kiss her pouting lips. Then he backed away, waved an arm and toed the Sheban horse to a gallop.

Jezebel waited until Ahab was a dust cloud to the north.

Then she turned on a cushion and fell sprawling.

Voices cried out in horror. She heard the pound of feet.

Hands were under her arms, lifting her up. She had a brief glimpse of Rael's tight face, white and drawn, before her head rolled back and she let herself relax more fully into his arms. He held her easily—she was pleasantly surprised at the strength of his slim body—as he carried her toward her litter.

As he put her on the cushions, he said to a man at his back, "I'll have to examine her. I don't think she's too badly hurt, but I want to be sure. Break out the tent. We'll camp here."

Rael slipped inside the litter and drew the brocade curtains for privacy. Never before had he been so close to Jezebel. The golden draperies through which the sun shone with an aureate lustre seemed to bound an entire world in which he and this woman were the only inhabitants. His heart was slamming so loudly he could hear its muffled thuds. His forehead glistened with sweat.

He fought to control his muscles.

His hands were shaking fitfully when he stretched them out to the slim white leg bared from red leather sandal to her upper thigh. There was a scratch of blood on the knee, no more; it glistened red and evil against the white skin. His mouth opened. He placed his parted lips to the little wound and drew at it hungrily.

"Oh," murmured Jezebel.

Rael whispered against her skin, "Sometimes there is infection when the cut touches dirt. Why this should be I do not know, yet it is so. I'll draw the diseased blood—if there is any—into my mouth."

He bent to her again and put his palms on her thighs as if to hold her leg motionless. He touched her not as a physician but as a lover, with gentle reverence, and he made a caress of his touching. Jezebel shivered suddenly and moaned.

"Your hands are trembling," she breathed.

"I have never put hands on a queen before," he answered. "I am afraid."

She smiled and put her hands over his. "They are cold, too. Perhaps the physician is in need of his own counsel. Here, let me warm them."

She drew his fingers upward toward the opening of her embroidered tunic. It was a garment designed to copy the *peplos* of the Mycenaeans, its linen so sheer that where the diffused sunlight touched it, it seemed to shimmer and vanish. As he looked along her bared thigh, Rael could see the inner slopes of her breasts where the garment had pulled apart.

Jezebel held his wrists in her clutching fingers, lifting his hands to the parting tunic. A moment she paused, smiling into his flushed face, then placed his palms on her breasts.

They were full and ripe, soft yet growing harder as his fingers closed about them. It seemed to Rael that all time hung suspended before the tactile delights of his hands. Her lips fell open to aid her deep breathing and her cheeks were flushed. Lazily she squirmed, making her breasts move in his palms, adding to his pleasure.

"Your hands are warm now," she whispered.

Before the steady gaze of her eyes and the command in

her voice, he let his fingers trail away from her bared breasts, down across her body to her thighs. Now he caressed her tenderly, all pretence gone, and bent to kiss her flesh.

Jezebel smiled. Ahab was her husband, her king. Rael would be her slave.

5.

Since the time of Solomon, Megiddo had been a royal stronghold, an armed fortress fitted out with stables and stalls to house war horses and chariots. In his day, Solomon had brought horses from Egypt to breed and multiply, the finest mares and stallions in his world, paying one hundred and fifty shekels for each animal; with them he had bought chariots, paying six hundred shekels for each one of those light, strong battle-carts.

In the sixty years since Solomon had died, the Egyptian horses had multiplied until now they numbered into the thousands. Israelite craftsmen had copied the Egyptian war chariots, handcrafting them almost as swiftly as they could work adze and awl. The chariot forces of King Ahab made a mobile army which could travel swiftly and easily in any direction.

"But how swiftly?" Ahab asked.

His guards captain could not answer his question. Perhaps no man alive could do that; his chariots must be tested in battle before any judgment could be made on them. Ahab paced the hot spring sunlight, head bared to its heat, clad in iron armor fitted with golden crescents, his feet kicking up puffs of dust at every stride.

The border guards on the northern strip of Israel, that curved northward from the Kishon River and Mount Carmel all the way to Mount Hermon and then down to Judah by way of Dan and the Sea of Chinnereth, reported large bodies of Aramaean horsemen along the border. They trotted back and forth, staring across the river waters into Israel, but they made no hostile move.

For two months they had patrolled the lands of Geshur and Bashan where they touched against Israel, ever since Omri had died in his sleep in his palace at Samaria. Like vultures hovering in the sky above a weak man crawling on the ground, their shadow lay over young King Ahab.

He wanted to hit back, but what man could fight a shadow?

31

He knew that an attack would come. He did not know where, could not know until it was begun. And once under way, it might be too late to defeat.

For the first time in his life, Ahab understood what it meant to be a king. He had seen his father pacing the palace gardens, brows furrowed with worry, but in his youth he had not dreamed that where Omri walked, he too would walk one day. He understood it now. Ah, how well he understood!

He beat his fist upon the curving handrail of an unharnessed chariot. Desperately, he wished that Jehu had not gone to Babylon. He would have put him in charge of the army, let him stake out his patrols, be responsible for the warning and the defense of the country.

Without Jehu, he must stand alone.

Zubral was no help. His eyes slid sideways to touch the muscular bulk of his war captain, a squat giant in brazen armor. Zubral was a good man to lead a charge, to take troops into battle; but when it came to planning the strategy of a campaign, his tongue clove to the roof of his mouth.

No, Ahab alone must map out a plan.

He kicked at the dust in his helplessness, remembering Jezebel and missing the fever of her embraces. He wondered what advice she might have to offer. It was stupid of him to turn to a woman in war counsels, he supposed, but she had shown so much wisdom in other matters that he felt curiously confident she would help in this. Was not her goddess Astarte also known as the mistress of horses and the lady of chariot? Astarte was a war goddess as well as the goddess of love; her prietess might be as wise.

His eyes touched a sundial in the stable yard. Samaria was only a score of miles away. A fast chariot would cover fifteen miles in an hour; he could be at the palace before nightfall.

A little of his despondency fell from Ahab.

This night he would sleep with Jezebel.

He found her in a large bedchamber the balcony of which stood out over the palace courtyard where it met the Jezreel wall. She was bent above a table on which rested the model of a building. As he approached her, Ahab touched the tiny edifice with his eyes; it was a temple of some sort.

He spared the plaything small attention, for Jezebel was clad only in a thin Egyptian kilt, no more. It was hot in this early summer of the year, and though the upper floors were free of the heavy drapes that sheltered them from the winds that roved the plain of Jezreel in the winter months, the air was heavy and sluggish.

He put his hands on her hips and drew her back against him. Jezebel cried out sharply at the touch of his armor, turning to stare up at him with something like fright in her eyes. When she recognized him she squealed in delight and opened her lips for his kiss.

"What interests you so much?" he wondered, when she took away her mouth. He followed her gesture down to the little temple model.

"A toy, my darling. I had it made in Tyre and brought it with me to Israel in my baggage. Some day I would like to build a temple such as that so I may worship my gods in Samaria as I used to do in Tyre."

"Some day," he agreed casually. "Right now I have other things than temples on my mind."

She drew him to a bench and pushed him down onto it, undoing the cuirass straps with her own hands, lifting off his iron armor and dropping it to one side of the bench. Then she seated herself on his thighs and began to kiss his throat and jaw.

"Solomon built a temple, darling. He even built temples for his wives. And he had a lot of them."

"I'm no Solomon," he protested, laughing.

She disarranged the quilted jacket over which he wore his armor, to lay bare his hairy chest and touch her breasts against it, she nibbled at his earlobe. Jezebel could feel her young husband responding to her advances. His breathing was faster, his muscles strutted by desire.

"A tiny little temple? One no bigger than a—summerhouse? Where only you and I may go to worship together?"

"If Ben-hadad permits us to live that long, we'll build a temple," he agreed grimly.

She drew back and stared at him, plucked brows meeting in puzzlement. "Ben-hadad? Does he mean to attack us?"

He told her of the horse patrols along the northwestern boundary of their country. "They could strike anywhere over a hundred miles of territory. We can't cover such a long borderline, even with all our chariots. The best we can hope for is that the invasion will come where one of our own patrols will see it."

"And that the charioteer can ride in time to bring a warning," she added soberly. The impishness was gone from her face, for Jezebel felt coldness stirring in her middle. To be queen of Israel only a few months, then to be overthrown, taken captive and perhaps raped to death as Shubadad had been—she shivered.

"What can we do?" she asked in a small voice.

"I don't know," he muttered gloomily. "It isn't just Aram that troubles me, either. Beyond Bashan is the land of Ammon and beyond that, Moab. My father conquered Moab but it's only waiting the opportunity to throw off its yoke. I suppose it thinks me weak, untried."

"As you are," she said flatly.

He nodded, sunk in his mood of self-abasement. Only to the west where lay Phoenicia, his ally, and the Great Sea, was there any safety in Israel. Even Judah to the south might strike a blow to reunite the twin kingdoms that had split apart on the death of Solomon. King Jehosephat was an ambitious man who would give almost anything for a chance to extend the shadow of his sceptre northward.

Jezebel wriggled from his lap and ran to a little tripod where a fire burned slowly. The tripod faced a wall niche in which was set a small image of the god Baal-Melkart, of red gold with rubies for its eyes. Ahab watched her lift a cone of natron incense, dip and hold it to the coals in the brass bowl supported on the tripod.

When a thin line of smoke rose upward she carried the lighted incense to an obsidian kylix standing before the god. With an obeisance, she dropped the cone into the shallow bowl.

"Baal-Melkart, hear my plea," she whispered.

She turned and beckoned him to join her. Sighing, Ahab got to his feet wishing he had the religious fervor that possessed his bride. If he could have gone to Yahweh in this manner, as Jezebel went to Baal, perhaps his own God might give him the help he needed so desperately.

Jezebel tugged him to the tiled floor where she knelt. Ahab joined her, staring up at the golden image. What was it the commandments said? *I shall not suffer graven images before me.* Yet while Moses had been on Mount Sinai writing down those laws, his brother Aaron had made such an image for the people to worship, a golden calf. He wondered what it was in the makeup of his people that enjoyed the ostentation of idolatry.

His eyes followed the black plume of scented smoke rising upward before Baal. Cold reason told him that this was nothing more than a statue of a man with the head of a bull, seated on a Greek klismos for the worship of deluded men who gave it, with their minds, the attributes of godhood. The statue could do nothing to help him. It was only the idea which counted.

34

"—sustain the thrones we sit so that—Ahab!"

"What? Oh."

"You're wool gathering, not paying the slightest attention to what I'm saying. If we were in Jerusalem before the Ark, you'd want me to show some respect."

"I respect your gods," he said firmly.

She looked at him, a slow stare that he could not face. At certain times, Ahab had the feeling that Jezebel was only using him, that almost any man would do for her worship of the gods, even for the pleasures of her body. It was not a nice thought and it made him uncomfortable as though he were in some manner unfaithful to her, but it hid away in the back of his mind and showed itself only when he was under tension.

So that he would not have to meet her eyes, he stared again at the statue. The black smoke stood out with startling clarity against the gold, even against the painted background of the chamber wall, where a scene out of the life of Abraham had been limned by some unknown artist.

A mountaintop had been sketched in the mural showing Abraham with the sacrificial knife in his hand, about to plunge it into Isaac. The clouds in the sky were very clear. It was almost as if Ahab were staring through an opening in the wall to Mount Carmel in the distance. If it were not for the incense smoke, he would imagine that the scene was taking place before him, so excellent was its composition, so vivid its colors.

Incense smoke, thin and black against the clouds.

If it were night, the black smoke would be invisible. Then, however, he would see the red fire that spawned it as the natron burned.

Ahab gasped.

Annoyed, Jezebel turned to glare at him but something about his expression made her curious. She frowned, touched her lips with her tongue; then asked, "What is it?"

"A way to warn my army when Ben-hadad attacks. The smoke from the incense shows clearly against a painted sky. It would appear as black against real clouds."

"Signal fires," she said, and shrugged.

"Not just signal fires. Oh, I know they've been in use for centuries, but these would be somewhat different. They would have the added merit of being holy fires."

"Holy fires?"

"In the old days where were the sacrifices made?"

"In the high places."

"Exactly. And on horned altars. Abraham would have of-

35

fered up Isaac on top of a mountain, as Jephthah gave up his daughter on a similar elevated shrine. Today the priests and the corybantes who worship the magna mater Cybele burn their offerings on hilltops."

Jezebel opened her lips, then closed them.

Ahab said, "You brought a number of priests with you from Tyre. Summon more of them. Send them to the western border, there to wait until Ben-hadad invades Israel. Let them send up a black smoke if it is day, a great red fire if it is night. It will be a warning. I will hold the army in readiness somewhere near Kedesh, to be midway of the point where I expect he'll come."

Jezebel nodded. "It might be done that way. Certainly the Aramaeans will not suspect holy men busy at their sacred flames for our spies." She glanced at him slyly. "Such a service to Israel would be deserving of a great reward."

He grinned at her. "A fine, big temple to Baal-Melkart, with possibly another one in honor of Astarte."

Sitting back on her heels, she clapped her hands. "I shall bring many priests to Israel so that their holy fires may protect us. I shall bring priestesses too, that they may dance when the fires are lighted and so distract Ben-hadad's soldiers from their duty."

Ahab glanced at her body, naked to her navel. "If the priestesses are half as attractive as their princess, Israel need have no worries."

He reached out and caught her, bringing her in against him.

Three: On The Banks Of The River Jordan

1.

Ahab stood with his feet braced on the dipping floor of the chariot, left hand to its rail, right hand firmly holding the polished shaft of a throwing spear. The wind stung his face but he reveled in its bite. It made him feel more vital, more alive. The black plume of smoke—the *mas'eth*—which was summoning him and the thousand chariots at his back was tall and dark against the eastern sky. It had begun an hour ago, first a little thin plume, then a darker feather, until now it stood like a finger pointing skyward.

Somewhere close to that black finger, Ben-hadad was attacking.

His horsemen would be churning across the waters of the Jordan, his footmen behind them, spears and shields held high to give them better balance on the slippery bottom stones. Brazen images of the Aramaean gods would be held high also, to encourage the men to victory.

Ahab grinned mirthlessly. The god Kemosh of Moah had been helpless against Yahweh when his father Omri had defeated King Mesha in battle six years before. Today, the gods of Aram would also be helpless against Yahweh. Or so, at least, he hoped.

He turned and ran his keen eyes back into the yellow dust cloud trailing his war cart. A thousand chariots filled with picked men from the Megiddo garrison, crack spearmen, expert archers, the best drivers in all Israel, were in his wake. The horses were the finest of his many stables. It was a hard, mobile force, manned by veterans of Omri's wars.

All they asked of him was leadership.

His hand tightened on the spearshaft. Yahweh, aid me. Be as my right hand this day! He wanted to be a great leader in the tradition of such fighting men as Joshua and David; Ahab was no king to sit a fat rump and let others do his work.

He scowled. They were approaching the rocky lands of Naphtali, great gravel flats stretching empty, barren miles from Chinnereth north into Dan. Beyond the row of hills, from the tallest of which was rising the black smoke of the sacrificial fires, was a sloping spread of ground that ran to the river. Across the river lay the land of Aram, out of which Ben-hadad was hurling his army.

A slow climb to the hill crowns, then a mad dash?

Ought that be his strategy? Or should he conceive a better plan, something with cleverness in it? Could he even think of a better plan? He was no warrior lord tried in battle. He was a fledgling king, untested; otherwise, Ben-hadad would not be invading his country to win back the land which he had lost to stronger men than Ahab.

Ahab bit his lip. It was hard to put your mind on serious matters with a chariot floor rocking and jouncing underfoot. Trouble enough to stay upright, without working out a battle campaign in a matter of minutes. And yet, that was what a king was supposed to do. If you took the glory, you took the troubles.

Ahab scanned the hills. They were low ground swells, part of the mighty mountain chain that divided Israel and her neighbor to the west, Phoenicia, from the more northerly lands of Aram. No help there. They were good only to hide him and his chariots until . . .

Ahab touched his driver. The youth responded instantly, jerking back on the red leather reins, chirping to his animals. An excitement was flaring in Ahab. Impatiently he turned, gestured Haran and Issachar, who had been commanders of a thousand—the *sar'eleph*—under Omri, to his side, together with his captain, Zubral.

He told them his plan, crisply, asking no advice.

Haran looked wise, but said nothing. The older Issachar shook his greying head in dismay. "Divide our forces? When already the Aramaeans must outnumber us ten to one? No, no, Ahab. It's a mad scheme." Zubral merely waited, noncommittal.

The king opened his mouth to argue, then closed it firmly. *I am king in Israel. I argue with no man.* I am convinced in my mind I do the right thing. It was Ahab who stood to lose the most, if his plan failed. Zubral and the others could always run away, but a king had no place to run and still be king.

"Mad it may be," Ahab snapped, "but perhaps it is of such a madness that Ben-hadad will think it hard sense."

To Haran he gave the five hundred chariots which would filter through the passes of the hills and spread out on the Jordan plain. Zubral he kept with him, lest his gloominess infect others. And because he might need advice from him, he bade Zubral follow in his chariot dust.

"The hills will hide our five hundred," Ahab explained. "Where the river bends it is sheltered by hills on the other side. Ben-hadad will not see us." By the time he did, it would be too late to stop. Ahab risked everything on this insane gamble.

As his chariot rattled past the hill slopes close to the river, Ahab told himself he had no other choice. His force was too small to meet Ben-hadad on the plain of Jezreel; he needed time to form an army for such a massive battle, and Ben-hadad would give him no time.

The water came closer, the sunlight turning its surface to the sheen of molten gold. Then the hooves of his matched whites were driving into its ripples, splintering that aura, driving on through the shallows. In the summer of the year, the Jordan was not deep this close to the sea of Chinnereth.

38

Zubral rode at his right wheel. Ahab could hear his deep bellow calling out instructions to the following chariots.

"Keep a line there. Come up, come up!"

Gravel rattled underwheel. Ahab firmed his grip on the rail, letting his eyes assess the hills to his left. Just the other side of those ground swells, Ben-hadad was sending his army into Israel, first the chariots to smash a path if there was opposition, then the foot troops and last of all the supply train and the royal litter.

Ahab grinned. Ah, if only Ben-hadad were with his troops!

Nervousness went away from Ahab, this close to the enemy.

He found himself filled with a strange awareness of little things, of a striped pebble flung sideways by the rear wheel, of the flicking tails of the handsome white horses in their red leather harness and traces, of the red and gold magnificence of the royal chariot. No man could say Ahab hid his identity behind the plain garb of a common man, this day! He would be in the forefront of the fight, the first to smite, the first to draw Aramaean blood.

His driver drew back on the reins to slow the progress of the chariot, guiding it into the narrow pass which would bring them out onto the trans-Jordanian plain. The high rock walls picked up the sounds of their passage and flung them about in echoes until in Ahab's ears it was like thunder rumbling overhead.

Surely the Aramaeans would hear them!

All Aram and a laughing Ben-hadad would be waiting as Ahab came out of the defile, spears and arrows smiting. Ahab would die, his chariots would be penned in the gorge and held there until Ben-hadad could move his army to its other end and pin them here for slow destruction.

Ahab shivered. Yahweh, hear me!

He thought a moment of the priests of Baal, worshipping in the high places of Israel as man had worshipped in the high places ever since there had been men who believed in gods. He may have made a mistake, there, giving over the lands of Yahweh to the adoration of a rival god.

But—it was the only thing to do. There would be no suspicion of the priests of Baal, naked except for a hairy pelt at their loins, or of their priestesses, naked but for the fertility symbols at their bellies, dancing, chanting, making the burnt offerings as close as possible to the sky where the gods lived. This had been a war measure, not a religious affair.

The gorge widened.

The plain grew outward to the eye as the chariot rattled

from shadow into sunlight. Ahab drew a deep breath, conscious of fire in his middle.

Yahweh, my thanks! You have delivered my enemy to my hand!

The Aramaeans were laughing, joking as they pulled and pushed at the royal litter, a huge wagon of red cedar from Lebanon and mighty gold bands. It was far away from the river that teemed with foot soldiers, with chariots, with men splashing one another and cavorting as if on holiday.

Ben-hadad kept a loose camp. But then, he supposed Ahab to be in Samaria, lolling away his time with Jezebel. Let his men enjoy themselves. They were going to fall upon Israel like hawks on a fowl. There would be loot and women to be had for the taking with no opposition to speak of—Ahab was no Omri!—and the world wagged just for Aram.

Ahab went forward slowly, letting his five hundred war carts from behind him. He realized that the hills hid him in the shade cast by the sun at the angle where it stood in the sky. He would appear to spring out of the very air itself, with his chariots and his killing spears.

The chariots picked up speed, rumbling swiftly.

Now Ahab balanced himself lightly, forsaking the rail to lift the small shield buckled to his left arm and raise his javelin. The noise of their coming was a whip flailing his blood to molten excitement.

An Aramaean looked up, eyes bulging. An arrow took him in the throat. Then the sky darkened as more archers went to work. Their shafts whispered and men died, caught in the middle of a laugh or curse.

Ahab roared and hurled his spear, saw a man go down with the point protruding from his back. Another spear he hurled, and then another.

They were on top of the Aramaeans then, with no room to throw. Ahab yanked out his long iron sword and slashed at a face with it. His shield picked off an axecut and the axeman died before his return thrust.

The Aramaeans were trying to regroup but surprise had driven the wits from their heads. Their officers were either on the far riverbank, trying to get back, or in the water itself, slowed by its gentle embrace.

His driver was turning the war cart in a tight circle. Issachar was beside him, white teeth flashing in delight through his grey beard, yelling something Ahab could not make out. Ahab chuckled. Apparently Issachar had changed his mind about the madness of his young king.

No more time for thinking! It was up spear and throw. Grab a second and throw that, see men go down kicking under those iron points. The Aramaeans in Israel were coming back now, into the water jammed with men.

A shofar blew, its notes making throbbing, stirring echoes.

Now! Out from his own concealment in the foothills of Israel sprang Haran. His chariots seemed to fly to Ahab as he risked a glance. Their spearmen hurled their javelins, their archers shot coolly, accurately. Men died by the Israelite riverbank so thickly that the water was red with blood.

Haran drove through the thin ranks like a scythe through ripe grain. Now his chariots watered their wheels while his archers' bowstrings grew warm with use and the Aramaeans in the river fell and died like impaled geese. Those who tried to get at the archers had to come within reach of the taunting spearmen.

A cry went up from the cedar litter.

"The king flees. Ben-hadad goes!"

Far across the plain, Ahab could make out galloping horses and men crouched low on their backs. The king of Aram was no man to make a last stand when all he had to fight with were men demoralized by astonishment and terror. The surprise had been so overwhelming, it bordered on catastrophe.

Though Aram boasted the greater number of men by far, half of them had been out of weapon reach when Ahab had driven across the river plain. They had gone down like pins when children play at bowls in a city street. The others had been in the river or in Israel, lost men without their knowing, with Haran at their backs.

Ahab yelled to Zubral, "Give them a chance to surrender, to be taken as slaves. Tell them that with Ben-hadad fled away, they have no hope of victory." To his driver, Ahab said, "They will yield. Life is too sweet even in slavery for a man to risk it, when by his dying nothing will be gained."

Zubral leaped from his chariot and ran to Ahab. He threw his big arms around his king and hugged him like a son, forgetting royalty.

"You did it. By Yahweh, you smashed him as I might smash a bug under my heel. Ahab, this day you have won yourself a kingdom!"

He remembered that his arms held his king and looked embarrassed but Ahab only laughed and hugged him in turn. Zubral had been his father's friend since boyhood. To him Ahab was no king but rather like a nephew.

"Moab will think twice about invading us now, as will the

41

land of Ammon. I think Ben-hadad will respect our borders, too—for a little while, at least," Ahab nodded. "As you have said, Zubral—today I am king in truth."

There was much booty to be taken. The Aramaean soldiers threw down their weapons, swords and shields, mail shirts and helmets, shields and belts and daggers, on the ground before Ahab in his chariot. They stood naked save for their cotton loincloths, helpless in the hot sun.

The red cedar litter would belong to Ahab, now, and all the supplies and spare armor and weapons in the baggage wagons. A man ran up to Ahab and told him that Ben-hadad had left behind his wooden coffers filled with jewels and monies.

"And—his women!" the man added, laughing.

Ahab grinned down at him, making a sign with his hand. "Let's take a look. Bring them forward."

All work ceased as the women—over fifty in all, the concubines and dancing girls with whom Ben-hadad was wont to while away the hours while on the battlemarch—were pushed into full view. Some of them were sobbing, some stood with heads drooping, others raised their chins defiantly. Each of them knew her fate, rape and death on the blood-wet battlefield or a lifetime of slavery in Israel.

The men shouted in glee as more women were pushed to join the first group. There were more of these, by far. They numbered into the hundreds. Camp followers, prostitutes, cooks, it made little difference to them what man they took between their thighs.

Only the royal concubines looked frightened.

"There will be no fighting over them," Ahab said to Zubral. "I'll not have men die because of a fever in their loins. Dole out the women after the evening meal. Until then, it's work. Let's get everything out of Aram and into Israel." He chuckled, then added, "—where it belongs by right of conquest."

Ahab tilted his head sideways. It seemed that he could hear music, the rattle of tambourines, the thup-thup of goblet drums, the piping of reed and silver flutes. And singing, the voices of women and men lifted in joyousness.

He shaded his eyes, staring toward Israel.

Out of the hills they were coming, the priests and priestesses of Baal, the smoke of the sacrifices behind them, gold images of their god held aloft on wooden poles. Ahab felt his blood drive faster in his veins. He could understand now how his people had bowed down and worshipped a golden calf, why Jeroboam had given Israel golden bulls to adore instead of the

42

Ark of the Covenant, which remained in Jerusalem when the old kingdom divided itself.

There was an old lust in Ahab's blood, a remembrance of ancient tribal ways, when the winning of a battle was followed by the feasting and the soft loins of a woman locked in combat of a different sort. This was a sacrifice to the fertility gods, to the magna mater, the great mother who helped the women spawn new children that the tribe might be strong and terrible in battle.

And from the fertility gods to the war gods, to the deities of weather and wind and water was but a short step. All false, of course; Yahweh was the true god, the only God; but the others were exciting.

The worshippers of Baal were halfway across the plain, now. His troops in the chariots along the water's edge were turning and cheering, shaking their weapons. Ahab frowned. The men were in a mood for revelry.

He spoke to his driver who yelled and shook the reins. The chariot lurched forward. Ahab shouted to Zubral to speed up the disarming and the taking of prisoners. He wanted everything in Israel long before nightfall. After that, he would think about celebration.

He left Zubral roaring in his bull voice.

As he held to the rail while his chariot splashed across the Jordan, Ahab found his gaze caught and held by sunlight on raw gold. It was not a golden image that made such a shine in the afternoon sunlight. It was something else, something worn by one of the priestesses of Baal.

He craned his neck to see, then swore.

It was a Phoenician helmet with a high crest and red plumes to it after the Greek manner, with cheek-pieces and a nose-guard. It was worn by a naked woman who came striding through the dust of the plain as if she owned the world.

Jezebel!

Ahab could not decide whether to be angry or delighted. No queen of Israel had ever paraded herself before her people like this, naked and shameless as any street corner harlot. He knew she worshipped Astarte, and to that goddess the nudity of womankind was holy. Did not the women who worshipped her give their bodies to strangers as a tenet of their religion? The coins they received for the enjoyment of their flesh, they donated to the temple.

Just the same . . .

Ahab pushed the driver from the chariot as it slowed to climb the riverbank. He would handle the reins, go to meet his queen himself, as a royal conqueror! No driver should see the smooth white body belonging to his wife.

The flutes piped louder as he neared the little cortege. Jezebel threw her arms wide in delight at sight of him. She came running, breasts swinging wildly, the flesh of her thighs quivering.

"Ahab! Ahab!"

Yahweh forgive me! I cannot resist her beauty!

He swung her up against his armor, threw his cloak about her nakedness as he kissed her pouting lips. He bruised her tender nipples on his cuirass, drove her soft belly against the iron of his scabbard and something savage in him gloried in her pain.

Her own pain stirred her sexuality, Jezebel found.

With her hand she touched her husband, this big man who had just smashed the forces of Aram, and laughed in the delight flooding her veins. "This night we worship Baal-Melkart," she breathed. "We shall set up tents and build fires. The men and the women shall drink and know one another to the glory of Baal and his consort, Astarte!"

With his right hand stroking her smooth flesh, Ahab could refuse her nothing. She was witch and wanton, sweetheart and mother, all in one.

Eternal woman. Astarte.

At her cry, the priestesses of Baal came to the chariot, drew Ahab from its floorboards and began to strip him of his armor. Jezebel clapped her hands and laughed at his expression. Soldiers were approaching with the royal tent that had belonged to Ben-hadad, and the great cedar litter. The plain would be the scene of orgy this night.

Excitement flamed in Ahab.

His own tent was flapping in the wind, tasseled fringes bright red against its stark whiteness. A priestess was lifting the flap, gesturing him to enter. Jezebel was watching with feverishly bright eyes, a smile turning the corners of her ripe mouth.

Ahab glanced at the river, at the far bank where his army labored to bring the prisoners and the great heaps of loot to this side of the river. Zubral and Haran were on horseback, towering above the field, gesturing and shouting, bringing order out of chaos.

The victory was won. There was no chance of any more fighting. It was time to forget he was a king and to be a man.

He let two redheaded priestesses catch his hands, drag him laughing inside the tent. A number of carpets had been spread on the ground. A brass tripod coiled sweet incense into the air near his broad couch. Several chairs had been placed here and there, and a table where Ahab was wont to look at maps and read reports.

Deft fingers undid the thongs of his quilted tunic while other priestesses carried in vials of oil and ointments. Ahab wondered what . . .

His tunic fell away and then the cloth which hid his loins. Naked he stood in the tent while a woman bent her back and unfastened his sandals. Jezebel was lifting off her golden helmet and tossing it aside, coming to stand in front of him, kicking away her footgear.

The priestesses poured oil from their vials and began rubbing it over his chest and back. Ahab felt their palms and fingers slip wetly across his skin. Sterile caresses and soft laughter as feverish eyes roved his strong body, seeing his maleness respond to their touches. Other priestesses were laving Jezebel while he watched.

For a long time the priestesses prepared them, scenting their flesh, rubbing dry their skin, tinting Jezebel's eyes with green malechite and with kohl, putting henna on her soles and on her fingertips, reddening the jutting nipples of her breasts with salve. A woman shaved Ahab with a razor while Jezebel laughed at the sight and clapped her hands.

A bowl of fruit was brought and ewers holding wine chilled in the waters of a hilltop spring. They ate and drank while the priestesses attended them, while other priestesses brought a golden image of Astarte and set it up close by the headboards of the couch with a censer for incense before it.

Ahab knew that he was being teased by these corybantes. Skilled from girlhood in all manner of erotic arts, they delighted in brushing his cheek with their soft breasts or in standing so that their bellies must press into his arm or shoulder where he sat for their ministrations on a wooden klismos. Sometimes one would kneel before him, swollen breasts thrust out for the enjoyment of his stare while another smoothed his bared thighs with scented perfumes.

And Jezebel watched, saying nothing.

Before they were done with him, the oil lamps were being lighted and there was the sound of singing and men shouting from the strand beyond the tent. Ahab was clad in a soft cloth kaunace that gripped his hips tightly, leaving his chest naked, his muscular legs bare. The kaunace was tasseled in the Phoenician manner, being red with black braidings, while matching sandals hid his feet and calves.

Jezebel wore a thin *mafortes* of purple linen so fine the eye could see her flesh through it. It was belted with golden chains from which hung tiny doves carved in silver, sacred to the goddess Astarte. On her feet she wore the upturned *mulu,* so popular in Babylon.

A golden circlet, symbolic of his kingship, was lifted and set on Ahab's black hair, then firmed down so that it shone in a wide band across his forehead. Instead of a crown, Jezebel wore the golden headband which denoted her attachment to Astarte.

He was a king, this night.

But Jezebel was a goddess.

She put her hand in his as a priestess lifted a tent flap. Together they walked out onto the plain and stood there while their soldiers bellowed with delight. What is it in our natures that make us respond to the glitter of gold and the color of Tyrian purple? This love of show, of ostentation, of ornate symbolism, was a weakness, Ahab supposed, but could not check the indrawn breath and uplilt of jaw by which he showed his reaction to that outcry.

The concubines of King Ben-hadad were being brought forward in all their finery, as they might have come before the king of Aram himself. In their wake walked the camp followers, the playthings of the common men. Some of these women were already half drunk from wineskins which had been slipped into the women's compound by eager soldiers.

Jezebel clapped her hands.

"Dance for us," she commanded.

Musicians ran forward, fell to their knees before the royal couches. Their stringed instruments sounded wildly, a baccahanal of music that made the soldiers roar. A concubine stamped her foot and slid forward. She was graceful, small but lithe, and her ebony hair was so thick and full it shadowed her face where it hung beside her cheeks. She made a twisting movement of her shoulders and part of her tasseled candys began to slide groundward.

Ahab could hear the stir of interest among his officers. They were not used to these perfumed women of foreign lands who were so expert in the amatory arts, but their bodies responded to their appeal, leaning forward on the edges of chairs or stools.

The fringed robe slid further down the writhing woman so that her shoulders gleamed like marble in the torchlight. Her breasts came into view, rounded mounds tipped with scarlet. Slowly her hips shifted back and forth, while her arms seemed

46

absolutely boneless as they moved like wriggling snakes in perfect timing with the slipping tunic.

The tasseled garment still clung to her hips. The woman gave a soft cry and held her arms straight out. Slowly her white belly revolved, around and around as if possessed of a life of its own. Ahab had never seen a belly dancer before and felt the heat of the moment grip his throat and fill him with a wild hunger. Soft womanflesh quivering and shaking, stirring his manhood.

Downward moved the candys.

Her upper thighs were bared, and the dark fur of her groin. Always her belly shifted and jerked and her heavy breasts swung and quivered. She was crying out softly now, little plaints that might be made by a woman in her need for a man.

The officers bellowed. The woman was naked except for thin leather sandals, red as fresh blood against her flesh. Now she flung herself into the spasmodic fury of a pagan dance as old as man himself. So might tribal females have performed long ago, to excite the lusts of men in the fertility rites. It was as one with the sacrifices in the high places and the burnt offerings. Her hips rocked and her soft middle convulsed. She made her breasts stand outward, arrogant and rousing.

The performance went on and on until the woman was wet with sweat and weak from exhaustion. She collapsed on the ground, writhing and twisting, moist hips gleaming in the torchlight.

"Bid!" cried Jezebel. "Bid for this woman."

Men roared their offers while Jezebel sat straight and smiled her triumph. With the gold which these Israelites would pay for the concubines of Ben-hadad she would begin the erection of a temple to Baal in Samaria. Baal-Melkart had given the victory. The temple would be his reward.

Four: In The Royal City Of Samaria

1.

The banging of spear-butts on the wooden street door roused Mordecai from the handsomely scrolled sheepskin which he was reading, lips moving swiftly as he spoke the written words beneath his breath. He was a handsome man, a Nazirite and a priest of the great temple to Yahweh that stood just beyond the marketplace. He lifted his head, the fringes of his head-shawl brushing his cheeks. He allowed no interruption during the reading of the prophetical texts that took place in his home at the hour preceding the evening sacrifice.

Sighing, he rose to his feet. From below he heard the ripping of hinges, the frightened scream of a woman. His wife, Deborah? Or his daughter, Esther? Or one of the maidservants? Suddenly angry, he dropped the parchment on a small table and went hurriedly to the door of his bedchamber.

As he opened the door the voices came to him more clearly. Soldiers were below and a man was groaning as if mortally wounded. Mordecai cried out and put his hand against the hall wall.

"There's the one we want," someone bellowed.

Feet pounded on the wooden staircase. Three big men, heavyset in copper armor with highcrested helmets in the Grecian fashion came storming up the stair.

The priest fell back in sudden alarm. "What's this? What's this mean? Who are you? Who sends you into the home of a priest of Yahweh?"

One of the soldiers grinned. "Baal sends us, son of Mordecai! And we come with a gift." His speararm went up.

Beyond him in the crook of his elbow, Mordecai saw the face of his wife framed for a moment. She was struggling with the hands that held her, that ripped loose her tunic to disclose her flesh beneath; her mouth was distorted with a scream, her eyes wide and bulging in terror.

The spear came forward. It flew swiftly, yet to Mordecai ben Mordecai it went slowly so that all the years of his life paraded before his eyes in moments. He saw the child he had been, and

48

the boy in the school of Ethan the Court Scribe, and later the student at the Temple. He walked with Deborah in the early years of their marriage and stood with her when Jacob was born, and Esther, and Joachim and . . .

The metal sank deep into him, giving no pain at first. Only when he fell back off his feet and into the wall of the upper hall did the pain come in blinding red waves that flooded him with agony. He bit his lips against the cry that waited on his lips but he groaned thickly and his body convulsed so that he flopped about on the floor like a gaffed fish.

Above him his wife was shocked to silence. She stared down at him; only the fingers of her extended arms, gripped by the soldiers, made any movement; they writhed like maddened snakes. She whimpered and a sob came up from deep within her body.

"Yahweh," she breathed.

A soldier chuckled. "You call on the wrong god, woman," the man said. "Baal is lord here. Jezebel worships him, and Jezebel is queen in Israel."

Deborah scarcely heard him. She was remembering stories she had heard of late, ever since Ahab had gone out of Samaria with his army, leaving Jezebel to rule behind him. Many of the homes of the priests of Yahweh had been broken into by bands of drunken men. No one knew just where to place the blame, or on whom. The priests were slain and their families disappeared as if the ground had opened up and swallowed them.

A few of the priests had gone to complain to the queen, to ask that she use the household guards to patrol the streets of the city after dark, but Jezebel only sat quietly on her high throne in the palace and smiled down at the complainants and made little gestures with her hand, promising that the matter would be looked into. It never was, of course; Deborah understood that, now.

Her husband lay bleeding out his life with the spear protruding from soft middle. He had not been a man of war but he was dead by a weapon of war. He was a priest of Yahweh, a good man, unused to violence. Yet violence had come to him and he was unprepared to meet it.

A hand touched her side, bare below the torn *kolbur*, stroking her gently. The woman whirled, startled. The soldier was grinning down at her.

"Come along, sweetness. Now it's your turn."

"No," she whispered. "Oh, no!"

The other soldier put his hands up under her ripped garment

49

to caress her heavy breasts. "The other two have your daughter, wife of Mordecai. You belong to us."

She screamed as they stripped her naked.

The captain of the palace guard moved his forefinger about in the pile of golden rings that lay spread on the wooden tabletop in the guardroom. He was a Phoenician; his black beard was curled and scented, his armor ornamented by silver plates. A crested helmet lay beside his sword and scabbard on the table, to one side of the golden rings. There was a scowl of dissatisfaction on his face.

"Is this all? Out of the four houses you visited this night? A mere handful of gold? Do you take me for a fool, the lot of you?"

A soldier scuffled his feet on the stone floor. "There is more, captain. This is but the first, from the home of the priest named Abram ben Jonah. He was not a very rich man, being a young priest."

The others snickered but ceased their mirth as burly Kition stared at them. "And his womanfolk? Were they young, too?" he asked wryly. "You know our agreement, made with the queen's consent. The priests are to die, their women enjoyed and slain, their treasure to be divided among us all."

"We know, Kition."

"The women have been denied me, since I must remain on duty in the palace lest any come to complain while our men are carrying out their duties. The most I can hope for is a bit of profit. And this I will not be denied."

The soldiers nodded, watching their captain carefully. He could be cruel, could Kition; they had seen him order men flogged for slight infractions of the rules he had laid down for their behavior; where treasure was concerned, he would be even worse.

"We will wait together, you four and I," Kition went on. "When the others arrive, we will learn how much loot they bring with them. If theirs tallies more than yours, we will consider your punishment."

The men looked at one another; one of them shrugged, saying, "It is possible there is more, that we forgot to bring some of it inside."

"Go and look again," Kition said with a grim smile.

They were back within minutes, carrying a leather sack which they upended over the table. Kition said nothing as golden vessels and jeweled baubles tumbled out before him, but his eyes glittered with a feral light. With his share of this

50

wealth, he could live in a small city of his homeland like a noble. He was very glad that he had volunteered to serve in Israel with Jezebel.

"This is better," he nodded. "I ought to whip you anyhow, as a spur to your memories in the future, but I do not think you will cheat me ever again. We understand one another, do we not?"

The soldiers nodded eagerly, their relief like a light shining on their faces. From the beginning, they had never quite believed they could fool Kition. Now they were convinced of the fact.

They waited for their fellows in a little silence as Kition lifted the golden vessels one by one into the light of a flaming torch and examined them, grunting from time to time in satisfaction at their weight and color. She will destroy the whole priestly class in Israel if she keeps up this blood bath, he was thinking. Four families a night for the past month, always in the dead of night and in secret, with no one to be blamed for the killing— it had been cleverly thought out.

Ah, Jezebel was a sly one.

2.

Jezebel stretched in the brilliant light of the flaming oil boats. Except for her physician, Rael, she was alone in the upper chambers of the palace. Long since, the evening meal platters had been taken away, leaving only tall silver ewers that held the wines of Gilboa. Rael was standing beside a tripod that held a smoking incense bowl, pouring the red Gilboan into two silver goblets.

"You make me angry with you," she pouted.

He turned and came to the low couch where she lay relaxed, her head on thick, scented cushions, one naked leg bent at the knee. Jezebel wore only a thin film of linen; under it her body made fleshly curves. Lazily she stretched up one arm, caught the goblet he handed her in ringed fingers.

"Why do you?" she asked again, gazing at him over the silver rim as she began to sip. "It's such a little thing I ask. A phial of poison, no more—with which to kill the dogs that bay beneath my window of nights."

Rael sat beside the lounge on a footstool. He looked down into his own goblet. "Jezebel, strange things have been happening in Samaria of late. Armed men have been roaming the streets, breaking in upon the holy men of Israel, slaying them and their families."

Her eyes widened as she stared at him. "I know that and I intend to do something about it."

"You do?" he cried in surprise.

He is such an innocent, so young and so filled with faith in people! It is time he learned that when a man walks with kings or even in their shadows, he must follow the ways of royalty.

"I have invited Benajah bar-Simon the high priest to meet with me tomorrow. Together, we will work out a plan by which to beard these ruffians, who prey upon the holy men."

His delight was a brightness in his eyes as he leaned forward, putting a hand on the lounge for earnestness. "I am glad that you have made this decision. And Ahab will be happy, too."

She made a face. "Ahab, Ahab. He's so busy with his armies he's forgotten kings have other duties, too. He leaves all his cares to me."

Rael grinned, "And you love it."

Jezebel laughed throatily, letting him see her tongue in her open mouth. "I can never fool you, Rael. You see through me as if I were made of glass." She stretched beneath his eyes, turning on the couch so that her warm thigh pressed his hand deeper into the cushions. Smiling, she reached out and ran her palm down his shaven cheek.

"Dear Rael. Whatever would I do without you to advise me? You keep in contact with the people through your visits to their homes as a physician, and you keep me informed of what the people are thinking. It's important for a ruler to know that."

Rael was trembling, suddenly. The soft thigh weighting down his hand was smooth and scented, and as the queen leaned forward, a slit in her linen tunic parted, revealing a magnificent breast. He wondered if Jezebel knew how her nearness affected him. If she did, surely she would not sit in such disarray before him. Burned into his mind was the memory of the afternoon she had fallen and he had examined her for injuries.

His lips twitched as he recalled also how he had caressed her skin with his mouth. His lungs needed air, suddenly; it became hard to breathe. He would have sat back, away from her, but now her palm was moving away from his cheek to the back of his neck. Her hand tugged gently.

"Tell me of your people, Rael," she murmured, smiling, drawing him from the stool onto the carpet beside the lounge.

52

"Forget I am your queen for a little while. Pretend I am just an Israelite girl with whom you gossip."

She moved a cushion, twisting to make room for his head on her soft thigh. Rael quivered as he sat beside his queen with his cheek touching her fleshy leg; his nostrils caught the scent of her womanhood, and up this close he could see her body clearly through the linen sheath that covered it.

"What shall I say, Jezebel?"

"The people do not like me, do they? They blame me for the deaths of their holy men."

"I'm afraid they do. They have seen workmen come from Phoenicia to begin the temple of Baal. They watch the priests and corybantes walk the streets of Samaria as if they owned it."

"They helped Ahab win a victory!"

"No one denies that. We are grateful."

" 'We'? Are you one of them—and against me?"

"Oh, no—never that!"

In his agitation at her accusation he turned his head so he could look up into her face. She seemed about to weep to his feverish gaze. His heart thumped crazily as he caught at her hands and covered them with kisses, kneeling beside the lounge.

"I adore you, Jezebel. You know that. You must know it, being a woman. In your heart you know you are dearer to me than any living thing."

Above his bent head, the woman smiled. She enjoyed this adoration, she admitted frankly. It was important to her as a woman and as a queen. But she pretended anger, drawing her hands from him, shifting away from him on the lounge.

"Words, Rael. Only words!"

"I swear by Yahweh—I do adore you."

"Yet you deny my slightest request. I ask for poison—and you shake your head. Like a husband of twenty years! I thought you loved me."

He panted out words with which to tell her of the fevers that burned his body at the mere thought of her, his queen. Love was not a word to describe the way he felt about her. He was mad with desire, wild with longing. If she wanted poison he would give it to her. This he vowed on the very love of which he spoke.

Jezebel pouted. "Oh, I don't want your poison. I can get a poison anywhere—am I not the queen? My guardsmen will fetch it to me. Captain Kition, for instance. He'll be only too happy to serve me."

Rael drew a sobbing breath. "No, not the captain. I shall bring it. A lethal liquid which will kill swiftly—and leave no after affects by which anyone can detect its presence."

In his protestations, Rael had forgotten Jezebel was his queen. Holding her hands and kissing them, abandoning her hands to kiss her soft thighs as proof of his devotion, he had disarranged her tunic. Its slits were wider, baring the mound of her belly and the entire length of one pale leg. His queen did not cover herself but let him feast his eyes. A man who has been gratified in his desires is a man who lost interest. She would keep Rael at fever heat until after he had given her what she wanted.

"Is there such a poison, Rael?" she wondered.

"Yes, yes. It is concocted of the hemlock leaf and another ingredient from the land of Ind with which I have experimented."

"I would not like even a dog to suffer."

"Death will be almost painless."

Jezebel ran her fingers through the hair of the youth who bent above her thigh, running his mouth up and down its surface. "When will you bring it to me?"

"This very night, if you wish."

Jezebel smiled. "Tomorrow will do as well. I have no special desire to kill the . . . animals . . . this night. In fact, I'm rather tired. So tired that I must send you home so I can sleep."

"Yes," he breathed, and rose to his feet.

His eyes were glittering as he studied the woman who lay before him so indolently, a white arm dangling from the couch to the carpet, her tunic nothing but a mist upon her flesh. His every instinct bade him hurl himself upon her, sate the desperate hunger of his loins in her body, but he knew that this would be a mistake. Jezebel was his queen. If she wanted him, she would take him. He must be patient.

"Tomorrow, then," he said thickly.

Jezebel waited until he stumbled from the room before she writhed off the couch and out of the revealing tunic. She walked naked in her sandals to the window that looked over the plain of Jezreel. Below her she could hear the dogs snuffling, padding about the compound near the wall that took its name from the plain itself. Putting her ringed hands beneath her breasts she lifted them high, to let the cooling wind soothe their heat.

Tomorrow she would hold a phial of deadly poison in her hand. Tomorrow the high priest of Yahweh would come to visit her. Tomorrow she would receive Rael once again into her bedchamber.

Tomorrow, tomorrow. . . .

3.

Benajah bar-Simon, the high priest, was an old man. He had been born in the reign of Jeroboam, some years after the kingdom of Solomon had been divided into Israel and Judah. He had lived through the reigns of several kings, siding always with the priests of Judah who claimed the only true worship of Yahweh was conducted in Jerusalem at the Temple of Solomon. He was a disputatious, arrogant man, and he hated the queen of Israel with a sincere and honest fervor.

He would never have come to the palace except for the fact that the soldiers had made another raid the night before; Phoenician soldiers, he was certain, but he had no proof. All he could go on was hearsay and gossip and these were not enough to bring an accusation before royalty.

As he stamped over the anteroom tiles, shoulders bowed with age, his fringed *ma'aphoret* swinging to his strides, Benajah told himself that the most he could do was beg Jezebel for protection, for patrols of honest Israelite spearmen to walk the streets at night. Israelites respected their holy men; they would see no harm came to them.

Jezebel was waiting for him, very regal in a purple mantle over a white tunic belted with golden rings. Benajah was faintly surprised; tales had leaked out of the palace of Ahab that his wife was addicted to the pagan garments of her homeland, the thin linens of Cos through which her body could be seen and admired. He decided her modesty today was a tribute to his age and rank.

He came to a stop and bowed his head, waiting.

"Hail, Benajah bar-Simon," said Jezebel brightly, and clapped her hands. A slavegirl came running with a tray on which were two silver goblets filled with wine. She knelt before her queen.

Above the tray, Jezebel looked at the high priest. Her hand had come up to pause above a goblet. Then she gestured at the high priest. "Attend the holy man first, girl," Jezebel smiled charmingly. "Sanctity always comes before royalty. Is it not so, Benajah?"

55

The old man inclined his head.

When the girl was before him he lifted a winecup and held it between the fingers of his two hands. The wine was cool; evidently it had just come from the springhouse. He watched the girl cross to Jezebel, saw her stumble, lose her footing, go sprawling. The tray and the wine went out across the floor.

Jezebel was on her feet instantly. "Little idiot! For this you shall be lashed!"

The high priest extended a hand. "I beg you, highness. The girl is human. She made a mistake. Forgive her!"

Jezebel stared over the whimpering girl who cowered on the floor tiles, rubbing her forehead against them. She was flushed, she knew; she made the perfect picture of a displeased queen. In pretended anger she slapped her hands together, then drew a deep breath. There had been poison in both cups. Adala had only obeyed orders by spilling the poisoned contents of the second goblet, that the queen might not drink it.

She drove a kick into the side of the grovelling slavegirl. "You heard the holy man. Rise up, then—and fetch another goblet. See if you can carry it safely, this time."

When she had the cup between her fingers, Jezebel lifted it toward her guest. "Drink with me, holy man. To a better understanding between your people and your queen." Jezebel appeared to hesitate, then plunged on, "I know many of your people hate me. I am a stranger in Israel. I worship Baal, a god you abominate. And yet, this is how I was raised. It has become a part of my life. All I ask is your understanding."

Benajah frowned. Jezebel appeared honest enough. She smiled at him, then sipped from her goblet. After a moment, Benajah joined her. The wine was sweet to his palate and good. He drank more thirstily. When the goblet was empty, the slavegirl came with another. Politely, he accepted it and set it on a table. He wanted no more royal wine. One goblet had been enough; already he felt flushed, almost feverish.

Then the old man was gasping for breath. The face of the queen was oddly blurred, nebulous, as though water were washing across his eyes. Benajah put out a hand and moved it to wipe away that film.

"I—I feel faint," he murmured.

The ivoried stool rocked under him. The floor dipped and lifted in frightening waves. He was falling forward, unable even to cry out. His every muscle seemed paralysed. He lay there on the tiles and knew that death was catching at his body with cold and terrible fingers.

Jezebel breathed deeply, looking down at the high priest.

56

Triumph was a warmth flooding her veins. She came a few steps closer until her golden sandals touched the grey wool of his tunic. Just so must all enemies of Baal perish! In time, there would be no priests left in Israel to serve Yahweh. Then and then only would Baal rule supreme.

"Benajah," she whispered.

There was no sound in the room but the breathing of Adala the slavegirl crouching behind the curule chair, rubbing a hand back and forth over her side where Jezebel had kicked her. Adala did not mind the kick; she had been told that Jezebel would pretend anger with her; a kick was only part of it. She had done her job well, spilling the poisoned wine across the floor tiles after the old man had made his selection. There might even be a reward of sorts for her.

Jezebel turned from the dying man to the slavegirl. "We will wait a little while before we summon Kition. The old man must be dead when we give him back to his people."

Jezebel sat down and reached for her winecup.

She was grateful to Rael, very grateful. He must not suspect what she had done, though; not yet, at least. He must be brought to heel before he could be completely trusted. Ah, well. She had the way to do that.

"Adala. The dogs?"

"They have been poisoned, highness. As you requested."

"Good. I wouldn't want Rael to think I lied to him." She held out the silver goblet to the girl. "Fill it again. I find I am uncommonly thirsty."

As the slavegirl poured the red Gilboan, Jezebel smiled as to secret thoughts. This night, Rael would be alone with her again. It would be as good a time as any to begin his final enslavement.

4.

Rael saw the dogs as he walked up the steps leading to the pillared porch of the palace. Rigid in death, they were being carried away by slaves with nothing to indicate the manner of their slaying.

As he had approached the palace he had passed a small wagon draped in black on which reposed the body of Benajah bar-Simon, who had been high priest in Israel. Shocked, he had paused to question the attendants who informed him that the old man had died on a visit to the queen. Rael had gone white, remembering the poison he had brought to Jezebel only this morning.

Had Jezebel used his poison to slay the holy man?

The idea was unthinkable. It stabbed a shaft of horror deep into the young physician. He must see the queen at once, hear from her own lips her protestations of innocence. Ah, and if she admitted her guilt—why then he would fly to Ahab, confront him with the news that his wife was a murderess. Ahab, busy levying troops for a projected war with Moab and Ammon, was out of touch with events in Samaria. He, Rael, would fill in the gaps of his knowledge.

Seeing the dogs just now, however, had given him pause. Could this death of old Benajah be a monstrous coincidence? Jezebel had asked for poison to kill dogs; the dogs were dead. Without proof to condemn her, in the eyes of the world the queen would stand innocent of wrongdoing.

You know differently, Rael. You know she is guilty!
Confront her, then! Accuse her!

Yes, this is what he would do. In his eagerness he began to run between the tall earthenware jars holding oil, lined up along this lower hallway like soldiers at attention. A guard moved his grounded spear in a salute, but Rael had no eyes for him.

The queen! He must see the queen!

His whole attention was concentrated on Jezebel. On the wanton who had tricked him into murdering an old man! Fool that he had been, to let a glimpse of a pretty leg sway him from his sworn duties as a physician. He would hurl his accusation into her face and watch it crumple with dismay.

The last long hall before her bedchamber seemed endless as he raced its length, his sandals making light, slapping sounds. His tunic flapped at his ankles to the speed of his running and his heartbeats were a series of thunderclaps in his chest.

He came to a stop between two red columns that flanked a wide doorway painted blue. The bedchamber lay before him, its gleaming blue and white tiles reflecting back the shadows of unlighted oil lamps, of hangings shut against the fading daylight. The room was dark, silent as a tomb.

Rael frowned. Jezebel liked light and laughter, the sound of voices and people moving to and fro around her. This funereal darkness, this untoward silence, was foreign to her nature. Puzzled, he took a step inside the room.

Faintly, he heard a woman sobbing.

He turned toward the sound. A kneeling woman was bent upon the ground, her hair spread out like a pall where she rubbed her forehead on the floor. She wore a shapeless cotton tunic dyed black, a funeral garment.

Rael stared around him. The great bed with its golden posts and headboards, its brocade drapes gathered by satin cords, was empty. The lounge where she had lain last night was abandoned, its cushions fluffed and uncreased. Even the balcony where Jezebel walked of nights lay deserted.

He moved across the room to the kneeling woman.

"Where is Jezebel, old one? Where's the queen?"

The woman lifted her face to him, eyes wide. Her cheeks had been whitened with pigments and streaked with black char. The hair he thought to be grey was black as the wing of a raven, discolored with ashes.

"Jezebel," he whispered, in utter shock.

"Rael," she whimpered, moving toward him on her knees, flinging her arms about his legs. "Rael—you came. Ah, thanks to Baal for your understanding."

"My—my understanding? What are you talking about?"

Her warm hands were on the backs of his knees and moving up his hard young thighs as he stood before her. Her face she rubbed against his thighs, weeping, sobbing, moaning out her despair. Against his will, Rael felt himself stirred by her nearness.

"What's wrong? Jezebel—what ails you?"

She flung back her head so that she might stare up into his eyes. "Haven't you heard? Where have you been? The high priest is dead! Here in my palace—in this very room—he collapsed and fell over so swiftly neither Adala nor I could catch him."

Fresh weeping convulsed her. She pressed tight to him, gripping his thighs, kneeling before him. Her body shook to the convulsions of her crying, moving against Rael so that he felt the firmness of her breasts and the brush of her belly against his knees.

He put his hands on her head, felt the ashes she had scattered on her black hair like grit between his fingers. His heart slamming, he pressed her head to him.

Twice he sought to speak, and could not. This was his queen kneeling before him, shaken by despair, by sorrow for an old man. I doubted her! I came here in anger to accuse her of his death! Contempt for his own suspicions worked in Rael.

"Jezebel! My queen—stop this."

She was growing hysterical, clinging to him in this manner. If he had not known that she was torn by sorrow, he might have thought she was a woman frenzied by passion. Her face

59

appeared almost to caress him as she knelt with her breasts moving gently against his thighs. Cursing himself, he felt his flesh respond to her movements.

His hands went to her arms. He lifted her upward, still clinging to him, whispering his name, sobbing her thanks for his belief in her. "I was afraid—so afraid! I am a Phoenician here in Israel. A stranger. Alone amid many enemies. Without you beside me—I would be as nothing. Rael—oh, Rael!"

Her arms held her body tight against him. Frantically she rubbed her cheeks on his, kissed his jaw and the corners of his mouth with her lips. If anyone should see them, he might think they were making love. Part of Rael wanted to push Jezebel back away from him, another part wanted to draw her even closer so that she might understand the true nature of his feelings.

"Rael—they will think I killed him," she panted.

"No. No, they won't," he whispered.

"They will, they will." More sobbings caught her in their grip. "The poison you gave me—which I used on the dogs—they will believe I used also on the high priest."

"But—you didn't."

She drew her head back a little. Her tears had streaked the char and the whitening so that she seemed a creature out of nightmare. The hair befouled by ashes made her seem a witch.

"Rael, can you believe that of me? That I had any wish to harm that fine old man? I brought him here to tell him I would patrol the streets of Samaria with Israelite soldiers—yes, Israelites!—to prove the honesty of my intentions. And now—"

He hugged her to him. Over her disarranged hair, he said, "I know you'd never do such a thing, Jezebel. In my heart I know it. So put all thought of it from your mind."

"Are you—sure? You aren't just—saying that?"

Telling himself that he meant the gesture only as proof of his sincerity, he bent and kissed her on the lips. Beneath his mouth he felt her own loosen, open just a little. She clung to him with both arms about his neck in a fevered embrace that made Rael quiver like a sapling in a gale over Mount Carmel. Her lips were sweet nectar, firing his blood like wine and her tongue was a moist torch igniting the fibres of his flesh.

"Rael, darling," she breathed after a moment, "what would I do without you to lean on? I felt so alone, so betrayed by an evil fate that—that I donned this funeral attire and sorrowed for old Benajah—and for myself."

Her eyes were suddenly impish beneath their long black

lashes as she flirted up at him. "I admit it, you see. I was afraid of what would happen to me. I was terrified."

Rael sought to gather as much of his lost dignity as he could. He tried to smile, but decided that his lips were only grimacing in grotesque mockery at himself. "You've been overwrought, Jezebel. Even if—even had you—no, this is badly put. The high priest died because his heart failed him. No more." Under her upturned eyes, he felt a need to go on. "Any physician in Samaria will so testify, upon request. It was a trick of fate that let the holy man die before your eyes this afternoon."

She slipped back into his arms, nestling her head on his chest. "You've made me feel ever so much better, my darling. I'm not afraid any more. There are other things to think of," she added, now in control of herself and once again an exciting woman.

He could scarcely breathe, Rael found. Alone in this dark chamber with the woman his body hungered for, he found that he was fast losing his sense of proportions. Jezebel was his queen. He was friend to Ahab the king, her husband. Yet right now, standing before her, she was only a woman and he a man.

When he put a hand to the bow that held her black mourning garment to her breasts, he moaned. Jezebel heard it but paid him no heed. She loosed the tied sleeves, let the tunic fall below her firm breasts to her white hips. Naked, she stood proudly as his gaze went over her. Then she stepped from the fallen tunic and gestured at the handcloth on the table.

"Moisten it," she ordered, her mood completely changed. "Coat it with suds and bathe me. You will be my slavegirl tonight." She stood waiting, her back turned to him.

Rael was like a man in a dream. Numbly he reached for the cloth, did as she commanded. When his hand was moving the wet cloth across her back and down to her rounded buttocks, he felt as though his flesh were on fire. When she turned to face him fully so that he might lave her breasts and belly, he dropped the cloth and pulled her against him.

"Jezebel," he whispered. "Jezebel, I worship you."

Naked, she pressed against him, letting him cover her lips with kisses. Not until his fingers sank into her buttocks did she stir, her hands moving to his hips, fumbling for the white cotton garment that bound his loins. Loosing its knots, she cast it aside.

This night on her bed, she would wrap this young physician in fleshly chains, bind him fully to her side. From this night on, he would be alive only when he was with her or served her whims. Naked she moved against him, letting him understand the warmth of her body. When he moaned, she smiled and put her arms about him.

"The bed, Rael. Carry me to the bed."

His arms held her easily, cradling her. His eyes could not get enough of looking at her, Jezebel saw through lowered lashes. Rael was a man dying of thirst who has been given a glimpse of cool water. She would be that cool water to his lips and fevered body. With the arts she had learned in the temple of Astarte, she would bring him to new life through ecstasy.

When she was done with him, he would be hers alone.

5.

On the great desert that bordered the land of Gilead, a man came striding. Tall and gaunt, browned by wind and sun, his hair long uncut and blowing in the hot *simoom*, he walked with long steps. His large mouth was set in a firm line and his shaggy grey brows were drawn together over slitted eyes.

"Evil," he whispered between set teeth. "As a foulness in the sun is the woman from Phoenicia."

Reports had come to Elijah in his wilderness home of events in Samaria. Priests of Yahweh were being slain in their beds. The temples to the Lord God were being profaned by the priests and corybantes who had come from Tyre and Sidon to help Ahab against the Aramaeans. Men said that the priestesses of Astarte had set up their little tents within the sacred compound where for coins or other baubles they took the men of Israel to them in lascivious embraces to honor their own love goddess.

"Abominations," breathed Elijah. "Harlotries cursed by God!"

Someone must speak out against the Phoenician woman. He was the man selected by Yahweh to stand against her indecencies, against the pagan idolatries taking place in Samaria. His lips would thunder out denunciations of the queen. His tongue would speak the truth, as Nathan had spoken truth to King David when he whored with Bathsheba.

Elijah spat in disgust. Fertility rites! Ridiculous. The ancient fertility cults were an excuse to assuage the lusts of the flesh, no more.

In Israel they had never gone quite so far as they did in

Babylon and Phoenicia, where it was a requirement that well-born ladies lie with strangers once in their lives for money, and that this money be turned over to the god in the temple. Not yet, at least. Elijah grimaced. The way Jezebel was carrying on, killing off the priests of Yahweh and even tearing down His temples on occasion, it seemed she aimed at this in her own lifetime.

A people who had followed Jeroboam when he broke free from Judah and established his own kingdom of Israel in the northland after the death of Solomon—and who had bowed down in adoration before the golden bulls he had fashioned for worship—might as eagerly follow where Jezebel lead.

It was his duty to prevent this. And he felt exalted in the sight of Yahweh.

Elijah walked on without pause, without rest.

Five: On The Battlefields Of Ammon

1.

Ahab surveyed his host from the deck of a slowly moving chariot.

His troops stood unmoving, spears like slim young trees in a vast forest, their mail shirts and metal helmets glinting in the sun. These were his trained veterans, the experienced fighting men whom his father had led before him, whom he himself had commanded against Ben-hadad of Aram. Behind them were the new levies, the raw recruits who had joined his banner within the past two months. They stood as rigidly as did the veterans but they lacked their pride and confident bearing.

Well, he would give them confidence and pride before the year was out. Beyond the river Jordan the lands of Moab and Ammon waited his coming. With these veterans and trained newcomers he would sweep into their lands like a scythe cutting through ripe grain, felling everything before him.

Moab and Ammon thought to refuse him tribute. Let them refuse! He would go with his armies and take it from them. Ahab was conscious of a flood of pride in his body. He was strong: with youth, with hunger for conquest. Just so might Saul have been before these same Ammonites or David facing

Goliath of Gath. He would go forth in his might of arms and bring Moab and Ammon to their knees. Ah, and after them, Aram and even Hauran.

All was in readiness.

His right arm lifted. Head high, his great cloak whipping out behind him, Ahab went as was his due at the forefront of his troops.

Behind him the footmen lifted spears in response to their officers' commands. Feet lifted and fell, raising vast clouds of dust. Flanking them, the chariots were already in motion, speeding swiftly. The army that Omri had strengthened until its fame was a byword even in distant Assyria was on the move.

Ahab was moving first against Ammon for it was from Ammon that the tribute money was longest overdue. Invade Ammon, smash its king and its army in a fight, and Moab might yield its own tributes.

Ahab and his army was three days on the road, bypassing the waters of Merom to cover the higher ground near the Jarmuk. They splashed over the Jordan not far from the sea of Chinnereth and moved into Ammon with banners flying and shofars sounding. Not until they were close to Raboth-ammon did a scout come galloping on a dusty horse with news that Dareel, king of Ammon, waited just beyond the next row of hills.

"His patrols are out, highness," the rider gasped. "Each of them carries a parley flag."

"Parley? I want shekels, not speech." Ahab grinned at his little play on words. Behind him, Zubral growled into his beard.

"It's a trick of some sort," the officer rasped. "Dareel is like the bag of a magician. Put your hand to him and you never know what you're liable to find."

Ahab considered this, head tilted. After a moment he straightened and nodded. "I will go and speak with Dareel, king of Ammon—and learn for myself what can be so interesting he wants to talk about it."

Zubral did not like it, and said so.

"Am I afraid of a lard tub like Dareel?" Ahab asked with a grin. His hand shot out, closed about and lifted a spear into the hot sunlight. "If he plans trickery—before his men can touch me this spear will be in my hand and on its way into Dareel's guts."

Ahab squinted. "Besides, Zubral—while I make my leisure-ly, kingly way to hold parley with Dareel—you'll move the chariots into the hills and the foot soldiers with them, to attack suddenly if you deem it wise."

Zubral growled and muttered in displeasure, but he knew his young king better than to argue further; at times, Ahab could be as obstinate and as balky as a mule from Hebron; as a man did with mules, he would wait to see how Ahab conducted himself.

In the meantime, he shouted, "You, there—chariots! On your way. Into the hills with you. On the double! On the double!" he was bellowing at the captains of the hundreds to go after the chariots even as Ahab rolled out of the dust on his way to the pass between the hills.

A dozen men waited his coming, mounted on the sleek desert horses for which Ammon was so famous. They bore a pole fitted with a white flag, the traditional sign for a meeting of leaders during which there was to be peace between the armies. To within a dozen paces of the little group Ahab urged his chariot, then slewed it around in a shower of dust and pebbles.

With a grin he tossed the reins to his charioteer. He saw admiration in the eyes of the Ammonites. Their own king was a huge mountain of a man, all fat and blubber. They appreciated seeing a king who was also a fighting man, able to take his own chariot into battle.

"What words has Dareel for Ahab?" he called.

The man with the poled flag cried out, "He offers talk, Ahab. A bit of speech between rulers. He offers to let you bring a dozen chariots to the meeting."

Ahab pretended surprise. "Why? Isn't his white flag to be trusted? I could come alone and naked into his presence, protected by the pale banner, unless he would dishonor it."

One of the younger warriors growled and pushed forward, a hand on the hilt of his curving sword. The poleman whirled and brought the back of his hand across his face. "Fool! Have you forgotten the flag? Next time, you stay among the women in the tents."

The youth flushed and sat shaking in the saddle. The older man, holding the pole so its butt rested beside his foot in the stirrup, made a low bow. "Forgive him, highness. He's but a boy. Dareel knows the value of the white flag."

"I hope so," said Ahab easily. "For I intend to go see him just as I am, with only my charioteer to side me." He wanted to play for time, to enable Zubral to line these foothills, which afforded excellent protection for hiding men behind tall bay trees or clumps of high-growing labdanum, with battle-carts and archers. "What is it King Dareel wants to discuss?"

The patrol commander shrugged. "He says nothing to us, lord. He is one who keeps his counsel to himself."

A wise rule, thought Ahab, and reached for the leather reins. He called to his horses and urged them forward, between the pass-walls until the plain of Aphek spread out before him.

The scarlet and gold tent of King Dareel caught the eye at once. Tall and coned, it towered above the grey tents of his officers. Even from this distance, Ahab could see the carved and gilded throne where Dareel sat surrounded by men in armor and what looked like women wearing tinted linens.

A corner of his mind told Ahab he ought to surrender the reins to his charioteer; it was not right for a king to drive his own war cart to a meeting between rulers. On the other hand, it was not right for him to come alone; he should be surrounded by chariots and officers and by trumpeters blowing horns. In the eyes of a ruler like Dareel, this display of horsemanship might smack of weakness.

No matter. He was committed to his act.

Ahab made the best of it, urging his matched stallions to a hard run, raising dust, making the wheels bounce so that he rode the floorboards like a sailor the deckplanks in a high sea. When he was fifty paces from that gilded throne—how they stared, all of them!—he yanked back on the reins, crying out to the bays. The muscles in his arms and shoulders bulged to the power of his tug.

He made a barbaric, martial figure, he realized suddenly. Only a man secure in his own power, in his personal might, would come this way to meet an enemy. Before the wheels had stopped he was tossing the reins to his driver and leaping from the moving war cart.

He ran a few steps until he was in front of the gilded throne, then made a mocking bow, sweeping his purple cloak up and over a shoulder. "Ahab comes to Dareel as a man, to hear the words he has to say. Greetings from Israel to the king of Ammon."

Even the old lard tub was impressed, he saw. Dareel was leaning forward, pig eyes glinting through folds of flesh, a pudgy hand knotted into a fist and resting on a thigh that was hidden under the heavy brocade of his royal robes.

"Greetings to Ahab of Israel from King Dareel," he rasped in reply. "I had not expected you so soon—and without a royal guard."

"What need have I of guards?" Ahab asked lightly. "Your men carry a parley flag and I am speaking to a subject king, a king whose lands owe me tribute monies."

Dareel flushed darkly and sat so that the upright back of his gilded throne pressed into his spine. "You touch the heart of the matter at once, Ahab. I refer to the tribute which I have paid Israel in the person of your father, for the past fifteen years."

"Now you don't want to pay it any more."

Dareel looked surprised at such forthrightness. He shifted uncomfortably on his throne and nodded, "It is so. My obligation ended with the death of your father. My debt is not to you."

Ahab grinned. "Then let us discuss it, Dareel. Perhaps I can make you see reason." He gestured imperiously to a man seated on a stool. The man glanced at Dareel, who nodded; the man ran to Ahab and set the stool down before him. Ahab seated himself.

He took a while to straighten his garments, to arrange his scabbard so that his sword was thrust upright between his knees. There was an open path between himself and the gilded throne; at the slightest hint of treachery he could be through that path and at the throne with his swordpoint thrust against Dareel's windpipe. Meanwhile, his own men were gathering in the foothills.

"There is nothing to discuss," said Dareel peevishly. "I have made up my mind. I am refusing you so much as a copper maneh."

"I have brought a strong army into Ammon," Ahab said slowly. His glance told the king that the Israelite army was stronger than his own. "I would not like to turn it loose on your thousands."

Dareel scowled blackly. "You see only a small portion of my army, Ahab. I have soldiers as many as the sands of the desert."

Ahab shrugged elaborately, spreading his hands. "So many of your men are not in sight, Dareel. Before you could summon them, my own army would overwhelm this force you have here at your disposal. In a matter of minutes, I might add."

Dareel leered. "Don't be too sure of that, Ahab. Your chariots would founder in the soft sands with which we are surrounded while my men on horseback would be as mobile as a dancing girl on hot coals." His laughter came up through his throat, making his body shake all over.

His ringed hand made a motion. "And speaking of girls—Tallia! Fetch us refreshments."

Girls came running with wineskins kept cool by packing in springwater. They poured the red wine into golden cups—one for Ahab, one for Dareel. Ahab watched closely, thinking of poison, but the girls dropped nothing into the cups.

Nevertheless, he waited until Dareel had sipped half his wine before raising a goblet to his own lips. The wine was faintly tart, very tasty. It was a warm day and went down easily.

A Lydian girl holding a wineskin stood close to his elbow, so close her bare thigh brushed his bared elbow. Ahab thought of Jezebel. He had been long in Megiddo, training troops. This touch of flesh to flesh was like a fire lighted in his loins.

He gave no indication of his thoughts, rather saying, "You asked me to a parley, Dareel. Surely it was not to boast of the manner in which you would defeat me."

Dareel was a big man, with a large thirst. He emptied three winecups before speaking. "You are right, Ahab. I have given this matter of the tribute monies much thought. You are a young man, a young king, and are faced with a great task. Your father before you was a strong man, a fine soldier. He conquered Ammon with his armies and he held it as I hold this goblet. Easily and without strain."

King Dareel leaned forward. "Being so young, you have not Omri's gift for warfare. I should not like to see you humiliated. Go back to Israel, therefore, with your armies, and we shall let men say you and I worked out an agreement whereby you remitted the tribute in return for a treaty of friendship between our countries. Let Ben-hadad hear of this and you shall have peace in the north, as well."

Ahab turned his head to hide a smile. At the same time he lifted his winecup to the slavegirl at his elbow. As she bent to tilt the wineskin, her breasts moved forward, ripe and brown, tipped with dark nipples. Ahab felt the flush rise in his cheeks as he studied them, then let his gaze slide down over her mounded belly with its dimpled navel to her hips.

Yes, it was time he thought about returning to Samaria and Jezebel. Otherwise he might not remain so faithful to his wife as she might like. Almost reluctantly, he turned away from those firm hips so scantily hidden beneath a sheer linen girdle, back to Dareel.

"A fine scheme," he said slowly, staring into the goblet in order to gather his thoughts. "At any other time, I might agree with you. But—I have brought my armies so far—to turn back now . . ."

His voice trailed off. Dareel sat straighter, grinning. "Let me give you gifts, Ahab—not tribute, mind you—but presents as between friendly rulers. Take them back to Samaria as evidence of our friendship."

Dareel spoke out of an inner weakness, Ahab knew. The man was not yet ready to do battle. Why, then, had he come so close to the borders of his country? By playing a game of mouse with cat, he might have held Ahab off until he had gathered forces equal to those of the invader. There was no doubt about it: Dareel had a plan in mind.

Ahab shook his head. "I cannot consent to that. My people would make mock of me were I to accept anything but tribute." He flung his arms wide so that a little of the wine splashed out. "It must be tribute or—nothing."

Dareel looked disappointed. In a stab of pique, he flung his goblet from him. His fingers played up and down upon the arms of his throne. Heavily, he said, "There remains then, nothing to do but fight, unless—"

The king of Ammon swallowed his words so that Ahab could not hear them. Ahab leaned forward courteously. "Unless what, Dareel?"

"Oh, it is nothing. A passing thought only."

Ahab sipped the Arabian wine slowly, relishing its taste. By now Zubral would have coated the foothills with his soldiers. The chariot horses would be straining at their traces, hungry to run. The ground hereabouts was firm enough, being filled with shale and pebbles. Only a hundred yards away did the desert begin. Room enough here for a quick attack, if need be.

"I am interested in any contingency that might resolve this difficulty between us without bloodshed," he told Dareel. "So speak your mind freely."

Hesitantly, the king said, "It was only a duel between champions—your finest swordsman and mine. To the death. On the sword of him who wins would rest the answer to our problem."

Ahab relaxed. So this was his plan. Bold, audacious. Dareel must have sent spies into Israel to learn what manner of man sat its throne since the death of Omri. The spy would have heard the tale of how Ahab had met and defeated Ben-hadad, himself leading the attack.

A fighting king ruled the land to the west of Ammon. This meant a daring man, a man who might gamble to win high stakes. The challenge of the duel between picked men was an old one. His own people named it *'ish habbenaym*. So David had fought Goliath, so Abner had propositioned Joab when war stood between Saul and David.

As he sipped the wine, Ahab decided that Dareel had chanced upon some great swordsman—a slave, perhaps, or even one of his own people with a peculiar talent for handling a blade. Among the Habiru few men were trained in swordplay. Mostly, his soldiers used the spear—the *kidon*—and the bow. They carried the short sword, the *gomed*, but they were clumsy with it. Only the officers, who were mostly from the better classes, knew how to play the blade with any degree of skill.

He himself was probably Israel's finest swordsman, having been trained in its use by Omri's captains since boyhood. The knowledge was even more heady to Ahab than the wine he sipped. To ask for a volunteer from the ranks meant asking a man to go to his death.

With so much riding on the outcome of a duel, Ahab wanted no man to do what he himself did not. He would accept the tribute monies as king of Israel. He himself should fight for them.

As Dareel and his officers watched, Ahab stood and dropped his cloak, revealing his shirt of fine mesh iron plates. His sword was the finest money could buy, being a Greek blade of tempered iron from Mycene.

"I will fight your champion," he said softly.

Dareel stiffened, unable to control the glint of triumph in his eyes. He had staked much on this duel. From what his spies had told him of this young Israelite king, he was gambling that Ahab would risk everything on a colorful gesture. Omri would have laughed at him but his son rose easily to the bait.

"Reflect, Ahab," he said heavily. "It is to be a fight to the death. I want no Israelite saying I brought you here under a parley flag only to murder you." Then, lest he argue Ahab out of his dilemma, he added, "I do not question your courage, naturally. You are a brave man. That is understood even if you choose to back out of your pledge, once you see my champion."

Ahab felt the sweat stand out on his forehead. Dareel would not be so confident were his swordsman not a fine one; on the outcome of this duel he was risking his tribute money. Fiercely, Ahab told himself he was a fool; he was risking life itself.

Retire in shame, rather than risk defeat and death here before Dareel. Retire and bring up his army and settle the issue between himself and the king of Ammon. Forget this nonsense about a duel.

Ahab was a proud man. He told himself glumly, he was too proud. His hand drew the long iron sword from its scabbard while with the other he hurled the silver-chased scabbard flying through the air. "My charioteer will tell my people the truth, Dareel. He will say that his king accepted a duel to the death for the tribute money."

Ahab paused and looked across his sword at the king of Ammon. "That is to be the stake, is it not? If I kill your champion, you will pay the tribute monies due me? From this day on, as you did with my father Omri?"

Dareel nodded eagerly. "Win—and my tribute travels into Israel before the week is out. Lose and—Ammon is free of its burden."

Without waiting for any reply, Dareel turned in his seat and gestured; a soldier moved to a tentflap and lifted it. An instant later a man stood framed between those flaps, grinning evilly as he stared at Ahab, king of Israel.

Ahab felt his heart lurch. The man he saw was yellow, with slant eyes and a tuft of black hair growing from the top of his head and hanging down his back in a thick braid. He was naked save for a twist of cotton at his loins. In his hand he held a long, curving sword of a kind Ahab had never before seen.

The man cried out something in a singsong voice. At his elbow a smaller man, a trader, began to interpret his words.

"Chang Lun says that he will slice this man to gibbets and that if the great King Dareel wishes, he will sing a song as he does so. There is no greater swordsman than Chang Lun in all the world. He is a descendant of the Shangs who ruled his land of Chin in the long-ago time. He was swordsman to the emperor of Chin—before he fell in love with a royal concubine and had to run for his life."

The man from Chin was advancing as the trader spoke. On bare feet, lightly and with curious grace for all his bulk, he walked toward the gilded throne. Ahab watched closely. The man must have soles like leather to stride so on these pebbles. No hope to trick him by rushing him onto sharp rocks. The man was a head taller than Ahab, but he was not fat like Dareel; he was hard, muscular, a true fighting man.

He handled his curved sword easily, too, as one long used to its feel and balance. Ahab sighed. He had been king so

71

short a time! It was too bad. He would die this day and Jezebel would know his embraces no more.

The yellow man bowed low before King Dareel. Again he spoke in his singsong voice as the merchant behind him explained what he said. "Chang Lun is a great warrior. He has fought for many kings for the gold they pay, but Dareel is the greatest his eyes have ever seen."

Despite his gloom, Ahab chuckled. This Chang Lun was a flatterer. Dareel primped before his words, nodding as though they were his due.

"Chang Lun says further that his god, the great Yu, stands ever at his elbow, lending strength to his arm."

Ahab stirred. His lips opened and he cried out, "Tell Chang Lun for me that my god is a greater god, that his Yu is only one in a vast stable of lesser gods Yahweh keeps for his amusement."

It was blasphemy, perhaps. On Mount Sinai, Yahweh had said to Moses, There shall be no other gods before me. Well, this Yu, if he were a lesser god, could scarcely stand before Yahweh. Ahab squared his shoulders, whispering between his teeth, "Stand with me, Yahweh. For your people I fight this day." He wondered if Baal-Melkart would side with him as well.

A little space had been cleared before the throne as soldiers came and pushed away the serving women carrying food and wineskins. Dareel was leaning forward, eyes glistening. His champion from Chin was swinging his scimitar in vast sweeps, leaping and turning in mid-air to display his agility. Ahab did not seem impressed, only bored. Dareel frowned. The young king of Israel should be trembling with fear, the idiot. He was going to die today. His blood would spill and soak into the ground and Ammon would no longer pay out its tributary gold.

Dareel raised his arm, then let it fall.

Chang Lun leaped forward, curved blade straight out. A less agile man than Ahab would have been spitted on its point. Desperately Ahab leaped sideways, thrusting with his own blade, but the man from Chin seemed to stop and turn in the air, leaping aside.

A murmur grew from the onlookers. Few of the Ammonites would have been able to escape that initial lunge. This might not be the quick slaughter they had anticipated.

Chang Lun came bounding to the attack, his blade making blinding movements in the sunlight as he feinted and slashed. Twice Ahab met that blade, twice was his own sword almost knocked from his fingers. The shock of those two meetings ran up into his shoulder.

The man from Chin was never still, never flat-footed as was Ahab upon occasion, the better to get power behind his swing. The yellow man was in the air or leaping sideways or rushing forward, always on the move, always giving as little of his body to Ahab as he could.

The blades clanged together, again and again. Ahab was ever on the defensive. The man from Chin appeared to need no rest. He came in with sweeping strokes of his blade or used it to thrust, giving Ahab no respite. He would grimace and contort his face in an attempt to paralyse his opponent with fear; Ahab imagined that such tactics might work on certain men who believed him inhabited by devils. To him, it was a childish display.

His sword was no child's plaything. It wove back and forth and in and out and three times it touched the king of Israel. Once it glanced harmlessly off his iron mail shirt, once it slashed the skin of his forearm so that blood ran down it, and once it cut a wound in his thigh.

The wounds were painful but not serious. Yet the strain of this constant movement, this steady guard and feint were telling on his body. He was not used to such a steady give and take. Ahab realized he was tiring badly.

His left side was to the gilded throne, where Dareel was staring so intently. Before him Chang Lun leaped and swung; over his yellow shoulder Ahab caught a glimpse of the Lydian slavegirl who had served him the chilled Oethalian.

What he wouldn't give for a swallow of that wine now!

The thought of the slavegirl made him remember how her thigh had brushed his elbow as she stood beside him. From her his thoughts swung to Jezebel and—

Yahweh! The slavegirl!

There was a chance, a slim chance of victory. The idea had almost slipped from his mind but now it was fullblown, alive. Decision sent a flood of energy into his muscles. His blade met the scimitar, turned it. Instantly Ahab thrust in riposte at the yellow man.

The man from Chin skipped back, grinning.

Ahab advanced to the attack for the first time. The yellow swordsman shouted words which Ahab could not understand but by the expression on the flat face Ahab understood he was doing what the yellow man wanted.

Exhausting myself by attacking, he told himself glumly. But he stuck to his plan to destroy Chang Lun; he would follow it through, no matter if it brought his death or not. Biting his lip to quell the trembling of his tired body, he lunged forward.

His iron sword danced this way and that in the air and the yellow man gave way before it. Back he drove Chang Lun, back until Ahab could hear the breathing of the slavegirl just beyond the left elbow of the man from Chin.

Ahab slashed viciously.

The yellow man leaped back. His heel struck the stool where Ahab had sat as the slavegirl poured his wine. He reeled. His arms went wide in a furious attempt to recover balance.

Ahab lunged, his iron sword straight before him.

To the hilt he drove it into the middle of the yellow man. Chang Lun screamed like a woman, dropping his scimitar to clutch at the hilt of the sword which impaled him. The man stood a moment on widespread legs, mouth contorted grotesquely, fingers writhing feebly at the iron that drank his life away.

Then he fell sideways like a cedar of Lebanon dropping under the axes of the woodsmen. Ahab held onto his hilt and wrenched it from the dying man. He stood over the yellow man, panting harshly.

Ahab put out a hand, caught hold of the trembling slavegirl, yanked her toward him. He grinned down into her upturned face, then caught the wineskin and lifted it to his mouth. Thirstily he drank, knowing the delight of triumph, the sweet draught of victory against a personal opponent.

He swung on Dareel who was standing, staring.

"The tribute money, King Dareel," Ahab called out. "I'll be expecting it within the week."

"No," gasped Dareel. "No! You are my prisoner, Ahab!"

The king of Ammon turned and lifted his arm. "Soldiers of Ammon. Take prisoner the king of Israel."

"The man who obeys that order—dies!"

The voice came from behind Ahab, but he needed no glimpse of Zubral standing in his chariot to recognize it. During the fight when all eyes had been on the yellow man and the king of Israel, Zubral had brought his archers and his slingers forward. They stood now with shafts nocked to bowstrings, with round stones ready in leather slings, waiting for word from Zubral.

"Surrender, Dareel," cried Zubral. "Or you die first!"

Dareel of Ammon was no hero. Not for him the risk of death in an uneven struggle. Pale and quivering, he sank back

74

onto his gilded throne where he seemed to shrink inside his voluminous garments.

Ahab gave a glad cry and brought the wineskin to his lips again. He drank and drank while Zubral ordered the chariots forward with the foot soldiers, and the disarming of the Ammonites began.

The Lydian slavegirl would have gone with the others but Ahab put out a hand and caught her by the wrist. "Not you, little one," he grinned. "You stay with the king of Israel."

His hand slid from her wrist along her arm and about her naked back down to a plump buttock. He fondled her, holding her close, knowing that he needed a woman this night. The duel and the wine had made him drunk and reckless. Only soft female flesh could ease the swelling fury in his blood.

Zubral was on the gilded throne, manhandling fat Dareel, yanking him forward with such force that he fell to his knees. Zubral bellowed, "Crawl to Ahab, you treacherous scum! Beg forgiveness for tricking him with a parley flag!"

Dareel shook in terror. He knelt before Ahab and knew that he had doomed himself. There was no mercy in the hard eyes that studied him.

"I could forgive your refusing to give me tribute," Ahab said. "I could even forgive your arranging my duel with the yellow man. But for not honoring your given word—you showed yourself no true king."

Ahab grinned coldly into the flabby face of Dareel. At the same time his palm stroked the quivering buttocks of the smiling slavegirl as she pressed her breasts against his iron shirt.

"How shall I kill you, Dareel? In the manner of the Assyrians—by pegging your arms and legs to four stakes and ordering skinning knives to rip the flesh from your body?"

Dareel screamed and grovelled, burrowing his face in the pebbles before Ahab. "Not that way—not by torture!"

"The Assyrians rule their tributary people by terror," Ahab mused. "The lesser kings who rebel against the *patesis* they flay alive, to convince their successors that rebellion is a useless thing. Or I could impale you on a sharpened pole, high above your gilded throne. Would you rather die that way, Dareel of Ammon?"

King Dareel had fainted.

Ahab touched him with a sandalled foot. "Take him away, Zubral. Keep him under guard. Tonight we will have sport with the king of Ammon and send word of what we do to his son who follows him to the throne."

He lifted the slavegirl up against him and kissed her open lips. His soldiers bellowed at the sight. Just so should a warrior king behave with the property of the man he has defeated.

2.

From the distance, as Ahab rode the floor of his speeding chariot, his city of Samaria made a whiteness in the sun. Spread out upon the crown of a great hill, fortified by high stone walls and gates of solid bronze, it was a masterpiece of military engineering. Omri had planned it, Omri had built it, and Omri had left it as a monument to his greatness.

Ahab felt pride as he studied the city. This was his city, the jewel of the land he ruled.

It was a good feeling to be king in Israel, to be riding homeward with captives bound in chains behind him, with a boy-king—youngest son of fat Dareel—on the throne of Ammon and sworn to pay tribute to Ahab until the end of his days.

Ahab touched the thong of his cloak where it chafed his throat. It was hot. Hot! The sun made the sweat run down a man's chest and belly and put an itch in his loins. He glanced back over his shoulder at a following chariot where the slave-girl Iyannu rode with both hands clinging to its rail.

He had given Iyannu freedom the night after he had killed Chang Lun, on the cushions of the royal tent of Dareel. Dareel he had hung with chains and made to wait upon him, washing his feet in warm water and carrying platters to feed him. Dareel he had caused to be bound to a stake while the soldiers of Israel built high fires and revelled with his women.

Ah, that had been an exciting time, reminding him of the night they had celebrated the conquest of Ben-hadad. Then, Jezebel had sold the women of the Aramaean king to his officers and given the common women to the soldiers. Ahab had ignored payment. He had flung the women of Dareel to his troops and let them sate their lusts on them—while Dareel was forced to watch.

Ahab drew hot air into his lungs. It was good to be a warrior, good to be a king homeward bound with captives strung out behind him, with a king trudging in his dust and weeping bitter tears, with a plump slavegirl still breathless from his embraces.

Ahab grinned. The wench had squealed and shrieked when he had taken her on the cushions of the royal tent, when he had loosed the tensions in his flesh—born of his abstinence from Jezebel and the excitements of the fight with Chang Lun —again and again while his soldiers made sport before the tethered Dareel.

Yes, it was good to be a king.

Head held high as befitted a conqueror, Ahab entered Samaria, his land.

THE BOOK OF RAEL

Six: At The Victory Feast Of Ahab

1.

The viols and dulcimers made sweet sounds in the scented air.

From the couch where he lay idly nibbling at a fat Aramaean melon, Rael studied the banquet hall. It was alive with torches and with oil boats, making everything almost as bright as day, shining on the silver salvers carried by slavegirls between the couches. The girls bowed before the little tables where the king and queen of Israel, together with their guests, the noble men and women of Samaria and the high officers of the army, might hold out ringed fingers to the fruit.

There was laughter and expectation in the air. Ahab had come home from Ammon with gold and jewels in wooden coffers, with its fat king in chains. As Omri his father had done before him, so would young Ahab do. All Israel could look forward to a score of years of prosperity with Ahab to lead its armies to great victories.

Rael was sincerely glad for Ahab. And yet—

His eyes went often to Jezebel where she lay relaxed among the soft red cushions of her royal couch, only slightly smaller than the great golden lounge where Ahab took his ease. She wore a sheer garment girdled with gold rounds set with carbuncles and slitted to show anyone who cared to look the smoothness of her flesh beneath it. Her black hair was piled high on her head and threaded with golden chains and pins tipped by rubies. Against the scarlet pillows she gleamed like a living gem.

Rael eased the dryness of his throat with white wine, expensive Mareotic all the way from Egypt. He was glad for Ahab, yet he hated the man. After the feast it would be Ahab who would walk with Jezebel into her bedchamber, Ahab who would disrobe her, Ahab who would know her moans and sobs as he made love to her.

Rael swallowed bitterness with the Mareotic.

For the past few months, ever since Ahab had gone on his war against Ammon, he—Rael—had been the one privileged to do those pleasant things. Ever since the night when he had stumbled in on Jezebel covered with ashes and mourning garments, his had been the hands to remove her clothes his eyes to glory in her naked flesh, his the lips and hands and body that adored her beauty.

Not the eyes and lips and hands of Ahab.

His discontent prompted him to leave the couch, to plead tiredness, to seek escape in his own home. Yet Jezebel held him. Even now his eyes caressed the length of her bared thigh as it protruded through a slit in her Cos gown, right up to her soft buttock.

Yahweh, aid me! Grant me forgetfulness!

He drained his winecup and held it out to a slavegirl to be refilled. His hand was shaking with the fever that burned in him.

Just beyond him was another couch where Iyannu lay, the girl Ahab had brought back with him from Ammon. Rumor said that Ahab had enjoyed himself with her the night he killed Chang Lun. She was a pretty thing, Rael supposed, with big breasts and a soft haunch, but she was no Jezebel.

Like Jehu, Ahab could be satisfied with substitutes.

Rael could not. He loved Jezebel and only Jezebel.

There was a commotion at the far end of the room. Glad for a chance at diversion from his thoughts, Rael craned his neck as eagerly as anyone, seeing the flash of torchlight on iron armor as soldiers dragged Dareel forward.

The fat man waddled, naked to the eyes of the Israelites. A great shout went up at sight of the gross body that until now only his own womenfolk had seen. Only manacles at his wrists and ankles hid him from their view.

Behind him came little wooden carts, painted and set with silver ornaments that held the coffers and chests containing the tribute gold of Ammon. The shouts that had arisen at sight of Dareel became a triumphant roar.

To the royal couch the soldiers dragged Dareel and the tribute wagons after him. Jezebel was sitting upright, clapping her ringed hands together in enjoyment. Alanna ran at her bidding to a small teakwood coffer, catching it up in her hands and fetching it to the queen.

While Jezebel preened with a golden collar at her throat,

admiring her reflection in the silver mirror held before her by Alanna, Ahab spoke.

"What shall be the fate of Dareel, my love?"

Jezebel took her eyes from the mirror and looked at the weeping king. "Let him be staked out in the palace courtyard for the sun to cook." She smiled cruelly at the fat man who grovelled before her, crying out for mercy. "What mercy had you in mind for Ahab, Dareel? Let him who looks for mercy show it!"

The nobles shouted in delight. A helpless Dareel, spread-eagled on the hot courtyard pavings would make a pleasing sight in their eyes. He would provide fine sport before he died.

Ahab nodded. "Let it be as the queen has said."

As the soldiers pulled Dareel to his feet, screaming in terror, the tapping of a stick was heard. Heads turned toward the painted doors of the banquet hall to see what new entertainment was being provided.

A tall man in flapping rags came into the room. His grey hair and long beard seemed to toss with the vitality in his gaunt body, and the gnarled rod he carried in his right hand thumped to his every second step.

Ahab sat up and swung his legs over the side of his couch. "Who is this who comes like a beggar to my feast?"

"I am Elijah, King Ahab. Out of the land of Gilead, like the voice of the Lord Yahweh, I come."

Jezebel hissed in her throat, sensing trouble. She waved away the silver mirror and leaned indolently on an elbow as her stare assessed the holy man. Coldly she said, "Let him be taken out and flogged for his impertinence. No wandering beggar would dare interrupt the revels of Ithobaal, king of Phoenicia!"

Elijah came to a stop before the dais where the royal couches rested. His right hand was lifted, pointing at the queen. "Harlot! Worshipper of Baal and Astarte! Your sins are—"

Ahab stood, face dark and threatening with angry blood. "Hold your tongue, man of Gilead! You speak about your queen."

The old man smiled. "Queen, is she? A queen of blood, a queen of lust. Behold her hands—red with the deaths of holy priests, stained with the sweat of men she has taken in her bed."

Rael shivered, eyes wide. Could this old man see what was hidden from all other eyes? Could he see himself and Jezebel in the royal bedchamber, straining their naked bodies together

81

in frantic couplings? Or—was he only making a shrewd guess? Hardly daring to breathe, he listened.

"Enough, old one," Ahab growled. "I've seen your kind before. Go out to them, where you belong. Join them in their frenzies. Work off your energies among them—not here in my palace."

Elijah ignored his king. Leaning on his staff, he stared at Dareel. "You have done a fine thing, Ahab of Israel. You have conquered Ammon and reduced its king to nakedness. You have sacked its cities of their gold as a tribute to Yahweh and His land. Of all this, Yahweh approves, for it demonstrates to the world His might."

A dirty arm stretched out. "Go even further! Put away this woman named Jezebel and her harlot temples which she builds upon the sites of temples to Yahweh she caused to be burned and torn down! Her deeds are a stench in the nostrils of the Lord. Set her aside as you would an improperly made sword. Take another to wife!"

Ahab growled in his throat with fury. The room was silent as the nobles of Israel gaped at the ragged man. In their eyes, he was holy. Like Nathan and Samuel before him, he came from God, from Yahweh. His people professed sophistication but Ahab knew that deep inside they believed in the only god of all, in Yahweh.

He must not offend them, for he counted on their money-purses to finance new military ventures, enabling him to build an army that would sweep like a living flail on Aram and on Moab. He would raise Israel to the pinnacle among nations. He would be the greatest king in its long history, greater even than David, greater than Solomon.

This was his destiny.

He would not suffer anything to stop it.

So he must not offend the rich merchants and nobles. Let him show the fabled wisdom of Solomon in dealing with this sudden threat to his kinghood! His right hand balled into a fist as he struggled to master his rage.

"Old one, Jezebel is my wife, my queen. What you would advise me to do will offend her father, Ithobaal. Do you want Phoenicia to march on us with its chariots and footmen?"

Ah, that struck home. Ahab saw his rich nobles glancing at one another with suddenly troubled faces. They wanted no war with Phoenicia! Thanks to the peace that existed between Israel and that great coastal land, they could send their bronze and copper, their frankincense, their oil and wheat to foreign markets in fat-bellied Phoenician ships. And these goods filled their money chests, enabled them to wear dyed Phoenician linens and jewelry from Babylon, allowed them to purchase Egyptian horses and Assyrian ivories.

The merchants and the nobles were well content to be friends with Ithobaal of Tyre. They wanted nothing to disturb that peace.

As if sensing their thoughts, Elijah swung on them. "It frightens you, does it, this talk of war with Phoenicia? Better for you were you to put off your fine clothings, your rings and bracelets of gold and silver. Better for you were you to wear such garb as mine. It would make you look handsomer in the eyes of the Lord!"

His voice grew stronger. "Aye, grow your crops, your wheat, your olives. Gather them while you may. For the day of retribution is coming. Yahweh has held back His hand for love of the youthful Ahab. But now—now shall you feel His temper!"

The gnarled staff banged the tiled floor. "Your crops shall wither in the ground and on the vine. No rain shall come to nourish them, to bring them to bursting ripeness. They shall turn brown and hard in the heat of the day and the deadness of the night!

"As Yahweh is the living God, I tell you this—that there shall fall no rain in all of Israel until I myself shall speak the word!"

He turned on a sandalled heel and walked away, striding grimly and purposefully through the lane the merchants and the nobles opened to his walk. They saw his rags flap, they heard his staff thump and his sandals slap but none of them lifted a hand to stay his going. They were too filled with dismay, with superstitious dread.

No rain—until Elijah gave the word!

Why, this would ruin them! They had their shekels tied up in groves of olive trees, in fields of grain rippling in the breeze, in rows of juicy melons. No rain! It was unthinkable. The hot sun would bake their growing things, turn them to dry husks. They would become paupers.

Frightened, they began to mutter among themselves.

Ahab heard their words and knew that he must offer them diversion. His glance touched Iyannu and moved on to Dareel, trembling in his chains.

It was Jezebel who solved his problem. With an instinctive understanding of his worry, she came up from the couch to stand beside him. Her warm hand caught his fingers and pressed them.

"People of Israel," she called sweetly. "Ahab your king would prove his belief in his own strength, not in the cant of a hairy old man who stinks." Daintily she held her nose between forefinger and thumb. A few people smiled but there were many more gloomy faces than cheerful ones.

"As a token of his belief in that strength and in the might of his armies and his sword, he offers to share his wealth with you this night." Jezebel signalled and soldiers drew forward the wagons laden with the coffers of gold and jewels.

"A gift for every guest," Jezebel cried.

As though she had performed a miracle, the people surged forward, babbling in their eagerness to share the tribute monies. Such a deed was unheard of. Most kings and queens hoarded the gold their armies won for them. To fling it to their people was a gesture unparalleled in history.

On a Grecian klismos brought forward by a slave, Jezebel seated herself, reaching a hand into the first coffer and bringing out a golden bracelet. Imperiously she beckoned a woman forward, slipped the bauble over her hand and up onto her forearm.

"Wear this the next time we meet at the temple of Melkart, Salantha. It will enhance your beauty. And for Jonath, your husband."

She handed him a fistful of golden debens.

Rael watched her, thinking, She has brought victory out of defeat, cheerfulness out of gloom. She is a witch-woman, a succubus whose beauty is an enchanted thing that can make men her slaves.

As Jezebel gave away the riches of a kingdom, Rael saw the slavegirl Iyannu watching Ahab. She loved big Ahab, adored his heavily muscled body, just as he himself worshipped Jezebel. Rael smiled wryly. Life always held its little ironies.

He was about to slip away when Iyannu moved toward Ahab, leaning her shoulder against his arm. Ahab smiled down at her, put a heavily muscled arm about her middle, held her to his hip. All around them the guests were holding up their gifts for examination, exclaiming in delight over them. None had eyes for this little byplay between Ahab and the girl from Ammon. Only Rael saw the way in which Ahab stroked her flank through her thin linen tunic and the manner in which the girl touched the king.

Rael lay down upon his couch, curious. He signalled for more wine and when it was brought, sipped it thirstily. After a time Ahab seemed to tire of watching Jezebel play at generosity. He still held Iyannu by the waist; like that, he brought her out of the throng and into the shadows of the hall pillars.

Rael swung his gaze to the queen.

Jezebel still sat straight upon her Grecian chair, her back straight and untiring. Had she seen her husband walk away with the Lydian girl? Rael grew aware that his heart was thumping with unusual vigor. Excitement was a flood of warmth in his veins. If Jezebel had been abandoned, might she not be angry at Ahab, so angry that she would turn to him, to Rael her lover? He beckoned impatiently for the winegirl.

Ah, his motion had caught the eye of Jezebel.

The queen turned and gestured him to come and stand beside her. There were few guests left now to receive their gifts. In a moment they would be back on their couches, fondling the slavegirls and the wives of their fellows, growing drunk with the Mareotic and red Thasian.

The feast would be an orgy very soon.

Jezebel leaned her head against his thigh. She spoke so that only Rael could hear her words. "Go now. Wait for me in the bedchamber."

Though he had hoped for some such encouragement, Rael felt incredulity rise within him. The queen would not dare take him for her lover with Ahab in the same palace! It was unthinkable.

He choked a little as he said, "I will wait for you."

Like a man in a dream he walked the corridors of the palace, the echo of his sandals on the tiles beating accompaniment to the thudding of his heart. Would Jezebel dare to take him? Ah, no. It was madness. Ahab might come in upon them at any moment. The queen was not such a fool.

Frightened and worried, he paced back and forth between a standing candle and a handcarven chest. Ahab was with Iyannu, most probably making love to her. That much he could accept, knowing the ways of kings. But he would not spend the entire night with her. Or—would he?

He beat his fist into a palm.

Soft laughter echoed his gesture. Rael swung about and saw Jezebel standing in the chamber doorway holding her golden sandals in a hand. Her tiny feet were bare. No wonder he had not heard her as she had come down the hall. Giggling impishly, she mimicked his glum expression.

"Such a happy lover I have. Are you not sorry for me, Rael?"

"Don't tease me," he groaned.

She softened, running to him, hurling her body against his. She looked up into his face, writhing against him until she felt him respond to her thighs. Devil fires gleamed in her eyes. Her lips were slightly parted, breathing perfume in his nostrils.

"Do you want me, Rael? Do you? Do you?"

"I burn for you," he whispered.

"Ahab is with his little Lydian girl."

"But for—how long?"

"It makes no difference. I've told him I must worship at the shrine of Melkart this night until the dawn."

Understanding came alive in Rael, making him tremble. Slowly he sank before this woman he loved, his hands sliding down her back to her hips. Under the thin linen her flesh was warm cream to the touch. His lips kissed her through the Cos gossamer until he heard her moan.

His palms slipped through the slits of her gown to caress her thighs, her buttocks. Where his hands went his lips soon followed so that she stood like a living goddess for his worship, hands stroking his black hair.

"Rael—come with me to the temple."

"Yes—oh, yes! Anywhere with you."

He let her go and still on his knees watched her snatch up a purple cloak and throw it about her shoulders. It came to him that Jezebel was not so much a queen this night as she was a woman. His woman. No longer the property of Ahab.

He had been a fool to worry about his king. Jezebel might be wed to Ahab but she loved Rael. For him would her lips cry out this night, for him would she bare her hips, for him would she lift her breasts in her hands so he might kiss their nipples.

It did not occur to him that by going to the Temple, by laying with her on the cushioned couch below the gigantic golden statue of Baal-Melkart, he would be taking part in a religious ceremony. Every caress, every touch of his hands and lips to her flesh, was sacred in the sight of Astarte and of Baal. It would be as incense before the gods Yahweh had forbidden his people to adore.

Seven: Behind The Walls Of Babylon

1.

Babylon was a city out of legend in the land of Israel. The tales of travellers had built it into an abode where massive gardens hung in the sky, where gigantic stone lions guarded its gates, where wine flowed from street fountains and every day ·was as a feast. Now as he paced his mare through the Ishtar Gate, Jehu told himself those fables were not exaggerated.

All the world had come to Babylon, he thought. The hoofs of the horses and the padding of the camels made stirring echoes that were drowned out from time to time by the shouts of the drivers and the bellowed orders of the armed guards stationed to speed up traffic. That traffic flowed from the gateway onto a broad cobblestoned square that opened like a fan before the city proper.

Straight ahead was a broad avenue along which men galloped horses or rode in chariots. To his right, the gate market teemed with life. Scythians with yellow hair glinting like gold in the sunlight. Assyrians in fringed brocaded robes. A Greek in high-crested helmet and bronze armor, probably a mercenary. Mitannians wearing their typical conical hats and cloaks with rolled borders. His eyes could not see them all, nor pick out details fast enough for understanding.

Jehu let himself be shoved with his mare to a table where he gave his name and his country, his purpose for being here in Babylon, to a uniformed clerk. He was waved on impatiently to make room for the others crowding behind him.

With the reins in a hand, Jehu walked down an avenue paved with slabs of limestone, his eyes on the fabulous sights.

As dusk gathered shadows and hurled them this way and that among the buildings and on the street cobbles, he came to a small inn. There was a little courtyard and a stable in the rear, and here he took the mare, turning her over to a linkboy.

Even in the yard he could smell the roasting lamb. It made his mouth water. Not since breakfast at the caravan sheds had he eaten, and his leather belt was at its last loop. Throwing his bag over a shoulder he advanced on the inn.

Ten feet from the door he heard a cry and the ring of iron on iron. All his grown life he had heard such sounds as these. In the alleyway beyond the tavern, men were fighting with swords. Jehu grinned. It was no concern of his; he would ignore the fracas. A man with an empty middle has more to concern him than the problems of utter strangers.

Just the same, it would do no harm to look.

A boy stood with his back to a brick wall, fighting three grown men. He was a muscular youth wearing what once had been an expensive candys of black brocade worked with silver thread. It hung now about his waist so that his chest was bared to the blades that came at it.

Even as Jehu watched a sword bit into his side and the blood began to flow. The boy made no sound but his teeth glistened where they bit his lower lip. Sweat was running down his chest, diluting the red blood flowing from his wound.

Jehu rasped a curse. Three to one were no odds to his liking, especially when the one was a boy. His bag-ropes dropped from his fingers as he yanked out his own blade. He shouted and ran forward.

One of the attackers turned to meet him, a bearded man with long arms and hard eyes. "Stay out of this, you idiot. We're from the palace!"

Jehu never paused. He was coming in with blade held high and moving downward. As the bearded man lifted his blade to ward off the blow, Jehu changed the direction of his cut. His blade slid past that upheld sword and slashed sideways.

The man screamed as the iron went deep into his right side, almost cutting him in half. The scream changed to a gurgle of pain before death caught the man even as he stood upright.

One of the other men swung on Jehu, rasping curses. "Fool! This is no business of yours! Get out of here while you can."

The boy made no sound, possibly because his teeth were sunk so deep into his lower lip. Only his eyes flashed in his dark face as he risked one grateful glance at the big Habiru.

Jehu moved forward, blade held straight out. His new opponent circled, shuffling his feet, scowling darkly. He had seen the ease with which this heavily muscled newcomer had killed his fellow; he wanted no such death to come to him. All he need do was hold the stranger in play for a little while, long enough for his companion to slay the boy. Then they would both finish off this rash interloper.

Jehu was impatient. The boy was panting hoarsely now,

being close to exhaustion; his swordarm was quite obviously tiring and he was standing only because his back was propped against the alley wall with his legs spread wide apart. Jehu let himself be moved about by the feints and parries of his opponent, but each move he made brought him closer to the boy. The Babylonian gained confidence from the ease by which he maneuvered the Habiru. Evidently the stroke with which he had cut down Enkal was sheer luck.

Jehu let him think what he would.

He took two steps to his left as if to avoid a thrust. He was close to the boy, now. One more step and—

Jehu took the step in the face of an overhand blow from his opponent. His own sword stabbed straight out—not for the man slashing at him but for his companion, the man who was fighting the boy. His arm trembled to the shock of his blade sliding into the man's chest.

As the man went down, his own opponent stared in horror. For an instant he stood indecisive, then whirled and ran.

The boy moaned, "Don't let him—get away."

Jehu lifted his sword, held it back over his shoulder. His arm came forward, fingers tight to the braided haft. When he let it go the blade was a blur in the early evening dusk. It went like an arrow through the air.

It caught up with the man at the end of the alleyway and sank deep into his flesh below the shoulderblades. The Babylonian coughed and plunged forward on his face in the dirt. The point of the sword that impaled him made a scraping sound where it touched a partly buried rock.

Jehu caught the boy as he fell.

He lowered him to the ground, ripped at a linen tunic he wore under the brocade candys and made a bandage of sorts for his wound. A close examination showed Jehu the cut was not a serious one. A little rest and the boy would be as good as new.

When the bandage was in place he lifted and carried him out of the alleyway toward the inn. The doorkeeper took one look at the boy and began to shake.

"By the gods—is he dead?" he quavered.

"Only wounded. Get me a bed."

"Blessed be Shamash for preserving him. If—but I can't bear to think of that." The doorkeeper was an old man, shrunken with years. Jehu thought he shook very easily but then, perhaps, he knew who the boy was. He let himself be guided into the inn and past the stares of a dozen or more early diners, up a narrow wooden staircase to an upper floor.

The old man opened the door to a large, airy room lighted by half a dozen candles. There was a bed here and a table with two chairs as well as a painted chest of the kind used by travellers.

When the boy lay naked under covers, Jehu asked the doorkeeper, "Who is he? Has he a family? Someone to look after him?"

The old man nodded, eyes moving furtively into the shadows. "Two men. They will be here soon. The boy must have run away from them. They are his guardians."

Guardians, Jehu reflected, meant the spoiled son of a noble house. Why then, had his attacker announced he was from the palace? It made no sense unless the father of the boy had offended the Throne and this was the royal way of striking back.

Jehu made a wry face. He wanted no part of palace politics. He had left Israel to avoid seeing a queen. In Babylon, he did not want to become embroiled with a king. His hand fumbled at his belt purse.

"Look—if the boy needs care, a physician perhaps or—"

The old man grinned at him, showing toothless gums. "That one has no need for money. Save your coins. You did enough for him, binding his wound. His guardians will be grateful."

"I want no gratitude," Jehu growled.

The old man chuckled. "You're a wise man." His leathery palm accepted the maneh Jehu pressed into it. "All right, all right. I won't say a word to anyone. Go your way."

"I'm hungry. I'll eat belowstairs in the common room. If anyone asks, I just came in."

The doorkeeper nodded and led the way out into the hall and down the stairs. His hand gestured the Habiru to a table. Then he went back to his post by the door.

Jehu ate roast lamb and a bowl of fruit, drinking a cheap wine from Engeddi. He was wiping his fingers on a cloth when he saw two bearded Assyrians standing near the stairs and watching him. The hairs at the base of his neck rose upward under those cold, hard eyes.

Jehu had heard stories about the Assyrians. Their cruelty was a byword even in Israel. It had been their king Tiglath-Pileser who had built a mound of skulls from the bodies of enemies slain in battle, who had cut off the hands and feet of their officers, the noses and ears of others, who had burned out the eyes of still more foes. He bound children with rope, making a pyramid of their living bodies, then set fire to them.

And Tiglath-Pileser was only the first of the warrior kings

of Assyria. His successors had adopted his tactics. The man whom Assyria hated trembled for his fate.

Jehu would have liked to sink out of sight but there was no evading the cold eyes that studied him. When he rose to his feet and lifted his bag, the two Assyrians moved to intercept him.

To his surprise, they bowed low.

"You will come with us, please," one of them said in the halting lingua that passed for a common speech in the trade marts.

The other man smiled. "You have no need for alarm. You have done us a good deed. We are very grateful."

Jehu nodded, relief washing across his face. He let them precede him to the stair and up to the room where he had brought the boy. As its door opened he saw the youth sitting up, propped with his back to the wooden headboard.

The boy grinned at sight of him and waved him to a silver ewer holding wine. "Why did you leave me? You should have stayed. If Khabul and Nineser had not seen you eating, I wouldn't have been able to reward you."

The boy gestured. The man named Khabul went to a chest and lifted a small skin bag. He held it out to the boy with a bow. The boy had been watching Jehu; he laughed softly at his expression.

"You wonder who I am, eh? Why these men bow and scrape before me. All right, Nineser. You're bursting to talk. Tell him."

Nineser swung on Jehu with a smile. "Behold the heir to the throne of Assyria, Habiru. This is Shalmaneser, oldest son of Assurnasirpal." The man scowled and shook his head. "He is a headstrong youth, one given to wanting his own way. He ran from us today. We could not find him."

"The soldiers of Nabu-apal-iddin found me," the boy commented wryly. "They would have slain me, too—if you hadn't chanced along."

Jehu sat down.

He was weak with reaction. His fear had been so strong that he had been envisioning death by torture. Instead he was to be rewarded, given gifts by a prince of Nineveh. His eyes glowed as they saw Shalmaneser lifting out a heavy golden bracelet clustered with rubies. The armband was followed by a golden ring in which an emerald gleamed.

The boy tossed them through the air at him. Jehu caught them and drew a deep breath. He wanted to say that he did not deserve them, that he would have done the same thing for any youth in that much trouble. His lips pressed together, instead. A princeling does not like to be told the truth.

Shalmaneser laughed at him gleefully.

"Go on, say it. You didn't know who I was. You don't deserve these baubles."

Jehu grinned. He liked this youth and his forthright ways. "Something like that," he agreed lamely.

The boy turned to the two men. "You see, Khabul? Nineser? I was right about him. He's no opportunist. He never knew me. I appealed to—what shall I call it?—his ideals. I was a boy in trouble, no more. He would have done the same for a shepherd."

Khabul regarded Jehu carefully. "I believe you're right, highness."

"Certainly I'm right. Now go down and have some food sent up. I'm starved. And put my friend some wine, Nineser. We'll have a little feast in my room. At least it will break the monotony of this visit to Babylon."

At his eager questions, Jehu told the boy his name and the fact that he was a war captain in Israel. Shalmaneser wriggled at that; he was a warrior son of a warrior father. He knew and understood war and its allied arts. Within moments they were deep in conversation about the value of iron swords over bronze.

The time went away on wings, it seemed to Jehu, later. The tall candles were nubs in their sockets and Khabul dozed lightly in a shadowy corner. The boy might have gone on all night— he was intensely interested in Jezebel and in what manner of man Ahab was—except that a sleepy Nineser began blowing out the candles, telling Shalmaneser to go to sleep.

"In the morning, Jehu? You'll see Babylon with me? Belly of Ishtar! I haven't been this excited in a long time."

Jehu made his promise as the last candle went out. In the hall with the door shut behind him, Nineser explained that he for one would be only too happy to have Jehu accompany his prince. He had heard Shalmaneser describe his swordplay. He would make a fit guard for the boy in case of more trouble. Jehu was closer to his age than himself or Khabul. He would be able to keep up with Shalmaneser, see that he was amused.

"Princes, princes," he muttered, shaking his head. "Sometimes I think they're worse than wives. So headstrong, so occupied only with their own pleasures. This one," jerking his head at the closed door, "keeps me hopping, let me tell you."

"I'll be glad to see the city with him."

"You'll be paid and paid well. Assurnasirpal is no pauper

king. He will appreciate what you do for his son. Assurnasirpal has high hopes for Shalmaneser. Some day he will rule at Nineveh."

Jehu stumbled to a small room at the far end of the hall that Nineser had made ready for him. His muscles ached with weariness. He wanted to think over what had happened today and come to a decision about his future plans, but sleep washed across him as soon as he had stretched his big frame on the cot.

Sunlight and a hand on his shoulder woke him.

The boy was grinning down into his upturned face. "Marduk has been travelling a long time across the sky. If you were a soldier under my father you'd be a long time on the march by now—or have your soles whipped."

"I'm a soldier on holiday," Jehu grumbled.

"Well, so am I—but I can sleep at home."

Jehu put a hand on his head and rubbed his close-cropped hair. "All right, all right. You want to see Babylon."

"Especially the hanging gardens."

Jehu stared, then grinned. "You're no lover of flowers. What's her name?"

"I don't know—yet. But she has a friend."

The Habiru made a wry face. "I've known opportunities like that, before. The friend is always fat or ugly or marked by the pox."

"Not this one. She's young and pretty. But there are two of them, you understand—and one won't leave the other."

"What about Khabul and Nineser?"

"I sent them to buy wooden swords in the *agora*. I want to practise my swordstrokes with you, later. I watched while I could yesterday as you fought those palace guards. I've a notion I can learn something from you."

Jehu sighed. "Oh, well. He might as well throw back the covers. He was wide awake now. He wondered what the girls at the hanging gardens would be like.

2.

"There they are," breathed the Assyrian when they arrived at the gardens.

The two girls wore fringed shawls over their shoulders. Below them, Jehu could see tight, fleecy skirts wrapped about

93

their hips and fixed in position by little silver pins. It was a Babylonian style of dress, the candys, and it stamped the girls as city dwellers. He had to admit that the girls were attractive.

He wondered which of the girls Shalmaneser had picked out for himself. He was soon answered. The youth went up to the taller of the girls and made a little bow.

He explained that he had brought along this friend who was from a far-off place so that he might join them at a stall for a sugared bun. The girls giggled and looked at Jehu and at one another. Up this close, Jehu could see that their breasts were bare under their shawls, which was a custom the Babylonians inherited from the Sumerian peoples living here before them. It was a fine custom, Jehu decided, trying to see a little more the nipples that peeped out through the shawl fringes at him when the girls laughed.

While he was gawking, the Assyrian guided the taller girl away, leaving him with the smaller one. She was saying, "My name is Marda. Your friend is funny. He makes me laugh. Where is he taking Tallith?"

"For a sweet bun—such as you are," Jehu grinned.

Marda giggled and lifted her shawl to hide her mouth while turning away her head. Jehu wondered if it were a flirtatious act, for the rising shawl exposed her plump breasts, pale brown and firm, to his somewhat startled eyes. Flirtatious or not, Jehu found himself captivated. His hand caught her arm and he hurried her along beside him after the others. As they walked he discovered that her father was an official at the court of Nabu-apal-iddin, ruler of Babylon, and fairly well-to-do. She herself had stood in the great Temple of Shamash, the sun god, at Sipper, which the king had restored to all its old glory.

They munched sweet buns side by side, talking and laughing like old friends. There was a gaiety about the girls of Babylon missing in the Habiru women, Jehu found. His own people were more sombre, less given to casual laughter.

Marda and Tallith chattered on and on. They knew all the latest gossip, since Marda's father was at the royal court, and they bubbled it out as water from a fountain.

There was talk of war with Assyria—here the girls looked sideways at the grinning Shalmaneser—but nobody seemed to know just what to do about it. The queen was going to have another child. Veins of iron had been found in the mountains to the east. There was a great drought to the west in the land of Omri. There was no doubt about that, Tallith assured Jehu at his sudden interest. Merchants had told her father this, and her father had a shop in which he sold Phoenician ivories.

Talk of his homeland made Jehu remember Ahab and Rael with poignant affection. He wondered what they were doing, whether Ahab still loved Jezebel as much as ever, whether Rael had married Ruth to whom he was promised in marriage.

He had little time for nostalgia. He found himself swept along with the others toward the great tower that loomed above the city, Babil, a monument to the god Enlil.

Suddenly Tallith clapped her hands and cried, "The priestess is here! See her by the tripod, waiting for those who wish their fortunes told."

Jehu grinned and fumbled in his pouch. "Will she read the future of an Habiru? I'd like to know what's going to happen to me in the years to come."

"The priestess sees everything, Jehu. All it will cost you is a silver maneh." Marda pressed her hip against him. "Ask her what the future holds for me as well. It will be only a little more."

They crossed the cobblestones to a bronze tripod where herbs burned on red coals, raising a bluish smoke. The priestess was a beautiful woman with black hair hanging below her shoulders. She wore a black robe that shrouded her body from throat to ankles. Her eyes were sunken in her head as though they sought refuge from the world about her.

Jehu trickled two silver manehs into her offering bowl. "I am Jehu of the land of Omri. I wish to know my future and that of the girl with me, Marda."

One glance the woman gave them all before she leaned her face into the bluish smoke and breathed in, deeply. Once, twice, three times she inhaled that acrid smoke. Then she leaned back in her chair and let her eyelids fall.

They waited. The priestess breathed evenly, unhurriedly.

Jehu grew impatient but Marda was close against him and the touch of her soft buttocks to his groin was so pleasant that he waited as quietly as did the others. This is fakery, he told himself. I have seen the *nabiim* dance in the market squares of Samaria and Jezreel and listened to their nonsense. This will be more of the same.

The priestess sighed. Her lips quivered into speech. "This man is to be a king. Before him people will bow down in fear and in respect. His destiny shall be to establish a new ruling house. By death and by blood will he win his crown."

Jehu grinned. This was what he wanted to hear, nonsense on a grand scale! He squeezed Marda against him so that she could feel his hard muscles. Marda wriggled. The priestess was speaking again.

"The girl Marda will marry a rich merchant. She will have five children. But she will die when the city of Babylon is sacked by its enemies, of a spearthrust."

Marda gave a wailing cry and turned, burying her head against Jehu. He held her trembling body against him, whispering, "You don't believe this fribble, do you? Me—a king? Have you no better sense?"

"A spearthrust," she whimpered.

Over her bowed head, Jehu saw Shalmaneser dropping coins into the silver bowl, so many they made metallic music. His voice, hoarse with emotion, rasped, "Tell me of myself now, priestess. I am Shalmaneser, an Assyrian."

The priestess opened her eyes. She looked drugged, almost lifeless. Twice she tried to speak and could not. Then she shook her head.

"I must rest a little while. Take back your coins."

The Assyrian stood undecided. Then he gestured fiercely. "Keep the manehs. But remember my name. I shall be back after you have rested. Then you can tell my future." He stared hard at Jehu. "If you are to be a king, I shall be an emperor. This I swear—no matter what the priestess says!"

Jehu nodded soberly, reading the pride and arrogance in the youth's stare. "I'll never be a king—but if I am, you will surely be an emperor."

His words mollified Shalmaneser. The youth snorted and drew Tallith closer. "I tire of this play. My throat burns with heat. There are wineshops beside the tower. Come, let's find one."

He and Tallith ran ahead while Jehu followed more soberly with Marda, who still trembled in her terror. He tried with words to comfort her but when they failed, decided on a different course.

The Assyrian had found an unoccupied cubicle and was standing at its doorway, holding open the leather curtains. "In here, Jehu, where we can be by ourselves." With a hand he signalled the temple wineseller to bring them a plump skin and four clean leather cups.

Jehu said to Marda, "Drink to your future husband—and your children. Forget about the spear. By then you may be old and wrinkled and glad to die."

She giggled through her tears. "Easy for you to say—you're going to be a king."

"Not I. I'm only a poor soldier."

Shalmaneser leaned across the tabletop. "Tell me, do you

believe in the priestess? That she can see what's going to happen?"

"Of course not," Jehu snapped. "She wanted an offering for the god. To get them, she tells people what they like to hear."

"I didn't like hearing about that spear," sobbed Marda. She broke off her weeping to look at the Assyrian. "Assyria has always been an enemy of Babylon. If I thought you might be the man with the spear—I'd scratch your eyes out."

They were interrupted by a serving woman with a wineskin and four cups. Hurriedly, Jehu poured wine and handed a cup to Marda. "Drink deep, my dear. In an hour you won't even remember your name, much less anything about a speartip jabbed at you."

With trembling hands Marda caught the leather cup and tilted it to her mouth. She drank eagerly, thirstily. When she was done the cup was empty. Jehu tugged her closer along the bench and refilled her goblet.

Here in this cubicle they were encased in privacy. Shalmaneser could stroke the smooth thigh of Tallith beneath her fleecy skirt and none could see. Jehu could fondle the plump breast of Marda while she became drunk with wine and tears. Beyond the leather curtain moved the world but it reached into the cubicle only with its whispers, with the harsh cries of the foodsellers, with the slap of sandals on cobblestones, the rattle of chariot wheels and the clink of coins being paid in the marketplace.

The Assyrian was leaning above Tallith now, disarranging her shawl and the sheer tunic she wore beneath it so that both her breasts protruded naked, small but hard, with long nipples. He bent his head to kiss them. Tallith sat with her head resting against the back of the bench, eyes glazed and mouth a little open to aid her hurried breathing.

Jehu watched, fascinated. He had never seen a man and woman make love before. The Habiru were strict about these things but here in Babylon there was a festive air at all times, as though the city played eternally at holiday. Beside him he felt Marda stir.

"Love me too, Jehu," she breathed in his ear. Her teeth caught his lobe and bit gently. It was a spur to his blood.

His hands reached up under her shawl and caught her breasts, which were larger and softer than the breasts of Tallith. She moaned at his touch and writhed so as to fit more of her flesh into his palms. When he kissed her, he found her lips parted and avid for his caress.

"King Jehu," she giggled drunkenly.

97

He was too excited to laugh, but the words whipped his spirit like a flail. It was fribble—but nice fribble. King, indeed! He wanted no kingship. It was enough for Jehu to be alive and strong and halfway drunk so that it was easy for him to push away the fleecy skirt that Marda wore and draw her naked thighs to him so that she might sit upon him as a rider on a horse.

—

3.

Two weeks Jehu spent in Babylon with Shalmaneser and his retainers. The days were filled with weaponplay in the courtyard of the little inn, with walking about the city until it became a part of them.

Sometimes they met Tallith and Marda at the hanging gardens, sometimes other girls. Once Jehu went with Shalmaneser to the priestess at the tripod and listened as she told Shalmaneser that someday he would rule the world. It was in line with the other hogwash, Jehu thought privately, though he said nothing of his beliefs to the Assyrian who was enamored of his destiny.

"The world," he said one night to Jehu as they sipped wine in a Tower cubicle with two priestesses of Nergal. "I shall own the world. You heard the seeress, Jehu."

"I heard her."

The Assyrian grinned. "You—a king. Me—ruler of the world. Of what kingdom shall you be king, Jehu? No matter. But this I promise. That if we ever meet in battle, I will spare your life. This I swear."

Nothing would satisfy Shalmaneser but that he lift out his dagger and cut his wrist and that Jehu do the same. They put their wounds together, then dribbled a little blood into a cup of wine, mixing the blood with the wine, then drinking it.

"The only way to make a vow of blood brotherhood," the Assyrian told the woman beside him. "Now I am bound by Dagan to do as I have said."

Jehu said nothing, being already drunk, but he wondered how he could ever set himself up in battle against mighty Assyria. It was of a sameness with the prediction that he would be a king. It made absolutely no sense at all.

At the end of the two weeks. Shalmaneser told him it was time he returned home to Nineveh. He wanted Jehu to go with him. In the great palace at Nineveh the Habiru would be an honored guest. His father, Assur-nasir-pal, would want to reward him for saving the life of his oldest son. He would hear of no arguments, he assured Jehu.

Jehu intended not to argue. There was no homesickness in him for Israel or Ahab. Jezebel was still the queen. He had come to Babylon for forgetfulness; he could also find it in Nineveh. Besides, the generosity of a king might be worth traveling to see.

From Babylon to Nineveh lay more than two hundred miles of flatland broken only by the twin rivers and their waters. A fast rider could cover fifty miles in a day, but Jehu and the others were in no hurry. They were still on holiday. When they came to a lonely way station they bought half a dozen fat wineskins and sacks full of food so that they might feast at the night camping and tell tall tales.

It was a strangely happy time of life for Jehu, a period on which he would look back later with a wrenching of his heart. He was young, filled with strength. The future lay before him— the promise of kingship had been all but forgotten by now— and offered its allurements as might a lovely woman behind sheer veils. Something of this future seemed to rise up out of the level plain early one morning as they galloped past a river bend. It was a long, low blackness he saw ahead of him that stretched on and on as far as the eye could see.

Jehu reined up with a curse. "What is the thing?"

The others laughed at him. "A wall, ninny. The wall built centuries ago to keep the Babylonian dogs in their own kennels and out of ours," replied Shalmaneser. "In those days we were not nearly as strong as we are today. It was something to hide behind."

It was a massive structure, Jehu saw as they neared its brick walls. Thirty feet deep, its walks were patrolled by men in the iron mail and conical helmets and fringed shawls of Assyria. The sun sheathed them as if in fire as they strolled their beats.

"It stretches from the Tigris westward almost to the Euphrates," Khabul added. "One division of Assyrians can hold off a hundred regiments of Babylonians behind its bricks. It is the greatest man-made object in the world."

Jehu believed him as he trotted his mare between the huge bronze gates that opened to a cry from the gate commander. A wall this big might enclose all of Israel. Awe worked in him. He had gone out of Israel to avoid Jezebel, preferring to see the world in her stead. His dreams were fleshing themselves out with a reality that took away his breath.

99

It was Shalmaneser who dug toes into his mount's ribs, shouting out a challenge to a race. "Nineveh is only a few miles away. A bag of golden manehs to him who beats me through its gate!"

The others rose to his bait. They galloped headlong through the dust of the mighty plain, past flocks of sheep and the moving wooden hoes of tillers of the ground. A merchant drew back with curses on his lips, not recognizing his prince. A girl squealed and dropped her water jar as four horses brushed her skimpy tunic. Jehu bellowed and hammered at the gelding but the animal could not catch the white stallion which went as with the wind. Behind him he heard Nineser shouting but he paid no heed. His eyes were concerned only with Shalmaneser ahead of him and looking back over his shoulder. Jehu did not like to be beaten by anyone, even by the son of a mighty king.

He wondered if it were symbolic.

Eight: As The Rains Fell Not In Israel

1.

From his balcony high above the city, Ahab could look out over the valley of Jezreel. As the sweat ran down his legs, he let his eyes assess the distant fields of millet and barley. He need go no further than his balcony to see that the stalks of grain were brown, withered from the lack of rain. As it was in the valley of Jezreel, so it was in the lands around Bethel and in Dan to the north, and all across the plain of Sharon.

His kingdom burned before his eyes.

Anger flushed King Ahab so that he hammered his fist on the balcony rail. Elijah! It was the fault of that cantankerous old man spitting out his venoms. The thought had come to Ahab more than once that Elijah might have timed his threat at the precise moment when he knew a long drought was to come upon Israel. Reports from travellers told him the parching land was everywhere, in Egypt and in the coastal lands, in Moab and Ammon, and even, to a degree, in far off Assyria.

There were those who could foretell the weather. In his youth he had known an old slave named Abijath who could predict the weather with uncanny and sometimes frightening accuracy. His system was based on a twelve day forecast toward the end of any given year, each day corresponding to a coming month. At first Ahab had scoffed with the others, but when Abijah kept records at his insistence, his accuracy became astonishing.

Could Elijah have stumbled on the same method?

Or had Yahweh actually spoken with him?

Ahab was no agnostic. He accepted Yahweh as the god of Israel and Judah just as he accepted Osiris and Isis as gods of Egypt and Marduk as the god of Babylon. Privately, he wondered if there were any such things as gods, though he did lip service to Yahweh from political necessity. His priests were a power in the land; it was best to conciliate them, to have them always at his elbow in friendship rather than in hate. As a king it behooved him to tread warily when it came to matters of religion.

He had allowed Jezebel to build her temple, remembering the manner in which Solomon had allowed his wives to worship as they would. Besides, there were certain factions even among his own people who preferred the orgiastic ceremonies of Baal-Melkart to those of Yahweh. A popular ruler knows what his people like, and gives it to them. Since a popular ruler is so often a strong ruler, Ahab wanted his home front to be solidly behind him in his wars.

Ahab snorted. His wars!

Right now his soldiers had been demobilized, sent back to their farms and little towns to lend their strong arms and backs to the tasks of fetching water and digging new wells so that something of the crops might be saved. Israel needed food more than it did conquest at the moment.

Yet Ahab itched to take the war road.

His fingers opened and closed on the balcony rail where he rested his hand. A week ago he had sent officers and men out into the back country of Israel, to Kedar, to Phoenicia and to Aram. Somewhere, Elijah would be found. He must be found, to remove this curse from Israel.

Ahab scowled, wondering what the price for lifting that curse might be. He turned his head, staring back into the shadowed room where Jezebel lay upon the royal bed bathed in heat. She wore no garments. Ahab could see the sheen of sweat across a thigh and the smooth skin of her belly.

Suppose Elijah insisted that he give up Jezebel, as he had done months before in the banquet hall? By Yahweh Himself! He would not. He loved this Phoenician woman. She was everything in his eyes! His love bordered on madness, he knew.

She put a fever in his veins, the way she did with so many other men.

Oh, he had seen them staring at her, his officers and his stewards, the merchants and the traders of the Israelite towns when they came to the palace for favors. Lust was a glint in their eyes that turned their lips slack and hurried their breathing. Ahab grinned, suddenly. It was good to have such a woman to wife, to know that he and only he had the pleasures of her body in the bedchamber.

A blast of heat from the valley floor came at him. Hot and dry, this wind was brother to the Egyptian *khamsin*, to the dreaded *simoon* of Arabia. It burned the skins of men and killed their crops and ate at their spirits. A man could stand it for a little while, but these past few months had been intolerable.

Somewhere, he must find Elijah!

He turned on a heel and walked into the bedchamber, moving toward the draped doorway. Jezebel heard him, turned her head. Her eyes were glazed, dull.

"Ahab—find Rael. Tell him he must minister to me. My skin is so hot, I feel feverish. He must have some way of giving me relief."

He nodded, studying her. She had grown thinner in the last few weeks. Her former plumpness at thighs and waist was gone, yet she lost none of her allure. If anything, her lean middle and slender legs emphasized the firm breasts which appeared even larger.

He paused, tempted to forget his kingly troubles with his wife, but she seemed to ignore his lazy stare, turning away her head. Ahab sighed and walked on. He would visit the barracks, jest with his officers a little while, find out if any of his riders had come in with word from Elijah.

Behind him, Jezebel smiled wryly. Her big husband was easy to lead. For a soldier, he was uncommonly sensitive, at least where she was concerned. The mere lifting of a hand, a twist of her lips, could bring him to her side or send him scowling away to some other part of the palace. She was too wise to keep him too long from her bed, however. Satisfied after a night of revelry with her, he was a changed man, happy —often singing as he strolled the palace halls—and content with life.

Lately, though—

Jezebel frowned. Was it her imagination or did Ahab seem to seek her bed less and less? She knew well enough that he had lain with Iyannu, the little Lydian wench he had brought back with him from Ammon. Well, that was all right; his attentions to Iyannu gave her more time with Rael. Still, her womanly pride was piqued. She did not want him panting after her like a hound behind a bitch in heat, but he might show a little more interest in her as a woman.

A footfall interrupted her thoughts. She extended her arms above her head in order that her breasts might stand more firmly. The heat was making her blood bubble these days. Ahab had his soldiers to keep him amused. Yes, and Iyanna. She only had Rael.

When he stood in the doorway staring in at her nakedness, his satchel of vials and instruments forgotten in his hand, she knew with sure instinct that this man belonged to her even more fully than her own husband. See how his eyes touched her flesh with caresses. See how the red flush stained his youthful face. See the trembling of his hands, the tip of his tongue touching his lips.

"I burn, Rael," she murmured, stretching.

"It is hot," he agreed, moving toward the bed.

"I sent Ahab to find you. I'm glad you were so close. Those liquids of yours that cool the skin. I need them."

He sat on the edge of the bed, placing his bag by his feet. "I was coming to leave some with Alanna. I met Ahab in the lower hall. He's worried about the drought."

His hands shook as he unstoppered a vial. Under his breath he swore at himself. Why must his hands quiver so when he came near Jezebel? She was only a woman. If he needed a female so desperately, he could always buy one in the slave mart. It was more than mere womanflesh he wanted, though.

Cupping a little of the liquid in his hand he put his palm to Jezebel, rubbing it up and down on her thigh. Hungrily he stared at the body lying so close to him, watching the flesh move and ripple to his stroking hand. She preened at his touch, writhing slowly.

"It is so good. So cool!"

"It is comprised of fermented wine mixed with the juice of green strawberries. Even as it cools, it softens the skin."

"When will this heat end? When will it rain again?"

"When Elijah speaks the word."

"Do you believe that old crank?"

"I believe in Yahweh."

"Is your god so cruel? So unjust?"

Rael considered his reply, aware that his thoughts were a chaotic jumble of impressions and prejudices in his mind at the moment. With his moist palms moving over Jezebel, a calm judgment was far from easy.

"Yahweh is—Yahweh. As Baal-Melkart is—Baal-Melkart."

"You think Yahweh is the true god?"

He nodded. Jezebel watched him carefully. Petulantly, she wriggled. "I believe in Baal-Melkart. Which of us is right?"

"Who can say? Yahweh sent the drought. Only Yahweh can remove it. You can pray to your god, if you want. If the rains come in answer to your prayers, only then is your god stronger than my god."

"If the rains were to come, then Ahab would go away to his wars," she pointed out. "He waits only for the rain. Everything else is in readiness. And he has riders out to find Elijah."

"Yes, I know."

A thought touched Jezebel. She drew in her breath suddenly, even as Rael brought his hands up to her breasts. She allowed him to stroke them for a moment, hardening their flesh, before she caught his fingers and held them.

"Rael, someone in Samaria must know where Elijah is! Your priests! Surely Elijah would have left word where he might be found."

"It's possible," he nodded.

She lowered his hands to her hard breasts, writhing upward to meet the clasp of his fingers. As he held her, she whispered, "You could go to them, Rael. The priests know and respect you. If you were to learn the whereabouts of Elijah and were to whisper of it in my ears—I would be very grateful."

She was twisting about on the bed like an oiled snake, supple and almost boneless. Lips open and eyes closed, she used her entire body to caress him, to rouse the fevers in him to explosive force. Her knees and thighs rubbed against him. She moved so that her loins might touch him even as her scented hands went in under his thin undergarment to his naked chest.

"For me, Rael? Do this thing for me?"

"I cannot," he exclaimed hoarsely.

"Not even for—this?" she breathed.

He cried out at her caress. His entire body was alive with need. There was nothing in him now but this pulsing hunger. He put out his hands to catch and hold her but his palms touched only her unbound black hair as she slithered away from him, laughing softly.

"Tell me where Elijah is," she whispered.

Dumbly staring at her nakedness, he shook his head.

Jezebel let her thighs fall apart, lying stretched on her back with her arms behind her head. Lazily she moved one leg back and forth. Rael was in agony, staring down at her.

"Tell me, Rael."

His tongue touched his lips. "No. No."

She showed no anger, though rage blazed inside her mind. Jezebel only sighed and reached out for a black shawl draped across a corner of the royal bed. Slowly she drew it over her nudity.

"I am the queen of Israel. It isn't right that a common man should see my unclad body."

"I love you," he blurted. "I worship you."

"Then tell me what I want to know."

"I—I'm not sure."

She slipped out from under the shawl and put an arm about his neck, pressing her warmth and softness against him. "Find out, Rael," she breathed into his ear. "Learn where Elijah is hiding—then come back to me. I will be grateful."

He stood like a man in a dream and walked away.

It was dark when he returned. Over the city the sultry night lay like a heavy blanket under which men and women slowly broiled. As he walked, Rael plucked the wet garments from his flesh where sweat made them stick like a second skin. Josiah ben Seraph, who was high priest now that Benajah bar-Simon was dead, had been most helpful, assuring Rael that Elijah was in no danger, that the riders from Samaria dispatched to find him only hunted down the wind.

Deep in his heart, Rael understood that he was playing the traitor to his people. Yes, even to his God. He could not help himself. His body was a tortured longing for the flesh of Jezebel. Again and again he had told himself to flee from Samaria, to go south into Judah where Jehosephat was king, and to forget Ahab and Jezebel.

It was impossible. Already his lips were trembling to spill out the words he knew. His tongue could scarcely stay quiet in his mouth.

There was a dark shadow to his right, near a pillar. The shadow stirred as he came near, stepping out into a beam of moonlight. Jezebel stood there, wrapped to her throat in a dark cloak.

"Ahab sleeps," she whispered. "Come with me."

He went like a slave behind his mistress along the halls and down a flight of stairs into the garden. Jezebel reached behind her, caught his hand and held it tightly.

Beyond the terrace was a small shrine, a pillared rectangle fitted with bronze grilles and open to the sky. A drape hung between the entry pillars, hiding the interior. Jezebel lifted the drape, held it so Rael could move past her into the shrine.

There was an altar, Rael saw, that was almost as large as a table. On it rested a number of silver bowls holding offerings to the goddess behind it, an ivory and ebony statue of Astarte staring blindly out upon her domains. Tripods for incense stood against the dark grilles, stippled by moon shadows.

What better place in which to betray Yahweh?

Rael felt Jezebel touch his arm, felt her fingers climb up under his tunic to his shoulder.

"What news, Rael? What is the word on Elijah?"

"Elijah is in Zarephath in Phoenicia, close to the city of Sidon. He stays with a widowed woman named Amaleth."

Jezebel searched his face with hard eyes. "Your holy man seeks refuge near the city where I was born? In my own land? You ask me to believe in the impossible. Your god is a god in Israel, not in Phoenicia."

"Nevertheless, Elijah is in Zarephath."

Her eyes went around the little shrine as if seeking inspiration. "It is beyond belief. And yet—where else would he find shelter from Ahab's riders? There are Habiru people in Zarephath. One of them might willingly hide him from the world. Yes! By the sterile loves of Astarte! It could be."

She went to the long altar and removed from it the silver bowls, putting them on the tiled floor. Turning, she let the cloak slip from her shoulders so that the moonlight glistened like silver paint on her bared flesh.

From the woman, Rael lifted his eyes to the ivory statue.

This was her goddess, the deity she worshipped in her pagan rites. This thing of carven ivory, of polished ebony. As his people bowed to the Ark of the Covenant as symbolic of the presence of Yahweh, so Jezebel and all her people knelt to these idols. Even to stand here with Jezebel was a form of idolatry

With her fingers, Jezebel was signalling him to approach and lift her up onto the altar. The stone was warm, he found when he ran his palm over its smooth surface; it was as though the night had folded about it. It would make a comfortable resting place for the queen of Israel who stood so proudly naked before it.

She smiled and reached out for him. At her caress his spirit broke within him and he fell to his knees before her, clinging to her slim legs, kissing their smoothness and burying his face against her flesh, crying out that she was all his world.

"I am as nothing before you," he whispered against her

106

belly. "You are my goddess. My Astarte, if you will. Only have pity on me."

Jezebel smiled above his head, staring straight ahead toward the scarlet drapery shutting out everything but this man on his knees to her beauty. Gently she began to stroke his heavy black hair.

"I am Astarte," she breathed.

"You are Astarte," he echoed.

"I am the goddess of the flesh."

"Yes, yes—the lustful goddess."

"In me are all caresses sacred."

"Even the sterile ones."

The unholy litany went on with Rael on his knees to her like a worshipper, fingers and palms sliding up and down the backs of her thighs and gripping her buttocks. She chanted softly so that none might hear but him, while he whispered his answers to her body.

"My breasts draw all men to them.

"My loins can fertilize a world.

"My legs are serpents of delight."

Rael forgot where he was. He no longer understood the words he spoke. He was aware only of the woman in his clinging arms, of her voice touching his ears. He was Rael no longer, only a man and from the earliest day man had adored woman as a symbol of strength and fertility, as the bringer-forth of children, especially the boy-child who would grow to manhood and so strengthen the tribe. He knelt and he made love to his queen and to his goddess.

After a while Jezebel drew away from him, sitting on the altar and extending her arms, causing him to rise and come over to her. Beneath the idol goddess he joined himself to her again and spent himself over and over in maddened frenzies which Jezebel told him were pleasing both to Astarte and to herself. Their echoing cries rose upward to the ivory figure even as their bodies lunged together.

2.

Ahab woke in the dawn to find Jezebel beside him, eyes wide and staring upward. He turned to her, resting on an elbow.

"Have you slept, my wife?"

"I have slept—and dreamed of Elijah."

Ahab smiled. "What was your dream concerning that wild man?"

"He hides in a town called Zarephath near Sidon."

The king laughed and rolled over on his back. "Truly, this was a nightmare."

"It is the truth. Send a rider into Phoenicia. Learn for yourself what is nightmare and—what is truth."

Her voice told him she was in deadly earnest. Ahab lay a moment, considering. His riders had failed so far to uncover Elijah. As well try a dream as do nothing.

"It is so ridiculous a notion that it might be true," he said at last. "This morning I will summon Obadiah and send him to Zarephath."

"Then Obadiah will find Elijah."

Ahab only nodded, not speaking. The heat was a weight on his giant frame. It was going to be another scorching day.

3.

Elijah walked the road between Zarephath and Samaria with resolute will, glancing occasionally at the copper sky. There were no clouds in that sky, only the sun like a yellow ball baking everything it stared on. Dust rose from his sandals in tiny clouds, so dry was the earth. Parched was the soil for the rain, as was Israel for the word of Yahweh.

He would bring both to the land of Ahab.

Soon would the rain come down in torrents. When it did, he must be in Samaria, speaking with the king and his harlot queen. He knew that King Ahab had dispatched riders to seek him out. Travelers in Zarephath had told him as much, not knowing his name or that he was the old man sought by Ahab.

The king despaired, those travelers said. He went daily to the lone temple to Yahweh that Jezebel had left standing and he prayed. He made offerings of myrrh and gold to the priests. He was like a man bereft of his senses.

In the north, in Aram, Ben-hadad was gathering an army.

In Israel, Ahab would be helpless unless the rains came. His soldiers were scattered like seed from the hand of the sower. They labored in a land turned to desert by an unrelenting sun and the lack of water. Their strong arms were busied with well-rope and bucket rather than with spear and shield.

Elijah did not want Israel to fall victim to the Aramaeans. The Aramaeans worshipped Baal, too. It would do no good to deliver Israel into pagan hands. Jezebel was a pagan but she was only one woman. It were better that Jezebel lived than that Ben-hadad should conquer the land she ruled.

The dust was stifling. Elijah breathed in the hot air together with the stink of his unwashed flesh. Water was too precious in these days, even in Phoenicia, to waste it by cleansing the body. Water was needed to stay alive. Men and women—except those of royal or noble blood—went about their tasks bathed only by their own sweat. Never had the land known such a drought.

He was close to the river Kishon which watered the plain of Esdraelon when he saw the horsemen before him, topping a little rise and reining up to point at him excitedly. Elijah paid them no heed. He walked on, serene in his own strength, which was from Yahweh. That first glance was all he needed to understand that these men were royal riders. Their armor flashed in the sun and was set with the device of the house of Omri.

The horsemen waited for him.

As Elijah came near, their leader threw up an arm. "Hail, Elijah. I am Obadiah of the royal household, steward and captain of the king."

The old man slowed his stride. "Go back to the king and say that Elijah is coming to his palace. Say also to him that I will cause the rains to fall in Israel."

Obadiah nodded solemnly, "Yes, I will go and say this to Ahab—for my men will bring you behind me. On your feet and walking, if you so prefer it. Otherwise bound hand and foot and carried on a wooden pole."

Elijah did not let his gaze waver. "I come on foot. I am a man of Yahweh and it is not proper that such a one travel like a dead animal felled in the hunt."

The old man started his trip and every so often he would look over his shoulders to the west and upward to study the cloudless sky.

4.

Ahab was seated on his golden throne as Elijah was ushered into the Hall of Audience. Jezebel sat beside him on a smaller throne, also of gold and decorated with lapis-lazuli. She was petting a great saluki hound crouched at her feet, staring

109

straight ahead with hard eyes while a slaveboy moved a fringed fan back and forth above her head. Ahab had been admiring her profile, her heavy mouth and tilted nose. His gaze remained on her while his ears told him Elijah was approaching the royal dais.

Slowly the king looked away from Jezebel to regard the old man, dusty and hot, who leaned on his gnarled staff and stared back at him. There was pride in Elijah that shone out at the king from under his tufted eyebrows.

"Why have you brought this trouble on Israel?" Ahab asked.

Elijah seemed surprised. "The trouble is not from me but from you, the king," he said harshly. "And because of your harlot queen, Jezebel."

Jezebel went white. She tightened her fingers until the saluki hound whimpered but she did not look at Elijah.

Ahab fought to keep his temper under leash. "You caused the drought, old man. Only you can remove it. Or so you claim."

"As I have said, so it is. Only I can cause the rains to fall. Or rather—Yahweh, whose voice I am."

"Are you aware that Ben-hadad gathers a great army in Aram? That he intends marching into Israel to gut its cities, to sell its people into slavery?"

Elijah inclined his head. "You sent for me just in time."

"Only when the rains come can I order my soldiers off the farms and out of the vineyards, to arm them against the Aramaeans."

"Destroy the temple of Baal and the rain will come."

Jezebel stirred and for the first time turned her stare at Elijah. Livid hate was in her black eyes, in her rigid posture. "Never," she whispered. "Never shall the temple to Baal come down. I do not believe your god can send the rain, old one. Nor that he sent the drought. I believe that it is time for the rains to come—which is why you left the house of Amaleth and were on your way into Samaria when Obadiah found you."

Elijah said nothing. Let these people think what they would. It was true that the rain was due very soon. His own forecasts had told him this, and the growth on his big toe was beginning to pinch. But not yet, not just yet.

Jezebel leaned forward, chin jutting aggressively. "I have suggested to my husband that he chain you up and whip you every day until the rains come. When they come—and so prove you a false prophet—then he shall boil you alive in oil."

Elijah blinked. He had not foreseen any such possibility as this. He was a holy man of God. Respect was his due in Israel,

110

the land of Yahweh. He turned to Ahab, who was watching him closely.

"Is this the order of the king?" he asked. His voice was not under full control. It broke and showed the momentary terror his face was hiding. "Am I to be flogged like a common thief? I, who am the voice of Yahweh in the land? Must I curse Israel ever more than I have done already?"

The noblemen and women in the hall began to murmur and move restlessly. The lack of rain had been catastrophical. Their fortunes had shrunk with the grapes and grains on which it was based. They wanted no more curses from Elijah. Breathlessly they looked at Ahab.

Ahab pondered. He had no wish to offend the priests of Yahweh. At the same time he did not want to cast out the priests of Baal, which would be an act of desecration in the eyes of his wife. To tear down the Temple of Baal was impossible. If that and that alone were the price for the word of Elijah to send the rain, it was too much to pay.

Something of his thoughts showed on his face, for Elijah stirred and lifted his staff, shaking it in the air. "Turn from the harlotries of the Phoenician god, Ahab—before it is too late!"

"Would you threaten me? Would you dare?"

"I dare to threaten all who are the enemies of Yahweh!"

"What man accuses me of this? I have gone to the temples and made my prayers and offered sacrifices that I should be holy in the sight of Yahweh."

"This is not enough. You must do more!"

Ahab shook his head, his stubbornness showing in the tightness of his lips. "I will not raze the temple I gave my consent to build."

Jezebel was half standing, pointing a quivering finger at the old man. "Hear the king, Elijah. This is his royal will. Let us make a test of your god! Let us chain and flog you for as long as the drought lasts and see if—"

Elijah straightened up. His long grey hair and beard seemed to rise and stand with him as he threw back his head and pointed his staff at the queen. "A test of gods—yes! I meet that challenge!"

"Chain him," screamed the queen.

Elijah lifted both gaunt arms. "Not in chains, no. As a free man I shall challenge Baal—and Astarte—and Moloch—and Asherath—any and all of the gods you worship, woman of Sidon!"

111

Ahab leaned forward, intrigued.

"What is this challenge of yours, old man?"

The Hall of Audience was hushed. Other than the rasp of Elijah's heavy breathing, there was no sound. Like a patriarch of old—as Moses might have stood before his people with upraised arms when he came upon them worshipping the golden calf—so stood Elijah. He seemed filled with fire and electricity crackled in his hair.

"Let there be a test between Yahweh and the false gods. On top of Mount Carmel let this test take place. Let two altars be built, one by the priests of Baal, one by myself. Then let the priests of Melkart pray down fire from the sky."

Jezebel snorted, "The man's mad!"

Elijah grinned at her, showing stained, discolored teeth. "I shall pray to Yahweh for the same purpose. I too shall pray down fire—fire which shall consume the sacrifice we each select—two bullocks on stone altars!"

Ahab turned from the old man to his wife. Jezebel was white with rage. He had never seen her quite so disturbed. A lock of her black hair had come loose from the golden wires that bound it and dangled beside her cheek. It gave her a curiously appealing look. She had released her hold on the dog. Her fingers were spread out on her thighs, deeply clinging as though she sought for support in this moment of insanity.

Then she laughed, throwing back her head and opening her lips so that peal after peal of humorless mirth flowed out across the chamber. Elijah grinned at her hilarity as though making a mock of it.

"So shall it be, old man. A contest of gods. Yours and mine. And when no fire comes from the heavens to devour your bullock, know that this shall be your fate! You shall be stripped and tied to a stake set upright on a wagon and you shall be taken through all the cities of Israel. In the great marketplaces shall you be flogged until the skin hangs in strips from your back. Thus do we treat false prophets in this land."

Elijah only bowed his head. "Let it be as the queen has said," he muttered, thumping his staff on the ground. Then he glanced shrewdly at Ahab. "And will the king see to the arrangements for this contest between gods?"

Ahab nodded. "You shall be housed in the home of the high priest and given garments better fitted for the occasion than those rags. I shall send men to you who will construct your altar according to your wishes."

"As the king has said, so shall it be."

112

Elijah inclined his head, turned and stalked from the Hall of Audience. Ahab watched him go with the odd feeling that he had come to a turning point in his life. Unaccountably, for the heat was still terrible, he began to shiver.

Nine: On The Heights Of Mount Carmel

1.

Twin mounds of wood and stone rose upward from the level stretch of ground that was the top of Mount Carmel. They towered high, for the wood piled around the dead bullocks on the twin altars was thick, and there was much of it. Double trenches had been built to accommodate the stone bases on which the hewn logs had been set.

The strings of zithers and lyres made the air sweet with melody. Naked corybantes danced and writhed for the onlookers as they cried their prayers to Baal. Naked priests prayed with them, whirling, skipping, hopping all around the altar dedicated to their god.

Staring at the posturing men and at the women who flaunted their loins in lewd poses, wrapped in a plain black cloak against recognition, was the queen of Israel. Rael stood beside her, the fold of his mantle drawn across his lower face. His arm held her hip to his own, as if her nearness and her softness might reassure him that he had done the right thing. It was not fitting that a man should interfere in the ways of gods, and Rael was troubled.

Seeming to sense his nervousness, the woman turned to him, smiling faintly. "You are sure you did what has to be done?"

He nodded curtly. She was whispering and it was hard to hear above the zithers and the outcries of the naked priestesses. "I gave them the powder as I promised you I would."

"Tell me again about this strange powder," she murmured.

"I found some papers in the effects of the man named Chang Lun whom Ahab killed in Moab. He came from a very far place, from the land of Chin which we in Israel have considered to be only a tale told by traders and travellers amusing themselves at our expense. But the marks on his paper were real enough. I could not read them—but some thoughtful char-

113

acter, probably his trader friend—had rendered them also into Greek. And Greek I can understand.

"The powder is black. It burns with a fierce flame and explodes in a violent manner when ignited. I do not know what it is called but it is made of saltpetre, charcoal and sulphur. It took me a long time to duplicate that powder. Saltpetre is not easily come by in Samaria. I had to send to Egypt for it."

She made an impatient gesture. "And now?"

"Now a small keg of that powder lies under the pile of logs and the bullock of Baal-Melkart. I have shown the priest how to light the fuse at a safe distance, unseen by anyone. It will burn in such a manner that its flaming will not be seen, since the priests have set up rows of sacrificial wine jars leading to their altar so as to hide it."

Jezebel touched the tip of her tongue to her upper lip. Her eyes gleamed with the light of triumph. "Go on, go on."

"When the burning fuse touches the hidden powder keg it will explode into a blazing holocaust. The sound will be deafening—like a god roaring in honest wrath. The fire will be so hot none will dare stand near it."

Jezebel closed her eyes under the stab of delight that rode along her nerves. Baal-Melkart would win this contest, be the supreme deity in Israel as he was in Phoenicia. Excitement was a pulsebeat in her body, jarring it with quivers. She pressed into Rael, reaching into his cloak to fondle him.

"This night I will make you scream with pleasure," she breathed. "For you will have brought my god victory. I shall never forget what you have done, Rael. This I vow—taking my oath as did Eliezer to Abraham long ago."

Her hand touched him and clung tightly a moment.

Soft laughter trailed up from her reddened mouth. "Am I so exciting? Or is it the dancing of the priestesses you find interesting?"

He could not answer her, his mouth was so dry. This woman beside him might be a queen but it was not her royalty that fascinated him. She was almost like a man in her direct honesty. There was no shyness about her as there was with the Habiru women. Ruth, for instance—to whom he was betrothed, but marriage to whom he kept putting off—would have died rather than take such a vow. Yet he would have Jezebel no other way.

She began to whisper to him now, calling his attention to the corybantes, to the plump thighs of one and the rotating belly of another, to the jumping breasts of a third. Her voice was like an aphrodisiac in his ears, as amorous incense in his

114

nostrils. He turned his eyes where she ordered and he saw what she wanted him to see.

From the painted nipples of a priestess his gaze fell on the twelve high priests advancing between the dancers toward their altar. They were stately men, imposing in cloth of gold garments and with horned tiaras on their heads. In their hands they held the sacred myrtle branches. Their chanting filled the air, overshadowing the erotic plaints of the priestesses. As the priests came closer, the women sank to the ground and lay prostrate, their white backs and buttocks gleaming in the sunlight.

"It is almost time," said Jezebel, pointing upward at the sun.

They could see Elijah now, striding forward with the wind ruffling his long white beard, his ragged woolen robe flapping at his skinny ankles. There was an exaltation in his face that made it seem to shine. Straight forward he came, long staff walking with him, up to the priests of Baal.

"Servants of Baal-zebub! Attend me." When they would have broken out into protests at his words, for *zebub* was the Habiru term for demon, his fierce gesture silenced them. "I came to give you the advantage—so there can be no doubt."

Elijah turned. His hand waved and pointed. A dozen young men came running with watersacks. They began sprinkling water over the wooden logs and the flesh of the dead bullock on the altar to Yahweh. Two of them ran even further—to the ground about the altar of Baal and spilled their waterskins.

Jezebel screamed in anger and dismay.

As if her cry had roused them the priests of Baal sprang forward. They caught the two youths and hurled them back away from the altar of Baal. But by this time the ground about that altar was soaked with wetness.

Jezebel screeched, "He is the demon—the *zebub*—that Elijah! He smelled a trick. He watered the ground lest it carry fire in some hidden way to our altar."

"The fuse is wet," Rael nodded. "It will not burn. The black powder is useless."

The high priests of Phoenicia understood this. They turned to one another in dismay. In some manner or by sheer guesswork, the old man had learned their ruse and had guarded himself against it.

"Now our fire will not light," snarled Jezebel.

"Neither will his," Rael consoled her, gesturing at the trench where the bullock of Yahweh lay drenched.

"I care nothing for that. I wanted Baal to win. I shall demand the contest take place another day." She would have gone forward but Rael caught and held her.

"Are you mad? To be seen like this in the garments of a temple priestess before your people? Well enough in Samaria but here in the countryside it will only be a scandal."

She glowered at him but allowed him to draw her back. Her body was shaking in a fierce rage and her nostrils dilated with the effort of her lungs to fill with air. Her lips were drawn to a cruel, cold line as she regarded Elijah.

The old man must die—as Benajah bar-Simon had died!

Golden trumpets were blowing and the sacred myrtle branches were being shaken. The high priests were chanting to Baal-Melkart and their singing was joined by the voices of the naked priestesses and lesser priests. Elijah leaned on his staff and watched them grimly.

Time went as if on silver wings. The sun climbed higher in the sky. The people gathered to watch the contest stared hard at the altar of Baal but even the most optimistic of them saw no spark, no burst of sudden flame. Yet the chanting went on.

After a little while the priestesses and the lesser priests began their orgiastic dancing once again. They went among the people, rousing them by their example to join with them in the worship of their god. Here and there a man and a woman cast off their garments and took their places with the holy ones, singing and cavorting. Soon hundreds were engaged in working themselves to a frenzy. To make their worship further pleasing to their god, men began to caress the women and women, the men.

Elijah cried out against this harlotry but his voice was drowned by the singing of the high priest and the sounding cymbals. After a moment, Elijah turned his back on them. This movement brought him almost face to face with Jezebel.

He did not recognize her. Gone were the golden baubles, the studied perfection of her queenly coiffure. Her hair hung long, her eyelids were tinted blue and her lips were thick and red with salve so that she looked the part of a sacred prostitute. As if to shelter her further from the prophet, Rael yanked her back into the crowd.

"Hide yourself," he growled in her ear. "Would you have him point you out to everyone?"

"I care nothing for myself. I want Baal to send fire!"

The fire did not come.

The priestesses were stained with sweat, their muscles slack with exhaustion. Some of them had sunk onto the ground, a

116

prey for the men who had joined the dancers or for the lesser priests who hoped by this demonstration of their manliness to induce their god to reveal his powers. Their example was a stimulant to others who fell to the ground or stood together hidden by cloaks against the eyes of the onlookers.

A cymbal clashed.

Then there was silence on Mount Carmel.

The holy men of Baal-Melkart stood with hanging heads in acknowledgment of their failure. Only where the men and women and the priests and priestesses occupied themselves with one another was there any sound or movement.

Elijah stirred. He lifted his head and stared around him. His right arm lifted to shake his gnarled staff.

"You have failed, men and women of ungodly faith! Your god is no true god. Only Yahweh the Almighty is the one god upon the face of the earth."

The black cloud was closer, filling the sky to the east with darkness. A streak of yellow shot downward in the distance. Elijah appeared to grow taller as he turned to point at the worshippers of Baal.

"My God comes, people of iniquity! You shameless ones shall see the vengeance of the true God. Remain and perish—or flee and live a little while!"

Others could see the black clouds and the lightnings and a murmur grew in volume among the people on the mount. With incredulity, they seemed to see a majestic face mirrored in those clouds. They did not need Elijah's pointing fingers and thunderous voice to tell them what this was they stared at in such awe.

The dark clouds came nearer, running before a moist wind. The yellow veins that were its lightnings stabbed downward with branching yellow ribbons. Thunder rolled across the hills and the plain of Esdraelon. Elijah stood now with both arms held high, his face turned upward.

"Lord God of Abraham and Moses—speak Your will to these unbelievers! Come in the majesty of Thy might and smite this bullock which I, Thy voice in Israel, have offered up to Thee!"

Lightning rippled downward. Thunder cracked.

"Let Your tongue speak again, in the lightning and the thunder! Speak, great Jehovah! Speak as I have spoken in Thy name!"

A forked tongue of blinding gold thrust groundward. Almost in midair it seemed to pause—to hesitate. Then it darted sideways, straight for the altar of Yahweh.

In the brilliance of that awful bolt, Rael gasped. The illumination was that of two suns. It hurt the eyeballs and made men cry out in terror. Yet before it struck, Rael saw a black rod thrusting upward from the logs of the altar of Yahweh.

An iron rod!

Ever since the discovery of iron it was known to the alchemists that lightning had an affinity for iron. It leaped to it as does the lodestone. Perhaps there was an affinity between this metal and the lightning and the magnetic properties of the lodestone. Rael did not know. He was not sure, though he could guess.

He chuckled so that Jezebel would not hear him.

The old man was sly, sly. He had known or guessed that a storm was coming. Perhaps his corns pained him or he might have some other, unknown way to tell when it would strike. He had estimated its arrival for this precise moment. And he was ready for it, with iron rods cunningly hidden in the logs.

Ah, and more than that—

Now Rael could see the purpose of the water! It was not to prevent a fire—but to hasten it. For lightning is attracted to water and the trench in which the log altar was built was filled with water, making a tiny lake.

If the iron did not draw the lightning—surely the water would! Elijah had been sly, clever, not above lending his God a helping hand!

For the lightning was playing steadily now, hissing and thundering and making the darkness glare like day as it played about the logs, drenching them with flames. Upward leaped that fire, higher, higher. Its sound was a thunder of its own, drowning out all else. Again and again and again the lightning struck the altar of Yahweh until its fire was an inferno.

Elijah gleamed red in the reflection of those flames. Like a scarlet fury he towered and his voice was a peal of fury calling down judgment on the worshippers of Baal. As if in answer to those ringing words—had the old man hidden more rods of iron here and there?—the lightnings played all around the top of the mountain.

A woman screamed as lightning enveloped her so that her hair stood up and her body became as rigid as stone. An instant she stood, then the lightning was gone and a charred corpse remained motionless on what had been its feet. A couple on the ground were next to be struck—and died in the same spasm by which they shuddered out their pleasure.

Jezebel was screaming steadily.

"Get me out of here. Get me out. Get me out!" she begged, long nails clawing into her companion. She was shaking in the intensity of her terror. Feverish eyes stared up at him as hysteria claimed her.

Rael threw his cloak about her shoulders and hugged her against him. With his left arm he brushed people away as he turned and ran with the queen of Israel beside him, across the level hilltop toward a narrow pathway down Mount Carmel.

Behind them was chaos.

The holocaust was spreading as sparks flew here and there, setting fire to cloaks and tunics. Men and women ran back and forth screaming out their agony as flames licked at their flesh. Always the lightning cracked and the thunder rolled and the yellow ribbons danced and jumped across the entire mountaintop. There were few Habiru left here for at the first sign of fire most of them had fled in superstitious terror. Only the Baalists remained and they were dying by the hundreds.

Rael cast one glance back over his shoulder, seeing Elijah standing with his arms held up and a glory of triumph illuminating his face. Perhaps he stood in a space where there was no water and no iron rods. Or perhaps he even hoped the lightning might consume him so that his people could say his God had come and taken him away in this most vivid moment of his long life.

Jezebel slipped and Rael forgot Elijah to catch her in his arms and set her feet upon the ancient stone steps that made a causeway up and down the mount. She was sobbing, shaking uncontrollably. Tears streaked her painted cheeks and a strand of her thick black hair was caught in the brooch that held her cloak. She clung to him as if he were the last reality in a world that had collapsed around her in smoking ruins.

Rael had no thought but to get his beloved to safety. He used a fist on one man, yanked his dagger and drove it to the hilt in the middle of another. He ran with the bloody blade in his hand and men saw it and drew back from him. As he ran his left arm brought Jezebel with him, slipping and sliding on the stone steps.

He had to get away from that holocaust above him. The stench of burning flesh was a nausea in his middle now and images of what he had seen ran before his eyes like those in a shadow lantern. The priestess who had stared upward as in a trance, until a ball of crackling lightning removed her head. The high priests who had run and stumbled full onto a blazing bit of tinder from the altar of Yahweh so that his cloth of gold vestments blazed around him while he screamed. The woman who had joined in the praise and dancing to Baal-Melkart, one of the first to remove her garments and stand naked in her pride, who had fled blindly, covering her eyes—only to trip and plunge into the trench where the bullock perished in the flames. He could still hear her shrieks ringing in his ears.

The vengeance of a god?

Or the cleverness of an old man who could foresee the weather and had made a terrible prediction which had come true?

Rael did not know. He lunged with Jezebel toward his chariot. Almost rudely he flung her to the floorboards and snatched at the reins. The chariot rattled and bounced as it ran along the Megiddo road. Rael was dimly aware of Jezebel huddled against his leg, clinging to it with her arms while her shoulders shuddered out the torrent of her fear.

"He made the fire. I saw him make the fire. The old man did it. He did what he said he would do." Her voice was like a litany of horror. "With my eyes I saw him. He called on his god to make fire and his god made the fire. I am lost. Lost."

A hand fumbled upward toward his belt. Too late, he realized her intention. His dagger was out of its sheath and firmly gripped in her hand before he stirred to reach toward her. The point was an inch from her skin when his fingers closed on her wrist. Silently she fought him, baring her teeth like an enraged cat.

Jezebel was strong, but she was no man. Rael shook her wrist until her fingers loosened and the dagger went flying. She broke free of him and huddled there sobbing harshly.

"I want to die. Why didn't you let me? I have been shamed in the sight of Israel. Don't you understand? My god has been defeated by your god. It was Yahweh who sent fire—not Baal-Melkart! I have failed and death is the penalty for failure when you are a queen."

"It was only a storm. Yahweh knows we're long overdue for one."

"The lightning struck the altar of Yahweh, not that of Baal. You saw it. You saw it."

"I saw more than that," he grinned down at her.

She stared up at him numbly, momentary puzzlement on her features. Then her eyes widened. She clawed at his legs, almost overbalancing him as she pulled herself upward off the floorboards.

"What did you see, Rael? What was it?"

He smiled at her, mentally cursing his tongue. He had no desire to expose Elijah. He was a physician, not a priest. These contests between gods were no affair of his except as they affected Jezebel. Yes, he saw how they might be his business

120

were they to cause this woman to kill herself. He could not endure to face life without her.

She pressed against him, fumbling with his clothing to run her smooth palms across his flesh, straining herself against him. Her cheeks were streaked with tears but the blue shadow on her eyes and the red salve on her lips were untouched so that he saw her only as a desirable woman.

"Tell me, Rael. Tell me what it was you saw."

A bare arm closed about his neck, drew his lips to her open mouth. She clung to him, caressing and stroking him until he was alive with need. And always her voice was a whisper in his mind.

"Tell me. Tell me. Tell me."

"Iron rods," he breathed against her tongue. "Iron rods cleverly hidden in the logs. And a trench of water, like a small lake."

She drew away slightly, frowning. "Iron rods? I saw no iron rods. As for the water, Elijah somehow discovered our ruse and guarded against it."

He explained something of the force within a thunderbolt and its effect on iron and water to her while the chariot rested by the side of the road. Jezebel still frowned, but gradually her expression relaxed as understanding dawned in her eyes.

"Yes," she breathed. "I saw the lightning curve to hit Yahweh's altar and thought it the will of your god."

"So you were meant to think. Everybody thought the same thing."

"Except you and Elijah."

He felt her move against him as a smile turned the corners of her mouth. She whispered, "My own Rael, my clever darling, was the only one who saw through the trick."

"The lightning showed the rods, it was so bright. It lit up the whole world."

"Yet your eyes alone saw the truth."

He wished she would stop her caresses. They were in the open here by the ruts at the side of the road. There was no cover under which he might take her as she seemed to want to be taken. And her fingers were making him alive with hunger, as they had done while he watched the priestesses dance on Mount Carmel.

Rael shrugged and sought to draw away but she held him too tightly, kissing his throat and upward along his jaw. "My lover. My sweet. My man." Rarely had he known Jezebel to be so amorous, writhing to him, quivering and soft, panting harshly.

121

Her cloak fell back, revealing her clad only in the transparent purple linen in which the priestesses of Astarte went to meet the visitors to their goddess in her love gardens. Cunning slits had been arranged to show her white, shapely legs, her curving outer hips, her middle. The swollen mounds of her breasts thrust from two holes in the garment, tipped with beautiful hard nipples.

Rael cried out as she drew him to her where she rested her buttocks on the chariot railing. Half suspended by his arms, she sank to him, crying out, her head fallen back. He felt an intensity of pleasure as she wrapped herself about him. His body shuddered in its spell. From far away he heard a man bellowing and a woman screaming. Not until much later did he understand it was himself and Jezebel.

They were still locked together as the rain came, first in a drop and then two, as if to warn the man and woman of the deluge hanging in the black clouds overhead. Within seconds they were wet from head to toes as the rain pelted them, drenching their skins.

Jezebel held her face to the sky and howled laughter.

To Rael it seemed the world was weeping.

2.

Assur-nasir-pal held two metal horns in his hands, pouring honey from one and oil from the other over the altar before the god Ashur. He was a fleshy man, strong with the thews of full manhood developed in the chase and on the fields of battle. His fringed candys was fashioned of golden threads. Tiny pearls woven into its fringes reflected the torchlight from the temple walls. His conical tiara was of beaten gold inset with rubies and emeralds. He was a living reflection of the might and wealth of the empire he ruled.

By his own admission, Assur-nasir-pal was the most powerful king in all the world. Standing beside Shalmaneser, Jehu admitted that there was truth in the belief of this Assyrian. He had been in Nineveh and Calah long enough to have seen examples of his might and his riches.

Greater even than Babylon was the Nineveh of Assur-nasir-pal. Everywhere the eye went, it saw evidences of the conquests of its armies.

A warrior, Jehu also appreciated to the full all he had

learned about the Assyrian army. Its organization—from the turtan, who commanded the armies, to the meanest slave who polished spearpoints—was a masterpiece of efficiency.

Jehu drew a deep breath, roused from his thoughts by the touch of a hand on his arm. Assur-nasir-pal was turning from the altar, rendering thanks for his latest victory. It was time for all to bow before the ruler of the Assyrian world. Jehu glanced from the ringed hand on his arm up the brocaded sleeve of a candys to the face that stared up at him.

"You are such a favorite of the king," the woman whispered, "I would not like to see you displease him."

The woman—her name was Asharra and she was cousin to the king, he recalled—bowed low, bringing him with her almost to his knees. His people bowed this way only to Yahweh, Jehu thought. It shamed him in a sense, such servile adoration; but he was in Assyria, a friend of its prince and of its king; it was best to follow custom when a stranger in a foreign land.

As he straightened, he read approval in the stare of this handsome woman. Heavily tinted lips smiled approvingly. "You did well, Habiru. It shows you are clever. I like clever men." Laughter glinted in her black eyes below the gilded eyelids. "Especially when they are young and strong."

A voice whispered. "Beware of Asharra, Jehu. She eats young men for breakfast." To one side of him Shalmaneser was grinning.

Asharra pouted, "Just because I don't lock myself in a cell now that my husband's dead doesn't mean I'm an ogress." She linked her arm with that of Jehu. "My husband was a great merchant, Habiru. After he was wounded in a battle, this is, and could no longer go to war."

Not wishing to appear rude, he strolled beside her rustling robes. For an Assyrian woman, Asharra was pleasantly slim. Most Assyrian women were short, and to Jehu's eyes, somewhat dumpy. Asharra was graceful and her walk was pleasant to watch.

"Since Khayani died, I have taken over his business ventures," she prattled as they passed between great red pillars towering upward into the darkness of a vaulted roof. "I converse daily with men from Malatiyeh and from Kue—even from your own Israel."

Jehu broke stride to the sudden pounding of his heart. Israel meant Jezebel and Ahab to him. What he would not give for an hour with them both! As though she sensed his excitement, Asharra murmured, "This very afternoon I hold converse with Micah ben Zebulun, who is a buyer of the alabaster tiles for which we Assyrians are noted."

"This afternoon? Is Micah ben Zebulun lately from Israel?"

She nodded. "He arrived only last evening by horseback with his armed retainers. He comes ahead of the other merchants, being not so old as some nor as fat as others. Since he arrives first, he has his choice of the finest tiles, the most exquisite potteries. It's smart business practice, don't you think? His caravan will set out for Israel a full week before the other traders get here."

They walked into the sunlight making dark bars of the portico pillars. The air was fresh and sweet, for springtime lay upon the land of the two rivers, and the scent of flowers and budding plants was everywhere.

"He will be filled with news," she added carelessly. "I encourage Micah to talk freely and so let me know what goes on in his corner of the world. It was a habit of my dead husband, who found that by learning news of a grain blight in Elam, he might profit by selling the Elamites some flour."

"I would like to meet Micah ban Zebulun," Jehu exclaimed.

There was a hunger in him for news of what went on in Samaria and in Jezreel. Too long had he been out of touch with his own people. Had Rael married Ruth yet? How many children had Jezebel given Ahab? What sort of a king did Ahab make, now that Omri was in his grave? Questions trembled on his tonguetip, questions he had forced down deep into his mind to remain unspoken while he was in Babylon and Calah.

Now this painted woman beside him was offering him that news. With a conspiratorial air, he closed his hand over the ringed fingers resting on his arm. Her dark eyes laughed up at him in understanding.

"I have my chariot waiting by the Gate of Nergal," she informed him, gathering up a fold of her heavy candys for easier walking. "It isn't so far to the warehouses."

She was like a child with a new toy, he thought, moving beside her. Laughter came easily to her lips, which was an odd thing, for most Assyrians were glum and morose by nature. She ran lightly beside him, her golden sandals winking into view and out of sight to each step. No one paid them any attention.

When they arrived she took command of the place at once, moving to the table, scanning the tightly written cuneiform, moving some to one side, some to another. Her ringed hand caught up a mallet, hit the gong a ringing note.

A woman entered, bowed low. "Inform Micah ben Zebulun we are pleased to see him," Asharra told her.

From the woman, Asharra turned to Jehu. "I'll leave you alone with him. You can chatter to your own content. I know how restricting my presence would be."

Jehu protested but she only shook her head. "No, no. An older woman learns consideration in her lifetime." Her dark eyes glistened beneath the gilded eyelids. "As well as—other things."

She moved past him, putting out a hand to touch his wrist. Her fingers closed, held him tightly. "Later, perhaps? After you've spoken with Micah ben Zebulun—you might share food with me at my home?"

Jehu bowed gravely. He was a little tired of palace formalities. A few hours freedom in a private home sounded pleasant. "Gladly. Perhaps you'd like to hear what news this Micah brings."

"Perhaps," she smiled over her shoulder as she went out of the room.

He had not long to wait. The drapery of the doorway swept upward and a lean man in a striped cloak stood staring at him. "Jehu of Israel?"

Jehu came across the carpeted floor to clutch the hands extended to him. "Asharra tells me you're in from Samaria within the past few days and that you might have some news of home for me."

Micah smiled. "I'm as filled with news as an honest measure with grain," he grinned. "Where do you want me to begin?"

Excitement flamed in Jehu. "Tell me all, everything you know."

Micah talked for over an hour. He made Jehu see the victory Ahab won over Chang Lun and the coming of Elijah. Of course, Jehu knew about the fight with Ben-hadad before that, and the help given him by the priests and priestesses from Phoenicia? No? Well, news travels slowly in the world. Only the Habiru merchants concerned themselves with what happened in Israel.

Ahab allowed Jezebel to build temples to her gods following this victory over Aram. For himself, he would not say whether this was good or bad. He was an understanding man, and realized that different people served different deities. But the prophet Elijah had not been so lenient. He had held back the rains from Israel for a long, long time. Only now, since his contest on Mount Carmel, had the rains come.

Gossip said that Jezebel had tried to poison the old man,

125

with a concoction given her by Rael, her own physician. This was or was not a cruel falsehood, depending on who told what story. For a foreign woman, Jezebel was popular in Israel but the priests of Yahweh hated her. Some said she was a good woman; others, that she was a harlot. To Ahab her husband who loved her, she was a helpmate and a staff on which to lean.

Only recently, for instance, just before he had left Samaria to go to war against Aram a second time, there'd been trouble about a vineyard belonging to a man named Naboth. Ahab wanted it, to enlarge his palace grounds.

Naboth was a stubborn man. He would not sell, though Ahab offered a more than generous purchase price. Ahab fumed and fretted; Jezebel acted. She conjured up a charge against Naboth of blasphemy against Yahweh, which was a laugh, considering how Jezebel herself felt about the god of Israel. She also managed a charge of treacherous words and acts against Ahab, which might have been true because there was no love lost between Ahab and Naboth. There were witnesses testifying to all this. Naboth was found guilty and was stoned to death beyond the city walls.

The sunlight faded across the floor and the room grew darker, yet still the merchant talked on, speaking of the submission Ben-hadad of Aram had made to Ahab after his second defeat and of the treasures that laden ox-carts had carried into Samaria as a result.

Oh, yes. One last thing. His friend Rael, the physician, had been married to Ruth, the daughter of Uzziah, in a great state ceremony. Coming as it had on the wings of Ahab's second victory over Ben-hadad, it had been the occasion of much celebration. Ahab and Jezebel had given costly gifts, as had several kings from Aram, from Moab, from Ammon, from Phoenicia. These gifts had not been to honor Rael so much as they had been to curry favor with Ahab, who was gaining quite a reputation as a military man.

Somewhere beyond the room a drum sounded, rolling out its rhythms. Micah came to his feet with a laugh. "I've babbled like the brook of Merom, Jehu. The warehouse is about to close."

They could hear the slap of rush sandals. A slave came into the room, bowing low, murmuring that if the visitors were finished, Asharra was waiting in her chariot for Jehu of Israel.

Micah winked and punched Jehu lightly. "Go have yourself a time, Jehu. Things are going well with your old friends. Rael is married. Ahab is a king in deed by this time. And Jezebel has her temples to Baal-Melkart. When I go back to Israel, I'll ask for an audience with Ahab and tell him you're doing all right yourself."

Their hands met, tightened. With small bows, they said their farewells. Ahab followed the slave down the long corridor and out into the warehouse square flushed red with sunset.

Asharra was standing in the chariot, watching him. As the dying sun touched her many rings with fire, Jehu realized suddenly that this was an important woman in Calah, wealthy and a relative to Assur-nasir-pal. He himself was a wanderer, a voluntary exile from Israel. Ashara might do more for him than merely introduce him to Habiru traders.

He bowed low before her, murmuring his thanks. As he stepped back onto the chariot floorboards he put an arm behind her back so she might brace herself against it. She leaned into him willingly, letting him feel her softness under the brocaded tunic.

After a moment she said, "Did your long talk make you homesick for Israel?"

"On the contrary, it only relieved my mind. My friends are well. I can go about my own business now with a glad heart."

"And what is your business?"

"To find a place for myself in a foreign land, first of all. As a soldier, preferably, since war is the only thing I know. Yet Assyria does not accept mercenaries in its armies."

There was a little silence after that, during which Asharra leaned more heavily to Jehu and seemed lost in thought. She roused herself as the chariot swung into an open gateway in a high wall surrounding a large mansion, turning to him brightly.

"If you would let me help, I might arrange a captaincy for you. I have a little influence with Assur-nasir-pal, being his cousin."

"I'd be grateful," he nodded.

She smiled at him, letting him assist her to the flagstones before a wide, airy portico. A fountain made splashing sounds in the middle of a garden filled in this springtime of the year with cinnamon and cassia. There was a fragrance in the air and the high brick wall seemed to cut off the rest of the city from this flowered sanctuary.

Asharra said, "I often walk here in the evenings. It helps me forget my loneliness." A wistfulness about her voice touched Jehu. "It isn't easy to be a woman and alone in a city like Calah."

127

Her eyes appeared to weigh him as he said, "It's even harder being a stranger, though Shalmaneser and his father have made me very welcome."

"Perhaps we might help one another forget our mutual loneliness," she said breathlessly, turning to stroll along a garden walk.

"If I could do that, I'd be happy," he murmured, following her swaying tunic. When she came to a stop beside the fountain and bent to dip her fingers in its waters, he added bluntly, "I'm a soldier, Asharra. No courtier to say the pretty speeches a woman likes to hear. My tongue stumbles over what I'm trying to say—"

She whirled, covering his lips with a soft palm. She was an attractive woman, perfumed and painted, and very soft under her garments. "Say nothing, then. Not yet. Let me dream a little."

He kissed her palm, relishing its pampered smoothness, telling himself that he and this woman were groping together toward a few moments of happiness in their otherwise empty lives. He had had enough of inns and taverns, of cold palaces where he was one of a number of visitors. Asharra was offering him a home, a pleasant place where he might be himself.

"There's roast lamb for dinner and melons from Aram," she said like a wife of long standing. "And wine from Khilbun kept chilled in the cellars."

"Wine with which to toast your beauty," he smiled.

She made a face at him, laughing. "Who says you aren't a courtier? Not even Bi-lubadad, who is *rabsak* to Assur-nasir-pal, could have made a prettier speech."

They walked toward the portico side by side.

Over the little round tables on which the steaming lamb and sliced melons were served, Jehu found that Asharra was a different woman in her own home. Gone with the heavy fringed brocades of court wear was her reticence and formality. As she had donned a simple linen tunic and loosed her long black hair which was gathered behind her in a circlet, so she adopted different manners. She laughed gaily and with obvious flirtatiousness. She made jokes about the king and his greed for power and wealth.

When the food was gone, she sipped wine with him, cup for cup, calling at last for a lyre on which her fingers made little melodies to which she recited poetry. Jehu was fascinated by her, a fascination she enhanced by casual disclosures of her body. When she bent to lift her winecup, her tunic opened at the throat to reveal a swollen breast. As she settled herself more comfortably on her cushioned couch and cradled the lyre to her middle, the tunic lifted to bare the insides of her slightly plump thighs.

She regaled him with Assyrian myths and folklore, speaking of Gilgamesh and Enkidu, and of the visit to the underworld undertaken by Gilgamesh in an abortive attempt to win life to his dead companion in adventure. She described the battle between the ancient hero and the monster Huwawa so expertly that Jehu found himself sitting on the edge of his couch as he listened.

When the oil boats burned lower and the chilled wine began to take effect, flushing her cheeks and putting a new sparkle in her eyes, Asharra turned to the more erotic poems of her people. She recited them gravely or with laughter as they seemed to deserve, playing out the part of frightened bride or amorous coquette in turn, with an aptitude which suggested an excellent ability at mimickry. Once she even came to her feet and danced about the room, the lyre held in the crook of a bared arm.

Under the thin linen *kalisiris* she was naked. Jehu saw her flesh tints where the light from the oil boats touched her body, shadowing it in darkness through the linen. Her breasts were large, heavy with maturity. Her waist was slim and her hips round and firm. Without conscious thought, he found himself roused by her nearness.

When she sank beside him on the couch, breathless and panting, he put out his hands to her, rushing his palms up her smooth arms to her shoulders, bending her slightly and drawing her down and into the cushions. She lay with laughter bubbling on her moist lips, eyes half closed.

"We have a legend in Israel of a female demon, Asharra," he whispered, "who takes the form of a beautiful woman to tempt men to madness. You are such a succubus. You make the blood bubble in my veins like flowing wine."

She breathed slowly, putting her hands up to his cheeks, stroking him. "I would be a succubus to you, man of Israel."

His head bent. His lips slid along her upper arm and across her naked shoulder to her soft throat. She gave to his caresses lazily, stirring her hips and giving forth concupiscent laughter, her pale legs uncovered where her tunic pulled back almost to her hips. Soft and warm beneath his stroking hands, she let him slide his fingers up her thighs and across her mounded belly to the soft flesh above her hipbones.

Holding her like this, he bent to take her lips with his. She clung to him with both bare arms, breathing harshly as

129

she drew him down across the couch with her. Their tongues played back and forth while she began to caress him, not with the touch of inexpert youth but with the assurance of a woman who has bedded more than a few times with a man.

His lips trailed into the opening of her tunic and across the upper swells of her breasts. Asharra was loosening his own short tunic, laying bare his hairy chest, fondling his hips, kissing his shoulders.

Just so might Jezebel have made love with me, straining and eager. A woman flushed with desire for my body, whose throat makes hungry moans that goad my flesh to fury.

As Asharra opened her linen *kalisiris* so that she lay nude from sandals to her long black hair, Jehu thought dazedly that one woman was very much like another. Jezebel surely had no more to offer him than this Assyrian woman who had begun to sob now with frenzy. In a way it was like winning freedom from galling chains.

The soft hands that parted his own garments and drew them from him were striking off the shackles of a doomed love, killing it, throwing it onto some psychic refuse heap. With her quivering flesh and anxious moans, Asharra was teaching him that he might forget Jezebel in the pleasure she would give him.

She cried out as he joined himself with her, as might a woman whose night dreams have become reality. Under his hips her own hips surged like waves, lifting high and still higher to the very limits of human endurance. As he shared her passion, Jehu told himself that Asharra asked nothing of him other than his body.

Jezebel would have demanded his soul.

Ten: Before The Walls Of Ramoth-Gilead

1.

The burial vault was cold and damp despite the many candleflames fluttering in the faint breeze blowing in through its single opening. It was a gloomy place at best, even when well lighted; it had been dug under the side of a limestone cliff that formed a part of the older portion of Samaria; it was always dark and murky, and its limestone walls, covered over by splotches of lichens, added to the atmosphere.

Rael knelt on the stone floor, shivering.

Behind him he could hear the chanting voices of the mourners as they walked away, leaving him alone for a little while, as was the custom, with his dead. In his mind and with his eyes closed as he swayed back and forth, he could see them with the ashes on their heads and their torn sackcloth garments. Their voices had been shrill and discordant in his ears for the past hour. He would rather have had them sing sweetly and with harmony, but this would have been a violation of tradition; the *qinah* was not heard except at the time of death.

For Ruth had been such a happy woman.

He wished he could cry for what might have been, but tears were denied him. The sackcloth garment that itched his naked skin, the ceremonial ashes on his shaven head and face, must take the place of tears for this woman who had been wife to him for less than a full month.

Perhaps it was horror that left his eyes and cheeks dry when they should be wet. His was the hand that had cut her down in the days of her bridehood, his the hand that had concocted the poison which she had swallowed in a golden cup handed her by Queen Jezebel.

Rael moaned low in his throat. The poison had not been meant for Ruth when he had stoppered it in a little glass vial and given it to Jezebel, but for—Elijah. It had been in those delirous days of desire, with Ahab gathering his armies for war and leaving him and Jezebel together so much, right after Elijah had confounded the priests of Baal on Mount Carmel, that he had made the poison for her to give the old prophet. Wisely, Elijah had fled away.

Would that Ruth had been able to flee!

A sob formed in his throat but Rael choked it back. He did not deserve to sob for his dead wife, did not merit the relief of tears. His relatives and the hired mourners had eyed him oddly during the short hours when Ruth lay wrapped in her cere-cloths before the burial. A husband should cry when his wife has died, especially when that wife is only a bride; Rael could not.

He remembered vividly the anger of Jezebel at his decision to wed Ruth after so many years of espousal. She had even thrown a winecup at him so that he had bled freely, cut deep enough for his wound to leave a fine white line on his jaw as a memento of the moment.

"Am I not woman enough for you?" her voice echoed in his head. "Are not my breasts firm to your touch, my thighs wide to your coming? Must you also bed this Ruth?"

At another time he might have gloried in her jealousy. Looking back, his misery came because he had not wedded Ruth sooner, had not taken out his hunger for the body of his queen on the body of his wife. If he had, Ruth might have been alive now. But unlike Jehu, he had never been a man for substitutes.

His head lifted. His eyes touched the body shrouded in white winding sheets, so still, so motionless. The candles beyond her head and beyond her feet made the whiteness seem more stark. Two days ago she had been vivid, laughing, alive with joy at the carnelian necklace and bracelet with the matching earrings he had given her so that she might be received by the queen in the finery so dear to the heart of a woman.

Jezebel had fed her wine as once she had fed wine to the high priest of Israel, Benajah bar-Simon. Ruth had sickened and died all in the space of three hours. The poison had been meant for Elijah. Rael wondered which might be the greater sin, to conspire at the death of a holy man of Yahweh or to murder your own wife.

His hands firmed into fists. Jezebel had dared do this to him. To him, who had been so much to her. Lover. Confidant. Conspirator. Fellow murderer. A man who had given up his God to avail himself of the sensuous delights of a foreign woman, a pagan, a woman who was no better than a harlot.

Yahweh, hear me! Give me Thy strength.

He could stay no longer in Samaria. Jezebel would send for him and he would go to her, having no excuse, and when his eyes touched her flesh he would once again be a slave to her will. He would forgive her for murdering his wife. He would draw her against him and cover her with kisses and caresses. He was weak where the queen of Israel was concerned and had no strength of his own.

Only Thy strength can help me, Yahweh. Give me of it!

How long he lay there before the bier of his wife he did not know. His hands were clasped and his head rested on them as his forearms rested on the cold damp stone. Perhaps he was in a swoon. He was never sure, afterward.

But when the hand of an uncle touched him, he stood up knowing what he must do. He would go with Ahab out of Israel and to Ramoth when Ahab made war against the hosts of Gilead. As a physician to tend the sick and the dying he would go, and perhaps in laboring to serve others rather than himself, he would find a new way of life.

2.

Two ebony chairs covered with the skins of wild animals had been set up before the gates of the city of Samaria. Here sat Ahab, King of Israel, and his fellow ruler, Jehosephat, king of Judah, to listen to the visions of the holy men.

Ahab was intent on these wild men, so intent that at times the older Jehosephat covered a smile with his hand. Ahab had a weakness for knowing his fortune. Well, that was understandable enough, after what old Elijah had done to him, denying him rain and then bringing fire down on Mount Carmel. Experiences like that put heavy lines on a king's face. Secretly, Jehosephat was just as well pleased that Elijah concerned himself only with what went on north of Bethel.

The king of Judah let his eyes roam out over the gathering. There must be several hundreds of the wild, ragged fellows who called themselves prophets met here by order of the king. Some wore the stinking hides of animals long since dead, some no more than mud daubs over their nakedness. Here and there a man stood better dressed than the others, eyes closed and lips moving in prayer. For himself, Jehosephat cared little what these ragamuffins said would happen to him. He believed a man wrote his own destiny.

He glanced at Ahab, who looked older than his years as he craned forward to see the cryptic lines a holy man was scratching in the dust. By rights, Ahab should be a happy king. He had an army second to none in this corner of the world. His military victories had won him fame and land and tribute. Yet there was a haunting melancholy about Ahab as though an evil spirit was astride his shoulders.

The shadow of Elijah?

A few months before he had demanded, almost with hysteria in his voice, that someone be brought before him who would dare to speak the truth. Was there a foreknowledge of doom in Ahab, a psychic understanding that his end might be upon him? Someone had mentioned the name of Micaiah, who was reputed to be an honest prophet, of the same cloth as Elijah; Ahab had sent for him, but Micaiah had not yet arrived. Jehosephat did not believe that one prophet was any better than the others; though from what he had done, Elijah seemed to be what he claimed to be, a man of God.

And Elijah had threatened Ahab with doom. Even in Judah, he had heard about the curse that terrified Ahab and his wife, Jezebel.

Ah, there was a woman, that Jezebel!

Jehosephat stirred, remembering how she had come to the feast to welcome him into Samaria, clad in those diaphanous Cos linens through which a man could see her body. He had looked freely enough, Jehosephat admitted, and had felt a stirring of the blood. As good as naked, she had been, with her fine legs and curving haunches veiled by black mist and her big breasts trembling to her every motion. He wondered what Ahab, as her husband, might feel when his wife displayed herself so publicly. It was a pagan custom in Tyre and Sidon, but here in Israel it seemed out of place.

Maybe that was why Ahab appeared so gloomy. His wife and Elijah were enough to give any man an apathy of spirit. He sought in prophecy a forgetfulness—or perhaps a simple hope of better things to come—that his ordinary life denied him.

"A great victory, lord king. I see captives without number and gold without counting. I see—"

"—blood! The blood of a king called Ahab!"

The voice was like a thunderclap in the sundrenched heat of midday. Jehosephat raised himself a little, peering over the heads of the crowd. Two officers were moving through the throng, bringing a man in their wake. It was this man who had called out in the stentorian voice.

When he stood before Ahab the man said, "You summoned me, lord king. You asked me to prophesy for you. I see blood. Your blood, spilled on the ground as death comes hunting for you."

Ahab chuckled audibly and the soldiers grouped about him laughed in echo to his amusement. "Am I not cursed enough by Elijah? Must you also croak as he croaked?"

The man stared back at him evenly. "I am Micaiah the son of Imlah. You sent for me to prophesy for you and the king of Judah. I do no more than you have asked."

Jehosephat leaned closer to Ahab. "The others have said we shall have good fortune. Why bother with this man?"

Ahab hit the arm of his chair. "Because I want the truth. Any man can say to me, 'You shall pull down the walls of

Ramoth in Gilead and know victory.' If these men can see the future, let their tongues tell me of it. Say on, son of Imlah."

Micaiah straightened slowly. "Once Elijah prophesied for you, king Ahab. There where you walked in the great gardens of Naboth on an evening with your arm about your wife Jezebel. The gardens you took from an honest man by stealth."

Ahab was stung to fury. "He was a confessed blasphemer, deserving of death by stoning. Such is the law."

"The law is only the will of the king."

"Have done, have done! Speak of the future, not the past."

No, not the past, Ahab. And especially not of that night in the gardens of Naboth—he could never think of them as his own, though his had been the orders that had made them over into an extension of the royal palace gardens—when he and Jezebel had sought relief from the summer heat beneath a plane tree. It was there that Elijah had found them, leaning more heavily than ever on his gnarled staff.

His eyes had been angry, overbright, as though he too tired of this role he played and wished to see it done with, finished.

"I come for the last time, Ahab. No more shall I stand before you to bring you the word of Yahweh."

Jezebel had looked around her as if for soldiers of the guard. Ahab knew how fanatically she hated the old man; he wouldn't put it past her to snatch a spear from a man and run it into Elijah; but there were no soldiers to be seen.

From under his bushy white brows, the prophet had brooded at them. "You enjoy the flowers and the shrubs of Naboth do you? By his death you gained them, by that death are you accursed. The Lord God has lost patience with you, Ahab of Israel."

"Get out," Jezebel had screamed. "You nasty old man— get out of my sight before I call the guard to kill you."

Ahab had sought to calm her but she was shaking with a rage that lent her unusual strength. She cast away his hands and faced Elijah with chin high in a fury that flushed her face.

"Naboth was a blasphemer. He deserved to die!"

"You forged the documents that convicted him. You bribed the witnesses. You ordered his stoning. And for all of this you have gained nothing. For the Lord God has sent me to you, saying,

"Here in this garden you have purchased your own death-bed, Ahab. Here where you stand shall you die, bleeding of wounds. And even in that place beyond the walls of Samaria

135

where the dogs licked up the blood of Naboth, there shall dogs also lick your blood!"

Jezebel screamed and flung herself at the old man, painted nails curved to rip and slash. Elijah warded her off with his stick, thrusting her back so that she staggered, but he also lost his balance and fell heavily to the paving stones of the garden walk.

He looked up at her and his eyes were feverish as his hand lifted and his forefinger pointed. "As for you, harlot queen and queen of harlots, hear what is to be your fate. For dogs shall eat Jezebel by the wall of Jezreel!"

Ahab had lunged to catch Jezebel and draw her back against him, pinning her quivering body to his own. She was breathing fiercely, like a bellows working at a forge, but she quieted a little when she heard the words of the old man.

"Leave us," she whispered. "Leave us, you who are our worst enemy. Would to Baal that my husband had the courage to kill you as you should be killed—or I the power!"

They had stood together—closer than they had been for a long time, Ahab reflected—and watched Elijah pick himself up off the stones and limp away out of the garden and their lives. Then Jezebel had turned and clung to him, shivering, not with tears and sobs for such was not her way, but in a frenzy of the spirit.

Now as he stared at Micaiah, Ahab hungered to know whether old Elijah had spoken truth or had merely mouthed his own private wishes. He leaned forward, gesturing at Micaiah.

"Yes, I sent for you, son of Imlah. Speak what you foresee in my future."

Micaiah stood straight, his head high. "I see as Elijaw saw, king Ahab. I see you dying in the gardens of Naboth, and outside the city walls, the dogs lapping up your blood."

Ahab smiled grimly. "And before that? Before I die, will I know victory over Gilead?"

"It is as the Lord God wills. You shall go to Gilead and victory shall be upon your arms. Ramoth shall fall and Gilead shall be taken unto Israel, to serve it."

Jehosephat held his breath, watching Ahab. Gilead to the east was a neighbor state of Israel, yet it was from Ramoth that armed men ventured forth to attack the trade caravans of Judah. For this reason, to rouse up Ahab against Gilead, he had come into Israel. His own armies were too weak for the task. By forming an alliance with Ahab, by giving him Gilead for his tribute, he would be insuring the safety of the caravan routes for his own people.

Ah, but if it meant his death, Ahab might not go to Ramoth. Jehosephat wished he knew the words that might sway his will, one way or the other.

The soldiers close to Ahab shifted, making room for a new-comer, a slim man with a hood over a shaved face and head, a man in mourning garments. Ahab looked up with interest at this new arrival.

"I have come to offer myself, Ahab, as physician to your troops when you march on Ramoth."

Jehosephat recognized the man, now. It was Rael, who had such a name for marvelous cures here in Samaria. Perhaps he could do what Jehosephat could not.

Ahab laughed suddenly and clapped a hand to his chair arm. "I sought for an omen and you came to me, Rael. With you at my side, what need have I to fear death? I shall stay far from the battlefront where no enemy can come at me. I shall thus test my strength againts the words of Micaiah."

The king looked at the man standing before him. "Take this man, Micaiah, son of Imlah, and put him in chains in the palace prison. Feed him only bread and water until I return from Gilead. If I die as he has said, he shall go free. If I do not die—he shall!"

Ahab rose and gathered his cloak about him.

The prophesying was at an end.

3.

The attack upon Ramoth was swift and deadly.

Ahab hurled his archers against its walls, showering them and the city streets beyond with flight after flight of arrows. From entrenched positions his war engines hurled flaming spears and massive stones against the rooftops of the buildings and the great stone towers rising upward from the sands. Smoke and flame began to plague the people of Gilead. From the wallwalks, their soldiery could do no more than stud the standing shields protecting the engineers with useless shafts.

For three days the assault went on before the gates of Ramoth opened and its troops came out in waves of spears and flashing swords. They hit the entrenched war engines with steel and fire. Destroy those—burn them to charred cinders—

and the attackers would be reduced to arrows. And arrows alone never took a city.

It was the move Ahab had been awaiting.

He hurled his chariots across the flat plains in three titanic waves. Each chariot held a bowman and a spearman. They fell upon the soldiers of Ramoth, cutting off their escape path into the city. Chariots were never made to stand and fight, so behind them Ahab crowded the massed spearman of Israel and Judah.

He watched the battle from a distance, chafing against his own safety, watching when Jehosephat went in gold and purple to lead the men of Judah as a king was meant to lead. At times the battle was hidden from him by clouds of dust, for this was the month of Ab when the sun shone hottest and the dust lay driest in the throat.

"Have we blocked their way back into the city? Can you see, Rael?" Ahab asked, standing on tiptoe in his chariot, straining his eyes.

"The dust clouds are too thick, Ahab."

Ahab hammered the chariot rail with a fist. "I must know. How can I fight from this far away? I'm like a blind man."

"You know what Micaiah said. Stay alive, Ahab. Let Jehosephat give the orders."

"Jehosephat is no general. He relies on me."

His eyes went this way and that, as if seeking the answer to his problem in the mounded ground which he had made his command post. There was no help in the dirt and pebbles nor in the soldiers who stood so quietly beside their horses, waiting to gallop into the fight with orders from their king.

But wait! Suppose Ahab were to go as a courier into the battle, to gallop as if bringing orders? Surely no one in Ramoth would recognize the king of Israel in the yellow cloak and tunic of a despatch rider!

"You there—Ahikam!" he shouted, stripping off his cloak, beginning to undo the straps that held his silvered armor to his chest. "Give me a hand, Rael. Hurry!"

Rael growled protests when he understood what it was Ahab meant to do. "You ride to your death, Ahab. Forego this madness. Let me go to tell you of what is hidden behind the dust clouds."

"I go where I should have gone in the first place. Easy, easy—that mail scratches! Ahikam, you put on my armor and my purple cloak. Stand here where all may see you and think you Ahab."

He laughed and leaped onto the back of a white horse. His

138

toes drummed its ribs. He was gone the next moment, galloping off the mound and across the plain toward Ramoth.

Rael stood undecided. He would have gone with Ahab except that for the royal physician to be so near a nameless courier in the midst of a battle might call attention to that courier. No, it might be better this way. Ahab would be unknown to the men of Gilead, and would be safe.

The arrow came by chance out of the melee.

It was not aimed, for the shaft wobbled as if spent, dropping out of the sky with only the weight of its metal head to give it force. If Ahab had been wearing his armor it would have bounced off harmlessly. As it was, it slid between two ribs and went deep enough to touch his vital organs.

His men put Ahab in a chariot and brought him swiftly to Rael. Tenderly, one of them held his king braced on a thigh and begged his physician to save his life.

Rael did what he could, cutting out the arrowhead—his men had already snapped the shaft—and cleansing the wound and bandaging it. Ahab bled freely so that the floorboards of the chariot were stained a deep red.

He will die here, not in the garden of Naboth, and no dogs outside Samaria shall so much as smell his blood, Rael thought. Elijah had only caught a glimpse of the future, he had not seen it clearly.

But Ahab clung to life, breathing heavily, propped up on blankets in the chariot that carried him home to Samaria. Rael rode with him, bathing his face with water, giving him wine to sip, marveling at the strength which let him live for that long journey.

It was evening of the following day when his servants carried Ahab into the royal palace. They went by way of the gardens of Naboth and when they were under a plane tree, Ahab cried out sharply.

"Rael! Friend Rael, where are you?"

"Here, Ahab—at your side," Rael said and made a sign for the servants to lower Ahab. The king looked up at him out of his heavily lined face, smiling faintly.

"We have been good friends, you and I, Rael."

Rael nodded, thinking of Jezebel.

"I am dying as Elijah said I would die, in these gardens and under the very tree where Jezebel and I stood the night—" Ahab stiffened, groaning to the pain in his body. After a moment he relaxed, staring blindly upward. "It grows dark. I am

139

afraid. If Elijah spoke the truth, if Yahweh is punishing me for—"

The voice faltered, fading to silence.

Rael bent closer. Ahab stared upward sightlessly.

A shadow from an upheld torch touched Rael. He lifted his head to look at Jezebel. She stood wrapped in a black cloak, only her pallid face visible, her hair uncoiffed and loose about her throat and shoulders.

"Is he dead?" she whispered.

Rael nodded and rose to his feet. He was giddy, light-headed, as though he had been drinking wine for days. He could not look at Jezebel, so great a hate was in him for her. She had killed Ahab as surely as she had killed Ruth. With her worship of Baal-Melkart she had brought disaster upon him, had alienated him from the God of his fathers.

She put a hand to his arm; he shook it off.

"You hate me, don't you?" she breathed. "For all that has happened, you blame me."

"You killed Ruth. Why deny it?"

"I was jealous of her. I love you, Rael. I wanted you only for myself. When I thought of you and her—"

The body of her husband lay between them. Rael looked down at Ahab, feeling nausea wash across him. So it had come to this between them, this stark reality. What had begun on that night so long ago in Tyre when they had climbed the god-wagon to get at Jezebel whom they had thought a priestess, was ended now. In death for Ahab, in despair and hate for him.

And for Jezebel—what?

He could not stand to face her, to read whatever was in her eyes. If he should see what he imagined he would see, lust and open desire, he would kill her. Better to turn away now, to avoid that last fatal glimpse of her face—as Lot's wife once should have turned away from Sodom and Gomorrah—and go on living out his days in expiation for his crimes.

Blindly he went through the gardens, seeking the open gate that lead into the street. Behind him, Jezebel was calling his name; he heard her but he paid her no attention. Let the others wrap Ahab in the cere-cloths, let them light the mourning candles and pour the ashes. He would mourn the rest of his days but it would be a personal matter with him, not a public one. He would permit no hair to grow on his face or head and always, under whatever garments he wore, would he endure the chafe of sackcloth.

He wandered the streets of Samaria all night long, his footfalls making empty echoes in his heart. He tried to think back, to judge where he had gone wrong, to guess at what he might have done so this guilt that ate in him as his wound had eaten in Ahab, might be eased.

There was no escape. Sooner or later he would have met Jezebel, whether he had gone to Tyre with Ahab and Jehu or not. It needed only that one glimpse of Jezebel to destroy him as a man. No more.

Morning found him at the gate of the city, watching the soldiers move about. There was the sound of water running. Attracted to it he went and stood outside the city walls where soldiers were washing blood from the royal chariot. The blood and the water was mixing and running red onto the ground, creating little pools.

Dogs stood there, heads bent, drinking the water.

And with it, lapping up the blood of Ahab.

THE BOOK OF JEHU

Eleven: In The Days Of Jehu's Homecoming

1.

Jehu rode swiftly through the early morning haze.

He straddled a big black stallion, a gift of Shalmaneser, with a talent for eating distance with its powerful legs. Jehu rode lightly, with only his weapons to keep him company on the long trip from Assyria to Israel. True, a leather sack fastened to his bedroll once had been plump with food and wine but it was empty now, flapping behind him like a clacking tongue urging him to greater speed.

Ahab is dead in Israel and her enemies are many!

The king was dead and his young son was dead after him two years later, but so slowly did news go in his world that Jehu had only learned of this within the past week. He had resigned his rank as turtan in the army of Assur-nasir-pal and kissed Asharra a long farewell. At heart he was still an Israelite. He had served the Assyrian warlords well and faithfully. He had no regrets on that score. The captaincy which Asharra had secured for him had been an honorary thing until his first pitched battle in the mountains of Andiu against the fierce Medes. After that even the warlike Assyrians respected his ability with the long iron sword.

He had displayed his leadership before the walls of Malatiyah, breaching a hole and holding it with half a dozen men until Assur-nasir-pal came himself to the breach, storming through—giving the weary and bloody Jehu a bearhug—and fanning out into the city to take it. The king had advanced him to the rank of lesser *turtan* amid the smoking ruins of this city of the Mitanni.

He had grown rich with loot. But his wealth could not compare with that of Asharra, naturally; she had a merchant empire at her fingertips; still two big wooden chests—following behind him by camel caravan—were heavy with carved ivories, golden cups and goblets, jeweled rings and bracelets, leather sacks fat with gold and silver manehs. During the battle with the Thamudites, Jehu had been lucky enough to win himself a great golden shield that was the sacred standard of their ruler. He had given it to Assur-nasir-pal as a gift, that it might be borne before his army as it marched in triumph through the streets of Nineveh. For this, Assur-nasir-pal had loaded him with his weight in rubies and sapphires.

As Israel measured wealth, he was a rich man.

And a famous man, he supposed. Words of his deeds had gone on before him, through Carcamesh into Aram and the lands about Naphta. It would have traveled on into Israel as well, by the tongues of merchants. He was a full general now, a turtan, with the right to have his own personal banner carried behind that of Assur-nasir-pal himself. Asharra had been very proud of him.

Ahead, Jehu could see the ancient stone fort that marked the turn in the great highway that ran from the Nile delta north and eastward through great Carcamesh and on to Babylon. He remembered, reining up and staring at the old fort tower, how he had turned in his saddle those years ago to cast one last look back at its black stones. Now a part of his life had come full cycle. He faced toward the fort tower rather than away from it.

Beyond the fort lay Israel.

And Jezebel!

Jehu grated laughter. He was a youth no longer but a man, hardened by a hundred battles, marked with the cuts of twenty wounds. Yet a throb of fear lay deep inside him when he thought of the Israelite queen. Had she changed very much? Were there any grey hairs on her head? Was her body as slim and as graceful as it had been that long-ago night in Tyre when she rode the god-wagon? He grunted and kicked a toe into his horse. He would know the answers very soon now.

Next morning a few hours after sunrise, Jehu trotted his mount through the gates of Samaria. The city was little changed, the same ragged holy men stood outside its gates offering to prophesy for a copper coin; watergirls walked with swaying hips from the great wall, chattering in their shrill voices; a merchant rode an ass on his way to market. The smells and the sounds gathered in his senses, stirring nostalgia in him.

No one knew him, even when he dismounted at the palace steps. A young officer came forward, staring curiously at sight of this big man in foreign armor and a rich red cloak trimmed with gold braid.

"I have come to see the queen," he said simply. "My name is Jehu. I was a friend of King Ahab."

The name meant nothing, Jehu saw, and grinned in honest humor. A man was never a prophet in his own lands, said the old proverb. The soldier was too well trained, however, to be other than polite. He gestured Jehu to follow him.

From the shadows of a canopy a man in silver mail cried out at the sight of Jehu and came running. The years had been good to Zubral; there was only a touch of grey in his black hair; he caught the younger man in his arms and hugged him while the young officer stared.

"Jehu! Yahweh is good to us in Israel, now that you've come home. I've heard things about you in Assyria—good things, lad!" Zubral saw the officer staring and bellowed laughter. "Here's your new general, boy. Salute him!"

"You rush things, Zubral," Jehu protested. "Jezebel may—"

"Jezebel prays with the rest of Israel," the Zubral growled, "though not to the same god, for the return of Jehu. Moab is arming to the east, with Ammon to side with her, now that Ahab and his son Ahaziah are dead."

"Ahaziah too?"

"From a fall out of an upper window of the palace. There are some who say he was pushed, but I wouldn't know about that."

"What of Jehoram, his younger son?"

"A wastrel who revels in debauching girl slaves in the temples where he worships Baal and Astarte." Zubral made a wry face. "A monster, that one. Cruel, vindictive, arrogant. His kingdom is collapsing around him and he cares only for finding some new sensation, which he says is only to honor the gods he worships."

Jehu scowled. It was hard to ask, but he said, "And Jezebel? How does she take to such a son?"

Zubral chuckled. "She hates the ground that holds him upright. Ahaziah was amenable to her advice but Jehoram scorns her. If you ask me, Jezebel would reward well the man who killed him."

"It would put her in power," Jehu nodded.

"No queen may rule in Israel by herself," the other man pointed out, "but it would put her in a position to choose a husband. Her husband—if he were a strong man—would be king. And Jezebel would regain her queenhood."

They were walking through the cool halls of the palace toward a staircase leading to the upper quarters. Jehu let his eyes roam, seeing an ivory inlay on a wall that brought memories, and a standing urn that he and Ahab once had overturned as boys while wrestling. Great red pillars ornate with gold towered above him; to their left was a portico opening onto the great inner court. A row of standards captured in battle hung on the wall to his right. He had stared at them often in his boyhood, visualizing the day when he could add to their number with his own hands.

Broad stone steps were underfoot. Above him was Jezebel, unaware of his coming. Jehu found his heart slamming in his ribcase, his palms beginning to perspire; he wiped his palms on his cloak, but there was nothing he could do about his heart.

A slavegirl bowed low as they went in through a stone archway to a wide chamber. She turned at Zubral's words and ran past a draped doorway to an inner room. Jehu watched that maroon drape, unable to take his eyes from it.

After what seemed hours, it moved to the thrust of a pale, ringed hand. It lifted and Jezebel stood staring at him.

She was no different. She was slim and youthful-looking and her black hair was cunningly bound up in golden beads, framing her beautiful face. A diaphanous tunic fell from her shoulders to her ankles and was belted by a girdle of golden links. Her eyes widened slowly and her lips fell open.

"Jehu! It is you!"

She came across the tiled floor, holding out her hands. He took them, kissed them, feeling his blood flow like molten metal in his veins. Her perfume was that of Shinar, musky and sensuous. Under the thin linen, her body was naked. In Assyria, women wore more clothes than this; Jehu reminded himself that this was a warmer climate.

He marveled that she remembered him. The only time she had seen him had been that night when she was on the pantechnikon, the night he and Ahab and Rael had climbed its sides to get at her. Or perhaps she only flattered him. It made no difference. He was here before her where he had wanted all his life to be.

"You're no Israelite, though. You're an Assyrian," she said with laughter in her voice.

"I came swiftly, without bothering to change garments."

"I like you this way. It makes you mysterious and—very forceful." She put up her hand, ran soft fingertips along an old swordscar on his cheek. "You've been fighting since you left."

"In many places, against many people. The Assyrians live to make war. It was a good school in which to study."

"We have need of a good general," Jezebel said slowly.

Zubral coughed. "I have my duties, Jezebel. Jehu, I'll see you later when you're free."

Jezebel never looked at him. She had eyes only for this big man standing tall and brawney in his cloak and armor. Ahab had been dead now over four years. Rael had absented himself from the palace, preferring to walk on a lower level in the city, among the common people who were his patients. Jezebel had abandoned the practice of frequenting the temples of her gods where a woman might give herself to a stranger as a sacred duty. And so nearness to this man made the blood run faster in her veins.

"You will be thirsty," she said suddenly, turning and moving away from him toward a tripod table holding a silver wine ewer and several goblets. As she bent to pour the rich red Khilbun her breasts came into prominence, highlighted by the sunlight behind her.

Jehu stared frankly at her, finding this momentary vision, with the linen turned to nothingness by the sun so he could see her upright brown nipples, honestly stimulating. He had tried to forget this woman with the girls of Babylon and with Asharra but he knew now he had only been fooling himself.

Beside Jezebel, those other females were as nothing.

Jehu sought to understand her appeal, standing there and watching her pour the wine. Asharra had been beautiful, too, her hips as curving, her breasts as full and heavy, her legs as shapely. And yet for all her good looks, his Assyrian mistress had lacked something. Something that—Jehu shook his head; he did not understand it. He only knew that Jezebel touched some well-spring deep inside him.

She came up to him, holding out a winecup. Her eyes were bright behind the long black lashes, glinting with an indefinable deviltry that seemed to flow out to him as did her perfume.

"I am a widow now, Jehu," she said slowly. "I have no strong man to stand before me against my enemies." She sipped the chilled wine, eying him above the bevelled rim of the goblet.

Tiny chills went over his flesh as those eyes regarded him. His mouth was dry so he lifted his own cup and drained it. Amusement shone at him from her curving lips as she added, "An ambitious man might aspire to be king of Israel these days. He might want to push me off my throne or—share it with me."

"I want no kingship," he said heavily.

"It's a relief to know that," she nodded. "I won't have to fear any coup by which you would come to power, then."

"I came back from Assyria to offer my services only as a military man. Zubral tells me Moab and Ammon are uniting against you."

"I'm a helpless woman, not a soldier. They see a chance to throw off the yoke Israel has imposed on them since the days of Omri."

"Make me your commander, Jezebel."

She did not answer him but went instead to the arch leading out to the wide stone porch balcony above the courtyard. She stood in the sunlight and put her hands to her thick black hair, rearranging the golden beads. Jehu watched her, unable to turn his eyes from the rounds of her buttocks so clearly delineated beneath her tunic. He wondered if she meant so to display herself.

"Why did you leave Israel, Jehu?" she asked suddenly.

"To learn my trade as soldier."

"Odd. I've always believed it was because of—me."

"Why should you think that?"

Rael had told her as much, over the years, in moments of rare confidence, but she would not admit this to Jehu. She only shrugged and turned to smile at him. What Rael had told her long ago was true enough; she could read the hungry devotion in his eyes that could not slake their fill of her body.

For the moment, she would be satisfied with his looking.

"This evening at a feast to welcome you home," she said, "I'll confirm your appointment as general of the armies."

2.

The place of honor to the right of the queen had been reserved for Jehu. He reclined on a Grecian kline, reaching out from time to time to sample a slice of roasted meat or a ripe fruit. Jezebel had walked with him among the guests—rich merchants, high officials of the kingdom, a few officers of the army—her ringed hand on his forearm, her voice praising him and announcing his new role as commander of her soldiers. She had been very gracious; almost too gracious, treating him as a favorite rather than as a general.

He did not know whether to resent or enjoy her attitude.

148

He was no pampered fop to be displayed because of his manly beauty or a musical talent. He felt more at ease in the battle-camps than he did in this perfumed banqueting hall. Yet he knew it pleased Jezebel to show him off.

Rael had been among the guests, in sombre garments of dark blue relieved only by a white *hazor*. He had responded to Jehu's bearhug with an odd stiffness. It was almost as if Rael resented him.

To his suggestion that they share the morrow together, Rael had been reluctant, offering his practice as an excuse to remain apart. Jezebel had explained in an aside as they moved away that Rael had not entered the palace since Ahab died. Evidently the death of their old friend had affected Rael as well as himself.

Jehu scowled, munching on a pomegranate. It was almost as if Rael hated him for coming home. Yet that made no sense at all. He was here only as a general, to offer Israel and its queen his military wisdom. He wanted nothing that Rael coveted.

Perhaps he was merely oversensitive.

His eyes went about the room slowly, finding that many of the guests were watching him, commenting on him. It was good to be the focus of attention in his home city. In the old days, it had been Ahab who was noticed, bowed to. He, Jehu, had walked in his friend's shadow.

It was this that had rankled him, he knew. Ahab always got the best horse, the finest sword. Well, he had been prince, so it was only natural. Ah, but now! With Ahab in his grave, Jehu was the most important man in Israel. On him depended the safety of the nation, the power of its armies. It was almost as if he were its king.

Jehu turned sideways, regarding Jezebel. If he were king, this woman would be his queen, his wife. She would make kingship exciting, he knew. His gaze went over a bare leg thrusting through a slit in her tunic up to her hip. The flesh of that leg was smooth, white, soft. His palm itched to caress it.

He growled low in his throat and thrust out a hand for his winecup. This very day she had hinted that she wanted a man beside her on the throne; he had not been deaf to the meaning of her words, but he had rejected the thought as unworthy. Ahab was dead but Ahab had been his friend. It was not his place to sit on the throne that had held him—nor to enjoy the embraces of the woman who was his widow.

Liar! Your flesh burns to know the embrace of his queen! Be honest with yourself! Admit that you are afraid of

Jezebel, of the attraction she holds for you. With all the other women you have known, you have been the dominant partner. None of them, not even Asharra, could have subjugated you. Ah, but Jezebel!

She might be able to twist him around her forefinger with a lock of her rich black hair even as she was doing now while she listened to the harpists with that dreamy look in her long-lashed eyes. Of what did she dream, lying there so indolently, exposing her body through her shameless Phoenician garments? Of Jehu as her husband? Her lover? He wished fiercely that he could peer inside her mind.

He was a strong man but he would be chaff before Jezebel if she so willed it, once they had joined their bodies. Instinctively he sensed this weakness in him where the queen was concerned. It was why he had run away.

The touch of eyes made him look up suddenly, catching Rael staring across the room at him. Was that hate he saw glaring at him? Hate for his old friend, Jehu? It could not be. Yet the face of the physician was sullen, angry as he glanced aside, not meeting the smile Jehu sent at him.

There were crosscurrents here he did not understand.

One thing he did understand: the need of Israel for a swift strike at Moab and Ammon. He lay here like a courtier sipping wine and eating his fill when he should be riding to Megiddo to evaluate the troops, to see what kind of fighting force he had inherited from Ahab.

Outriders should be appointed to patrol the river lands against surprise. Recruits should be gathered, trained. A hundred—no, a thousand things needed doing. Impatience came to him. His Assyrian friends would not be feasting when there was a war to fight. They feasted after a war, not before it.

"Why do you scowl, Jehu?" asked Jezebel sweetly, breaking in upon his thoughts. "The feast is in your honor—yet you frown as though you were a human sacrifice in Sidon."

"I should be in the barracks at Megiddo, not here. Moab may strike at any time. I want to interrogate officers, check equipment, learn the dispositions of the chariot corps. I want—"

"Tomorrow we ride to Megiddo, you and I," she interrupted. "I am not a fool, Jehu. I have done all these things. I am not entirely unready to fight for my kingdom. I learned a lot from Ahab."

Her smile was hard, suddenly. "Lacking an ambitious man, I must be an ambitious woman, eager to keep my throne, my

150

crown. I say 'my crown'—because I consider Jehoram unfit to rule. I must be the strength of Israel. And so I say—my army is fit, ready to fight. But it needs a leader, a man the men will follow as they followed and fought for my dead husband."

She turned about on her kline, putting her sandalled feet to the tiled floor, reaching a white arm out for her fallen robe. "You are that leader, Jehu. Don't fail me as once you failed Ahab by running away."

She stood, wrapping the white woolen mantle about her body, smiling down at him. By Yahweh! She looks the queen she is, right now! And who would have thought her sharp enough to understand that he had failed Ahab long ago? He himself was only beginning to realize the fact, after all this time.

3.

Jezebel was at home on the floorboards of a chariot, Jehu found before they had gone many miles. She clung to the curving handrail with her fingers as her legs bent and her body shifted gracefully when the wheels bounced or when the horses galloped faster. She had chosen a short Grecian chiton for her garb on this trip to Megiddo. Over it, when she left the palace, she had thrown a chlamys of Tyrian purple but the cloak lay now at her feet so the wind could find her flesh and bathe it.

She had loosed her black hair so that it fell behind her, making her seem like a young girl. It was a side of Jezebel he had not seen. She had as many facets as a finely cut gem, he thought glumly, and each new aspect of her personality was like another chain binding him to her.

Her laughter came easily, for she seemed to meet each new movement of the chariot as a personal challenge, as though its wood and metal were engaged in a combat of sorts with her strength.

Only once did she fall against him, when the chariot slid sideways where rain had washed out a portion of the road. And as she slipped away from him he felt her fingers reaching into his *kalasiris*, pinching his hip. It was a gesture no queen would make, but only a young girl alone with the boy she loved. Somehow it endeared her all the more to him.

Yet when the walls of Megiddo loomed in sight, she bent and

lifted the purple chlamys, putting it about her shoulders. From a bag she drew a thin golden fillet and set it on her head. And suddenly, so easily, she looked like a queen.

They were greeted by a dozen officers who had been expecting them, alerted by a courier to their coming, gathered in a group before the great gate of Solomon. Five towers made the gate almost impregnable to attack. Beyond it, in the courtyard, an armed guard was at attention in honor of the queen. Jezebel walked among the officers, smiling and nodding her head as she listened to their outpourings of information about men and arms, horses and chariots.

From the corners of her eyes she watched Jehu, who walked a little behind her, yet close enough to hear everything that was said. Not one word, not one iota of information did he miss. When he asked questions, they were always to the point. It pleased Jezebel when her officers gradually turned their attention from her to the man in the Assyrian cloak.

The troops paraded before the visitors on the level plain outside the citadel while slaves brought food and wine to the queen and her escort. Jehu ate quickly, as a task that must be done, but his eyes were on the soldiers rather than the platters put before him.

While the troops were still parading, he gave orders for horsemen to patrol the river lands, with relays of horses to be maintained for them along the chariot roads. Two horsemen were always to ride together, one to come to Megiddo, one to Samaria, in case of attack.

"Not that I think Moab and Ammon will venture into Israel," he informed his listeners. "The habit of defeat is a hard one to shake off. Having been beaten a number of times by Israel, Moab and Ammon will prefer to wait and fight us on their own land."

Jehu spent the evening with two captains, poring over maps and troop lists. He suggested that the captains mix the regiments, joining veterans with recruits rather than keeping them apart, so a trained man might bolster and inspire a new one in the heat of battle. He laid out his route for entry into Moab, too, when the time should come.

It was the hour of the midnight watch when he rolled up his last map and slid it into its metal case. His eyes smarted and there was a weariness in his body. He smiled gratefully at the officer who conducted him to the bedchamber allotted for his visit. Jehu felt that he had taken a long stride forward this day. He had seen the troops and talked with them, had heard their strengths and weaknesses from their officers. The weapon he would need with which to smite at Moab and Ammon was already shaping to his hand.

4.

Megiddo was a low black line on the horizon behind them. The chariot went slowly, at little more than a trot, for Jezebel held the reins and was inclined to laziness. Her head turned this way and that as she scanned the flat surface of the plain of Jezreel. To the man at her side, it appeared that she looked for something.

The sun on their faces was hot, for they travelled eastward to Samaria, but there was a cooling wind off Mount Gilboa, tingling the nerves, lifting the lungs so they might experience the sweetness of the air. It made a man glad to be alive, Jehu thought, especially with a lovely woman at his side.

Without a word, Jezebel yanked left on the red leather reins, sending the horses at a gallop and the chariot wheels bouncing over a stretch of pebbled ground. Ahead was a small stream of water, flooding downward from the hills on its way to merge with the river Kishor.

"In the sack at your feet, Jehu—two swords!"

There was laughter in her voice as Jezebel flirted a glance at him. Wonderingly Jehu bent, opened the leather bag and lifted out two wooden blades with braided hilts. Children used them in their mock battles; with them, veteran soldiers taught recruits the art of swordplay.

"You shall teach this craft to me, this day," she told him. "I would be a queen in truth, not just a figurehead. If I might walk beside you at the head of my troops—be an inspiration to them—why, together we could build a kingdom mighty as was Solomon's."

"A woman belongs in her home," he growled.

"What of Deborah who fought against Sisera at Mount Tabor? Or Semiramis who was a queen long ago in Babylon?"

He shook his head, thinking that a queen might indulge her whims where a lesser woman would be clouted alongside the head and tumbled back into her pots and pans. Swordplay with Jezebel! He thought to himself that he would rather duel with her in a sweeter way and one more suited to the softness of her flesh.

153

She drew back on the reins, making the chariot skid on the stones, then was out of it and striding toward the waters that tumbled through their bed of clay and rock. Her fingers loosened her cloak, let it slide from her shoulders. She caught it and draped it over an arm as she went to stare down into the stream.

"It's deep enough to swim a little here," she called back to him. "In the summer it would be only a trickle but in this month of Iyyar, it's a full tide."

She turned fully now and laughed at sight of his glum face. "Bring the swords, Jehu. Teach me as if I were a raw beginner in your army."

He grinned almost cruelly. "If I did you'd scream for mercy."

"Try me!"

Her head was thrown back so that the wind rippled her long black hair and blew the thin chiton she affected in the manner of the Greeks against her full breasts and gentle mound of belly. By Yahweh! She was a wanton thing, standing like that to show herself off. The blood stirred in Jehu. If she wanted rough treatment, he would give it to her. His fingers undid the silver pin that held her red military cloak.

With the wooden swords in a hand he came up to her, holding them out. "Take one, highness."

Her fingers closed on a braided haft, her other hand touching the girdle at her middle. "My clothes are too good to stain with sweat and dust, Jehu. I'll slip out of them, fence as do the men and maids in Sparta. Naked save for my sandals."

The chiton slipped from her shoulders, hanging a moment to the outer edge of her arms. Jehu felt the breath rasp in his throat. The neckline fell to the upper swells of her breasts, paused a moment, then went down. Her swollen nipples exploded into view on the tips of her heavy breasts. Then he was seeing the navel, her belly and the triangular darkness. Her thighs were somewhat heavy but the legs were slim and shapely.

She let him look his fill, knowing instinctively that he could not turn away. Her fallen garments were pooled at her ankles. "Now," she said.

He shook his head but she only laughed and added, "We shall pretend we are in Sparta, you and I this day. I'm a newcomer to the army, you're the tough sergeant. No royalty. No consideration for my rank."

"Is that a promise?"

She nodded, lip caught between her teeth. Slowly Jehu began

to doff his mailshirt, his short cotton tunic. When he whipped aside the loincloth, she closed her eyes convulsively.

"On guard, you brat," he grinned, lunging and whacked her thigh with the flat of the blade.

Jezebel cried out, hopping sideways. The blow had stung. Angrily she opened her mouth to rail at him but remembered her promise. She leaped forward, slashing with her own blade. Jehu seemed not to move, yet he was out of her path and turning, bringing his blade flat against her soft buttocks.

The whaaack was loud in the still air.

Jezebel jumped, her heavy breasts swinging wildly, and gave a sharp scream. Putting her hand behind her, she rubbed herself. Her lips were quivering, her eyes moist with tears of pain.

"Come on, come on, brat! I haven't all day to spend on you. Come at me—and keep coming."

He was enjoying himself immensely, Jezebel saw. She had thought that the sight of her nakedness would bring him to his knees before her as it had Ahab and even more so, Rael. Instead he was swatting her flesh and relishing the awkwardness with which she jumped and hopped.

He was a big bear of a man, huge and hairy. The muscles rippled on his arms and chest, even on his hard belly. Black hair made a thick mat on his chest, on his middle and lower down, on his thighs and calves. He was no weak reed to bend to circumstances as Rael had been, no man to yield to his passions and so be swayed by them as Ahab.

A grudging respect dawned in Jezebel.

She sidled closer, gripping her wooden blade more tightly, determined to get in one hard slash at least. She swung but he turned the blade easily, merely brushing it with his own. Her action had brought her close to Jehu. She let the edge of her blade slide down to his hilt and pushed.

Her naked body came against his own. For an instant they were crushed to one another, her breasts against his chest, her thighs against his thighs. His hard muscles on her softness made her senses swim. Her knees grew rubbery. Not since before Ahab died had she known the embraces of a man.

She did not need to see the fever in his eyes to know he wanted her. Suddenly Jezebel laughed and danced away, her own weakness forgotten before the hunger of the man. She thrust at him with her point, laughed when he leaped back.

He bellowed and dove for her, his wooden sword a blur in the sunlight. The flat of that blade landed on her thigh, on her hip, on her quivering buttocks when she turned, yelping. It came so fast she hardly saw it, only feeling it when it smacked against her flesh. Strangely, she felt intensely aware of the pain. It was almost as if this big, hairy man were caressing her in some unusual way.

Without mercy he pursued her, spanking her with his blade until she was roused to madness, turning and slashing the empty air where he should be standing but was not. Furiously she thrust and beat at his big bulk but did not find him. Sobbing, knowing the tears were running down her cheeks in anger and vexation but not caring, she rushed at him with her fury clear to read.

And then—

She felt herself swung upward into the air, the wooden playsword ripped from her clasp. His lips kissed her bruised and reddened skin while his great hands held her under her arms as though she weighed no more than a doll.

Jezebel writhed in pleasure. She cried out softly, brokenly.

He was turning her this way and that, taking his pleasure of her with his hands and mouth and she was swept away in a tide of delight that made her arch and scream out thickly. Panting, she pressed to him, urging on his madness. Never before had she wanted anyone so much. A fever of desire held her helpless in its flood, whipping her senses to a frenzy.

Not until much later did Jezebel realize that for the first time in her life, a man had dominated her in lovemaking. Until now she had always been the one to set the pace, the mood. Jehu would not stand for that; he had indulged her little pleasantry but when he had been stirred to action he had not waited for her word. He had simply taken her, treating her like a wallside harlot.

And oddly enough she had enjoyed it.

It was dark when they entered the palace compound. A boy came running to snatch the red leather reins and lead the horses to the stables. Jezebel walked with lowered head up the stone steps, her chlamys wrapped tightly about her, Jehu beside her with a hand on her shoulder as though he owned her.

She did not know whether to resent the hand or love it. Despite those feverish hours beside the little stream at the edge of the Jezreel plain, nothing had changed between them. She was still the queen of Israel, Jehu was its general. He had made no offer to marry her, to accept the crown and the throne as her husband.

Vaguely, Jezebel felt anger. Or perhaps it was only her pride that was hurt, she reflected. The least he could have done was ask her to be his wife. Not that she was a timid virgin with her first lover, but a man had a certain responsibility when he took a queen as his mistress. Especially a queen without a husband.

She had made a mistake with Rael, understanding now that he had not been the man to replace Ahab. Israel needed strength at its throne. Jehu could be that strength even more than Ahab had been, who had bowed down at last to Elijah.

Well, Elijah was dead—gone up to heaven in a chariot of fire, the story went—but there was another man who had taken his place. Some farmer Elijah had anointed and made his successor. What was his name? Oh, yes—Elisha. Jezebel did not think Jehu would bow to Elisha as Ahab had to Elijah. Though you never could tell with these Habiru. They were strong in everything but standing up to their god. It was their one fatal weakness in her eyes.

In her private chambers on the upper floor, Jezebel ordered food and chilled wine brought to them. When Jehu would have left her, she caught his hand, holding it between her fingers.

"We have much to talk over, you and I," she murmured, staring up into his eyes. "This day was only a promise of what might be—between you and me."

"I'm a general, not a stud."

She smiled wryly. "Israel needs a general, but she needs a king even more. You would make a good king, Jehu."

He snorted in derision. "Me? The son of a merchant? What sort of lineage is that to offer my people?"

"What heritage had David? Or even Solomon, who was a bastard out of Bathsheba? A king appoints his successor, but Ahab is dead. The throne stands empty. Yahweh also appoints a king—but Yahweh has not spoken of a new king here in Israel."

Jehu felt temptation. To sit in the Hall of Audience with the golden circlet on his head and Jezebel beside him, was a dream unthought of until this moment. Oh, he'd dreamed of Jezebel often enough, but as a woman, not as a queen—his queen. The sensual frenzy that had overcome him hours earlier might be repeated night after night. All he need do was nod his head.

King Jehu of Israel.

Why not? A strong man could carve out his own kingdoms, these days. Omri had done it, and Jerobaum before him.

"Yes," he said slowly, "that is true. Yahweh has not spoken. Until He does, there's no reason why I can't pretend to the throne."

"Not pretend only—but take possession."

She disarranged her tunic, baring her breasts, lifting his

hands and cupping his fingers over them. "As you hold these fruits of my womanhood, hold also the power I represent. As you took me on stones today, take me in the royal bed. As your queen, your wife."

He thought he had slaked his fill of this woman, but he had not even begun, Jehu realized. The instinct that had made him run from Israel to Babylon and on to Assyria was as alert as ever. He would never have enough of her. These firm breasts in his palms were even now rousing him as they would always have the power to rouse him.

Against their lure, against the temptation of Jezebel the woman he was like a newborn babe. Jehu groaned, not being a man driven by ambition. If he must accept the kingship to have her always available to him, he would become a king. Then at a thought, he frowned.

"What of your son Jehoram? I gather he's not much of a king from what gossip I've heard, but he wears the crown."

"Forget Jehoram. Baasha came to power here in Israel when Jerobaum died. Omri did the same thing, by killing Zimri who was king by reason of the fact that he in turn had slain Elah."

He could not think clearly with Jezebel so close to him. He knew only that he must have this woman at all costs. To get her he would kill Jehoram with his own hand, if need be. Long enough had he run. It was time now to make a stand, to declare himself. All his life he had fought battles for other men, for Ahab, for Shalmaneser, for Assur-nasir-pal. Now he would fight for himself.

He gathered her into his arms and covered her face and throat with kisses, "Marry me, Jezebel. Be my queen as I will be your king! My flesh starves for your flesh. I've tried to fight it long enough. I'm tired of keeping a tight rein on myself."

His hands slid over her nakedness beneath the chiton, caressing her hips, her buttocks. Jezebel felt herself half lifted, strained against him. She smiled to her thoughts as his lips fell upon her breasts. This huge bear of a man was not quite the iron man she had thought him to be. There was a flaw in his strength, and the name of that flaw was Jezebel.

She would not have it any other way.

Twelve: Beside The Wall Of Jezreel, In Samaria

1.

The lands of Moab and of Ammon lay before the armies of Israel, wide and flat, open to the wheels of its chariots and the marching feet of its spearmen and archers. Riding in a chariot decorated with gold and ivory, the same chariot in which Ahab had ridden out to his own military triumphs, Jehu stood like the king he had agreed to become. A purple cloak hung by silver chains from his shoulders. His armor was inlaid with silver. The scabbard at his side, where hung the long iron sword that had been a gift from Assur-nasir-pal and as a result was the finest of its kind, was encrusted with gold and carbuncles.

There was respect in the eyes of his officers, awe in the stares of his soldiers. The name of Jehu was like a legend in the land, already. His adventures in Babylon and Assyria, he was sure, had been enlarged upon and expanded until credit had been given him for the victories of Assur-nasir-pal and his professional troops; he never bothered to deny them, knowing their effect upon the men who followed him; the soldier who thought his general unbeatable, became himself unbeatable.

Somewhere up ahead his videttes galloped on fast horses seeking out the enemy. Jehu had learned too much from the Assyrians to be caught by a surprise attack. His flanks were protected by cavalry, his rear by a line of mounted bowmen. His army moved secure within its outriders.

Jehu was in no hurry to come to grips with the Moabites. They knew he was advancing to the attack. They would worry when and where he would strike, and worried soldiers are only half soldiers.

He gave the signal to make camp before the sun turned red in the west. His great felt tent came out of a wagon and was swiftly hoisted into place on its several poles. The standards were planted in the ground before its flaps and a chair brought so that Jehu might converse at ease with his officers.

It was dusk when a horseman came at the gallop, flinging himself from the saddlecloth and kneeling before Jehu.

"A holy man comes, Jehu—sent by Elisha."

Jehu scowled. He wanted no truck with prophets. From Jezebel he had learned enough to know their ways were not the ways of kings. Prophets thought only of Yahweh and kings thought only of their kingdoms, and sometimes the two were at odds.

"We will wait for him," he said dryly.

There was nothing else he could do, he thought.

The young man came a little after dawn, weary with his long walking, having refused the loan of a horse from an outrider. He was one of the holy men about Elisha, he informed Jehu, one of those who had seen him part the waters of the Jordan, who had watched as he cured Naaman the leper and as he had set the she-bears upon the children of the Baal worshippers. He had in his belt-purse a vial of holy oil blessed by Elisha, with which he was to anoint Jehu to be king in Israel.

Jehu sat stunned. This thing had been a secret between himself and Jezebel. How then had Elisha learned of it? Troubled, Jehu shook his head.

"It is true I have promised Jezebel that—"

"That bitch!" exclaimed the young man. "She is of the family of Ahab, which is to be destroyed by you."

Jehu half rose from his chair. "Is this madness I hear? Destroy Jezebel?"

"This is the will of Yahweh who sent me."

Jehu waved his hand. "I must think, I must think."

"There is no need of thought. Accept the will of the Lord God, Jehu—and be king in Israel with His blessing."

His officers pressed forward, urging his acceptance. None of them were favorites with the queen. With Jehu as king, a soldier, they would know more authority in the kingdom than they had since the death of Ahab. Instead of a woman, they would serve a man.

They could not know the turmoil of Jehu's mind. The woman he loved, he had been ordered to slay! No more to kiss her flesh, no more to enjoy the frantic embraces of her body! It was not to be thought of. It was too much even for his God to ask.

"If I were a king in Israel, Jezebel might be my queen," he said slowly, watching the young man. The lesser prophet shook his head, saying, "This is not the word of Elisha. Jezebel is to die and be eaten by dogs. It is the will of Yahweh."

Jehu argued until the sun was overhead and the heat of midday was upon them. The young man stood with shoulders back, facing this man in armor with the long iron sword at his side. With his hands alone Jehu could have broken his back but behind him was Elisha and behind Elisha, Yahweh.

And so at last he asked heavily, "What am I to do?"

"Turn back from Moab and from Ammon. Return to Israel and the city of Jezreel where Jehoram will be, with Ahaziah of Judah his friend. Jehoram you are to slay and after him, Ahaziah."

Jehu nodded. Yahweh could be a vengeful God upon occasion. Jehu would not be the first man who served His ends. Slay Jehoram, slay Jezebel, become a king. It was that simple. His hands had killed many men, though no woman.

"Kneel down," said the young man.

Jehu knelt before him and the holy oil was put to his forehead. When he rose to his feet, he was king of Israel.

2.

"King of Israel!" screamed Jezebel. "What madness is this?"

The servant kneeling at her sandalled feet quivered in terror. Only just now had a dusty rider come from Ammon with the news that Elisha had ordered the anointing of Jehu. As fast as his feet could carry him, the servant had brought this word to Jezebel. For a reward, he might well be flogged to death.

"Gracious queen," he choked, "I but repeat the words that were spoken to me. Elisha sent the holy oils and a young man to administer them in his name. Our spy in the camp came as swiftly as he could."

"Swiftly, yes," Jezebel muttered. "There may yet be time."

She put hands to her flushed cheeks, not yet quite believing what she had heard. She had counted so much on Jehu. He was not to be another Ahab, another Rael. He was her iron man, who would stand straight before the wrath of Yahweh and His prophets. She began to laugh hysterically.

"And—and what was the rest of the message? That Jehu was to kill Jehoram? Well, for that I'd thank him. Jehoram would have died anyhow, if he and I were to become rulers in Israel. But the other—about slaying me! Are you certain of that?"

She bent to catch the hair of the kneeling man, lifting his head so she might read the truth in his terrified features. What she saw confirmed her fear. She released the man and went striding up and down the room.

"So then! Jehu is to kill me. Ah—but to do that, he will have to be alive himself! If I send loyal men to Jehoram in Jezreel, warning him—bidding him to be on his guard—lay a trap for Jehu . . ."

Her words fell away as she paced from the balcony rail across the upper chamber as far as a table covered with lapis-lazuli work. There was one man in the palace she could trust: Kition, who was the captain of her guard. Kition had done ugly jobs for her in the past. True, she had rewarded him well; today he was a wealthy man; for one more reward, he might do what needed to be done.

"Send Kition to me," she snapped. "And hurry!"

Kition had grown heavy with the years of good living, she thought when he stood before her. Much of his muscle had turned flabby but he was still strong. In his silvered guards-armor he looked very much the soldier. There had been times in the past few years when Jezebel had thought of summoning Kition from wherever he might be and ordering him to serve her as a lover. She had hesitated, fearing it might give him too much power. The lover of a queen sometimes became prideful, and prideful men are an abomination to rulers. She might even have been compelled to remove him, and he was too useful to kill.

"Jehu marches on Jezreel where Jehoram is," she told him firmly. "Jehu has been ordered to kill him."

Kition waited stolidly. He was used to moving swiftly and secretly on the affairs of Jezebel. Since those years before when his roving patrols had gone into the homes of the priests of Yahweh, slaying them out of hand, he had devoted himself to serving this woman.

"You will ride to Jezreel at once, bearing news of this to my son. Only to alert him to his danger, however. You will take such steps as are necessary to trap and slay Jehu yourself. Do you understand?"

"I understand, highness."

Jezebel drew a deep breath. "It would be too bad if an arrow were to slay Jehoram during the trouble. There would be none left of Ahab's family to sit the throne."

Kition smiled grimly. "Jezebel would rule in Israel, then."

"No queen may rule in this kingdom by herself. A queen would need a husband, Kition."

The guards officer did not understand. He remained staring at his queen, the daughter of Ithobaal of Tyre, like a man struck dumb. Jezebel smiled encouragingly. "I am tired of dealing with Israelites who think of their god before they do of themselves. A god is a good thing for men to have, but only when the god acts or speaks as one would have him do."

"As you say, highness, these Israelites are fools."

"What god do you worship, Kition?"

"Baal-Melkart. And his consort, Astarte."

"If you were king in Israel—you, a Phoenician—and I were your queen, life would be very good for you."

Kition opened his eyes wide. Ever since he had come to Samaria with Jezebel as captain of her personal guards, he had lusted for this woman. At a safe distance, of course; he was too clever to let his feelings be sensed. As might any man, his eyes had devoured the swollen breasts, the fleshy haunches and the slim legs which she showed the world in thin Cos linens and transparencies from Byblos. He had never thought to own that body, as might a man who was her husband.

Impulsively, drunk with this new vision opening before him, he stepped forward, caught Jezebel in his arms. His mouth came down on hers, found her mouth opening and her tongue probing to meet his own. Under his palms her flesh was warm and smooth. She was a woman to make any man know the heat of his own blood. He held her to him for many minutes, reveling in her perfumed flesh.

Then her hands pushed him away, gently.

"Come back to me a king, Kition," she whispered.

His bellowing laughter assured her nothing could stop him.

Rael was soothing the flushed forehead of the boy when his father came through the door carrying a spear and a helmet. The man was a Phoenician; he had been in the retinue that had come from Tyre into Israel when Jezebel had married Ahab. Rael knew him well. His name was Allarbal.

"The boy? My son?" the man asked hoarsely.

"He will live. The crisis has passed. I will prescribe a broth diet mixed with certain herbs. In no time he'll be running around like the young rooster he is."

Allarbal looked relieved. "Good, good. I have to ride south with Kition to Jezreel. Jehu is—" He broke off, looking frightened. Men died when they babbled palace secrets. He muttered hurriedly, "With the boy on the road to recovery, I won't worry."

Rael nodded and sat on the cot to minister again to the child. Only half his attention was on his task; he tried to listen as Allarbal went into the next room to say farewell to his wife. They spoke in whispers so that it was difficult to hear anything more than snatches of their talk. But there was an undertone of the excitement in the air; Rael had been around royalty long enough to know that some important happening was about to take place. It sharpened his already keen interest.

". . . don't know when I'll get back. The killing of a man like . . . no, no, I'll be careful. Kition has thought this out, he and Jezebel . . . what harm can come to me? I tell you he won't suspect . . ."

The woman was sobbing softly The man was seeking to reassure her, but impatience was in his voice, increasing its volume.

"I tell you he won't suspect a thing. Like a lamb to the slaughter. All the way from Ramoth-Gilead . . . and he'll be tired . . . hasty, anxious. It will be over quickly."

Rael went white. Jehu was in Ramoth-Gilead.

Could he be coming to Jezreel?

3.

The young king of Israel looked up from the Nubian slave-girl he was fondling. He had disarranged her tunic so that both her breasts lay bare to the stares of the onlookers. She was plump and dark, and her thick black hair lay like a veil on her shoulders. A lazy smile twitched the corners of her lips as she writhed her body to meet the palm that sought her nakedness. She had no eyes for the King of Judah who lay watching, nor for the servants who moved back and forth with trays of food, nor even for the heavyset Phoenician guards—captain standing at attention before the royal couch.

Jehoram scowled and pinched the flesh he caressed, making the Nubian cry out. He said, "To kill me? Are you mad? I'm the king!"

Kition, being a wise man, allowed his head to droop. "It has been so reported to your mother, highness. A holy man sent by Elisha to Jehu anounted him king in your place. He—"

"By the gods!" Jehoram screamed, throwing off the girl and coming to his feet. He was a beardless youth, old before his time, his lips overthick and his great black eyes protruding in a heavily lined face. His features were marked with his cruelty and arrogance, his quivering voice bespoke self pity. He stamped his foot.

"I won't stand for it, do you understand? I'll not allow Jehu to come and slay me as he might a fat pig!" His voice rose to a scream. "Didn't my mother do anything? She always tells me she loves me. What's she done to prove her love?"

Kition told him of the plan he had concocted on his swift journey north from Samaria to Jezreel. Jehu would come into the city and would head straight for the old palace which had been the home of Jeroboam in the early days of the two kingdoms. He would not be anticipating an ambush; he would walk into it with his eyes open; Kition and his Phoenician guards would make short work of him.

Jehoram listened with his mouth open; after a moment, as understanding came to him, he giggled. "Yes, yes. I like that. Kill Jehu—and his soldiers will belong to me. He's half a foreigner anyhow, having stayed so long in Assyria. I shall put my foot on his neck as he lies dying and inform him that I am still the king in Israel."

Kition hesitated, then drew a deep breath. "It may be necessary for the king to let himself be seen—so as not to arouse suspicion."

"Of course, of course. I understand that. I shall be a bait. We shall have a feast—dancing girls—jugglers—sword swallowers—and wine shall flow—for all except you and your soldiers, Kition!"

He ran about the room like a child with a new toy, giggling and slapping his guests on their backs, inviting them to come see the usurper king die under his foot. King Ahaziah too, he asked to stay, to see the little drama. Not much older than Jehoram, Ahaziah thought it would be a great sport.

When he could catch his breath, the king swung back on Kition. "How soon does he arrive?"

"Not before tomorrow evening. I have fast riders along the roads to Moab to intercept him."

Jehoram clapped his hands.

Kition bowed low to hide his faint smile. This prancing, perfumed child—how could a man like Ahab and a woman like Jezebel have created such a little monster?—was applauding his own death. With his own hand Kition would loose the shafts that would make him, Kition, king in Israel. First Jehu, since he was the more dangerous of the two, then Jehoram.

He would need time to position his soldiers, to familiarize himself with the palace. He murmured of this to the king who gestured him off with a gay laugh—"Go, Kition—go. Where's that little devil, Shebusi? I haven't finished with her yet."

Jehu came in a cloud of dust from the east, riding a bouncing chariot behind two big grey stallions. He traveled with a small escort, no more than a dozen chariots, as nearly as the lookouts could discover, and there was no sign of his army anywhere about him. His purple cloak flapped out behind him in the wind of his coming; he looked every inch the king he claimed to be, Kition was thinking, looking down at him from a tower walk. He would not have minded following this man into battle, but it was not to be.

Everything was in readiness. His archers were distributed among the servants at the palace feast, their bowstrings at the ready. Let Jehu and his men walk into the palace and a hundred shafts would whisper through the air at them, whisper the words of Mot, god of death. Hearing those words, the men about Jehu would fall transfixed.

Ah, and then—then he would let his bowstring twang again —this time with Jehoram as his target. The boy-king would go down in a heap and Kition would be king in Israel with Jezebel the incomparable for his bride. He grinned in the teeth of the wind rising over the plain, staring at Jehu and his approaching chariots, then turned and moved away to take command of his troops.

Kition paid no heed to the man on the foam-flecked grey horse who trotted behind the chariot that held Jehu. If he had looked closer, he would have recognized Rael the physician.

All day and all night Rael had ridden to find Jehu on the road from Gilead into Jezreel. Short hours before he had caught up to him with his warning that Kition had left the palace at Samaria with the Phoenician guards of the queen, possibly to lay a trap for Jehu. When he learned that Jehu had been anointed king of Israel, he was certain of it.

Somehow, Jezebel had learned of this; she had sent Kition to Jezreel as her answer, to intercept and slay Jehu before he could take over the throne. Let Jehu scoff if he would; at least, let him be careful.

Jehu promised, mainly to soothe his old friend's fears.

He had an army at his back. What were a few Phoenician guards to his veterans? When Rael begged him to wait for that army to catch up to him, Jehu only grinned. He had been ordered by Yahweh to rid the world of the house of Ahab. He would do it as swiftly as possible. No palace guards captain would stand in his way.

For Jehu was a man in a hurry. He treated his chariot with disdain. Its wheels scratched sparks from the courtyard cobbles as it braced to a stop but Jehu was out of it and striding swiftly, his picked fighting men behind him, hands on their swordhilts and their shields strapped to their arms.

They came at a trot into the silent palace—too silent, a voice in his mind whispered to Jehu—and moved along the tiled corridor past the traditional basin. Of a sudden, as they were ascending the stairs, they heard a burst of laughter, a clangor of harpstrings too quickly brought to life. Jehu chuckled grimly and made a gesture with his right hand.

He growled, "It seems that Rael was right. We don't come unexpectedly. Go and fetch Rael. I want him beside me when I face Jehoram. He may have saved my life. He hates Jezebel worse than does a dog the cat. He would relish seeing what takes place in the banquet hall."

The officers saluted and moved away.

When Rael stood at his elbow, Jehu said, "Walk with me, old friend. But be on your guard. At the first show of violence, throw yourself on the floor. My men will be stationed to prevent this, but there may be a slip-up. You are no man of war, so be advised by me."

Rael only nodded, tightening his lips.

Jehu walked on like a man in his own home. There was no fear in him; no pampered fop like Jehoram nor toy soldier like Kition could frighten him; but he was no fool to rush headlong into danger. As he approached the great bronze doors of the banqueting hall he saw the guards on duty reach for the silvered handles and tug on them.

With Rael beside him, he walked into the feasting room.

All sound ceased when he put a foot inside the doorway. There were two couches straight ahead of him, he saw; Jehoram sat on one with a Nubian girl, Ahaziah of Judah on the other with a lean Edomite. Between them a dozen dancing girls stood frozen in terror, staring at him.

Jehu relaxed suddenly. Rael had been right in his warning. The fear in the eyes of the entertainers was proof enough to him. A trap had been laid for him, a trap on a large enough scale so that not only those involved in it knew about it, but even the servants and the slaves.

If further proof were needed, he had it from the smile on Jehoram's lips. The boy lay insolently stroking a Nubian girl, grinning at him. Jehu was no familiar of the boy-king, but he knew him well enough to understand that unless he thought himself safe, this dramatic appearance of the general of the armies would have made him babble hysterically.

Jehoram thought himself safe from danger. He would only do this because of certain knowledge that Jehu was no threat to him.

His skin crawled a little as Jehu moved forward. Were his

men where he had sent them? From the corners of his eyes he saw the armed guards in the shadows, bows in their hands. Bows? To feather their shafts in his body. Nor were these Habiru men, but Phoenicians. Even in the shadows he could make out the Dagon seal on their cloaks.

Scabbard clanking against its chains, he advanced.

He risked his life on the prompt action of his men, he realized. Yet they were veterans of a dozen battlefields, hardened by the sun, shrewd when it came to killing. Nor would they have any compunctions when it came to slaying the men of Tyre and Sidon. But would they be in time?

Jehoram was quivering with eagerness, the Nubian forgotten. He was rising on his elbow, eyes darting here and there in the shadows of the pillars flanking his hall of feasting. Impatience showed in every line of his body. It would be soon now, if at all.

There was a whisper in the air.

Rael cried out, threw himself against Jehu, knocking him off balance. In the same motion, he grunted; the unmistakable sound of an arrow driving into flesh could be heard. Rael fell on top of him. Against his arm Jehu felt the shaft which he could see protruding from Rael's chest.

There was movement among the pillars where his men were, but Jehu had no ears for them. Men were crying out, dropping in among the black shadows, the sound of their armor hitting the floor tiles like a death dirge played on metal.

Jehu knelt over his friend. His throat was choked so that he could not speak. He saw the eyelids flutter, lift. A smile touched the pain-distorted lips.

"It was—best this way," the physician whispered.

"No. You will live. I swear it. I need you, Rael. You must help me rule Israel."

The head on the floor tiles moved imperceptibly sideways. "You will be a good ruler, perhaps even better than Ahab. Of the three, you alone are strong enough to subdue yourself so as to—obey Yahweh. . . ."

He dies with the name of his God on his lips, Jehu thought, staring down at the white, pinched face. Whatever he was, however many his weaknesses, he had made his atonement.

The eyelids opened again, staring sightlessly. His voice seemed to come from a long distance. "Beware Jezebel, Jehu. She has a power no man can resist. She planned to slay you and Jehoram and take Kition for husband. I swear this is the truth. So beware her . . . . beware. . . ."

Rael shuddered and was dead.

168

A man in a mailshirt and metal helmet came out from behind
a pillar. His sword glinted redly in the torchlights. He cried,
"They are dead, Jehu. All of them, even Kition, captain of the
palace guard in Samaria." The blood dripped slowly from the
blade, making moist sounds in the stillness.

Jehoram screamed. He turned to run, tripping over the
cushions of his couch. The Nubian girl shrank back. To his
other side the king of Judah was standing also, staring to his
left and right, the fingers of his hands opening and closing.

A bowstring sounded. Jehu saw the arrow arch through the
air and overtake the running boy-king moments before he
reached a rear-wall door. His knees touched the tiles and he fell
sideways.

Jehu then watched Ahaziah stumble past but made no move
to stop him, merely gesturing two bearded warriors to follow
and slay him.

Jehu was now king in Israel.

4.

Jezebel admired her beauty in the silver mirror a slavegirl
held up to her. Tiny seed pearls on silver chains glistened in
her thick black hair that was piled high to reveal the loveliness
of her throat and shoulders. In the transparent purple tunic
edged with gold at hem and shoulders, belted by golden discs,
she was every inch the queen. Never before had she looked so
breathtakingly lovely.

And she must look her best, this day.

For Jehu was coming to Samaria in the might of his new
kinghood, to kill her. So much news had a spy brought only
the evening before, with blood from a dagger wound caked on
his upper arm and fever glinting in his eyes. Without stopping
he had come at a gallop from Jezreel where Jehoram and
Ahaziah lay dead of arrows in their backs.

She was all that remained of the family of Ahab.

Jezebel was not yet afraid, being woman enough to know
that Jehu loved her. He had always loved her, as had Ahab and
Rael while they lived. When he saw her like this, in purple and
gold and with her nakedness white to see beneath the purple,
he would not slay her.

Impatience was a fever in her blood. She crossed to the balcony from which she could see the great bronze sundial in the

courtyard. Her fist hammered on the balcony rail as if to hurry the passage of the shadow across the lines that marked the *sha'ahs* into which the day was divided.

The air grew cooler with coming night and still there was no sign of Jehu or his chariots. Jezebel summoned Alanna, bade her fetch meat and drink. With the passing of the day, a little of Jezebel's confidence waned. She felt cold now, a little fearful of what was to come.

Why did Jehu delay? Would he send an officer rather than himself to do this deed Elisha demanded? He must not! He must come himself and look upon her.

There! Surely that was the sound of chariot wheels? Yes, coming from the city gate along the Avenue of Kings to the palace compound! A rising murmur from the city streets told her that it was Jehu. The people would cry out like that only at sight of their new king.

"Alanna," she cried. "My mirror, my mirror!"

It was time for their meeting, perhaps the most important meeting in all her life outside that first one, long years ago, when she had stood on the god-cart and Ahab, Rael and Jehu had climbed its sides to get at her. She breathed a prayer to Baal-Melkart. As she had served him well all her life, let him stand by her now in this hour of her need!

Jehu came with a clank of metal and the slap of sandals on tile. He was a soldier always, she thought distractedly, a man of iron. Always he wore his sword, always he let his skin be chafed by the weight of mail.

She turned to face the doorway, her coldness gone before the pounding of her blood. She glanced sideways. The candles were placed exactly right so their light would turn the purple tunic to nothingness, baring her body below it. Let Jehu see her like this and he would be no more than soft clay in her hands.

Jehu stood there, staring at her.

He had come so suddenly despite the fact that she had heard his approach, that Jezebel started and put a hand to her bosom. She must make certain that her voice did not tremble, that she did not show her uneasiness.

"Hail to Jehu, king in Israel."

"Hail to Jezebel," he said slowly.

"Men tell me you have come to kill me."

"Men tell you truth, Jezebel. I have been ordered to slay you by Yahweh through Elisha."

"You aren't such a fool."

His smile was oddly sad, she thought through her fear. She tried to laugh against that queer smile.

170

"We are people of the world, you and I. We're not ragged holy men mouthing words about a God who has no existence. You're a king. I'm a queen. We are in love."

Jehu nodded slowly. "Yes, we're in love. At least—I love you, Jezebel. How much you love me is another matter, since it was Kition and your Phoenician guards who died in the palace at Jezreel before they could kill me."

"Kition aspired to the kingship himself. He planned to murder you and Jehoram my son—"

"Ahaziah talked before he died, Jezebel. And Rael—Rael came to me on a lathered horse babbling about some plan of yours to kill us all and take Kition as your husband."

"Where is Rael? I'll give him the lie in his teeth. I made no such plans. I—"

"Rael is dead, dying from an arrow meant for me. Even as he lay there in my arms, he swore that what he had said was truth—and to beware of you, that you meant to kill me."

Her smile was scornful. "And you believe that nonsense?"

"Not I. A man makes his own doom during his lifetime, by the way he lives. This business with you is something else."

"What is it, Jehu?"

"I find it difficult to speak of Yahweh when you stand so disbelieving before me, knowing you would not understand. So I'll put it another way. Say that to make my kingship a good one, my God requires a sacrifice. A human sacrifice, Jezebel."

She stared at him in horror, eyes wide. Now she was truly afraid, with her fear a dryness in the throat and a numbness in her legs. A sacrifice! Ah, this struck home to Jezebel, for her religion demanded sacrifice of one sort or another to her gods. One cult asked newborn babies to be thrown into a great fire before Baal. Another asked that war captives be slain in the temples. Astarte demanded the spilling of male seed. Until now, Yahweh had never asked such things.

Or—was it only Jehu asking this?

She ran to him, threw herself against his body. "You cannot," she breathed. "I am a priestess and a queen. You cannot sacrifice me! Listen, Jehu! We can have so much, you and I. A great kingdom! Power! Riches! We can ally Phoenicia to Israel, take over Judah. This will be a kindom to rival Assyria itself."

She felt him stir to her nearness, to her nakedness under the purple tunic. Triumph came alive in her veins. "With me beside you, your name shall sound through the ages. See how your body stirs to me. Let your mind leap also. Hold me close, Jehu!"

He put his arms about her and he kissed her. Jezebel did not see the dagger in his fist. She felt it only when it was buried to the hilt in her back. Then she stiffened and moaned. Her eyes rolled in her head. Only his arms held her upright.

"You misunderstood me, Jezebel. It was my sacrifice I was offering Yahweh. I love you. I shall always love you. It is my love I am offering up to Him."

There were tears in his eyes as she slipped and fell to the floor. Only Jehu knew that this day he had slain his happiness, that from now on he would be as a dead man inside his body.

He sent for three men to come and lift what had been Jezebel, queen of Israel, and throw her over the balcony rail into the courtyard. It made no difference what they did with her now. She was only meat.

Later that night, after he had eaten his simple meal, he sent for a burial detail. "She was a queen," he told them. "Give her a royal burial in the crypts below the palace."

To make certain that they obeyed his orders, he went with them. As they came out onto a pillared portico, they could hear the growling of dogs.

Jehu remembered the old prophecy. *And the dogs shall eat Jezebel by the wall of Jezreel.* He gave a great cry and ran across the courtyard to the towering wall that faced the plain of Jezreel.

The dogs heard him and fled.

All that was left of the woman he loved was her head, her hands and her feet. Jehu fell to his knees and wept.

Epilogue

Twenty years later, Jehu knelt in the dust of a battlefield and bowed his forehead to the ground before Shalmaneser III, king of Assyria and Babylon. Beside him on the bloodied ground knelt the kings of Phoenicia and Aram, Moab and Ammon. They had banded together to halt the onrush of the Assyrian juggernaut into the lands bordering the Great Sea. Their gesture of obeisance was an admission that they had been defeated.

As he felt the pebbles press into his cheeks, Jehu thought of Jezebel. Had it not been for her, he would never have saved the life of this man before whom he now knelt. Shalmaneser was no longer the youth Jehu had seen in Babylon, long years ago; he was a mature man in the full tide of his strength and power. In a sense, Shalmaneser was here because of him, Jehu. It was ironic.

"Stand, Jehu of Israel," said Shalmaneser kindly.

Jehu rose to his feet. His armor was dented by a dozen sword-blows. His cloak was torn and heavy with dust. Blood seeped from a number of wounds, staining his flesh and his garments. Yet there was a pride about him that made the Assyrian king smile.

"You fought well today, better than any foe against whom I have hurled my might. But in a sense, you are an Assyrian turtan." He hesitated, then said, "You are also my blood brother. Or have you forgotten it?"

Jehu smiled grimly. "I have not forgotten. I remember also how the priestess of Baal-Marduk prophesied that I would be a king and you a ruler over my nations."

"Even the nation of Israel, it seems."

"Yes. Even Israel."

"It has always been the custom of my people to slay the kings who oppose them. It is in my mind to change that custom, here and now. Israel and these other nations— Phoenicia, Moab and Ammon—are far from the boundaries of my country. It would cost me time and money if I appointed

173

governors from my people and yours rose up against them. Were you and these other rulers to swear allegiance to me and pay me tribute, I would spare your lives so you might rule for me, in my name."

Jehu said quietly, "I will so swear. The others will swear too, being sensible men."

Shalmaneser looked hard at him. "You are a proud man. Why do you yield so easily?"

"For the sake of my people. Once I fought beside you as an Assyrian, as you have said. I saw what happened to the peoples of the cities we sacked. I would spare my people this."

Shalmaneser nodded. "This I believe. And believing, I accept your submission and spare your life, and the lives of these others. I shall give orders that a tablet be created commemorating this event." *

For the first time, Jehu felt his wounds and the tiredness that ate into his muscles. Again he thought of Jezebel. There was a curse on every man she loved, born of the very nature of the love she inspired. Ahab was dead and his family was no more. Rael too, was dead, buried beside his wife in the family vault. He alone yet lived, but for the past twenty years he had been no more than a dead man himself.

Yahweh was finally avenged for the crime of loving Jezebel.

---

*This tablet, the Black Obelisk of Shalmaneser, may be seen in the British Museum.